BULLET TRAIL

BULLET TRAIL

WILLIAM COLT MACDONALD

WHEELER
CHIVERS

This Large Print edition is published by Wheeler Publishing, Waterville, Maine, USA and by AudioGO Ltd, Bath, England.
Wheeler Publishing, a part of Gale, Cengage Learning.
Copyright © 1936 by Allen William Colt MacDonald under the title BULLETS FOR BUCKAROOS.
Copyright © renewed 1964 by Allan William Colt MacDonald.
The moral right of the author has been asserted.

LIBRARY OF CONGRESS CATALOGING-IN-PUBLICATION DATA

MacDonald, William Colt, 1891–1968.
  [Bullets for buckaroos]
  Bullet trail / by William Colt MacDonald.
    p. cm. — (Wheeler Publishing large print Western)
  Previously published as: Bullets for buckaroos.
  ISBN-13: 978-1-4104-3203-2 (softcover)
  ISBN-10: 1-4104-3203-3 (softcover)
  1. Large type books. I. Title.
PS3525.A2122B85 2010
813'.52—dc22
                           2010031478

BRITISH LIBRARY CATALOGUING-IN-PUBLICATION DATA AVAILABLE
Published in 2010 in the U.S. by arrangement with Golden West Literary Agency.
Published in 2011 in the U.K. by arrangement with Golden West Literary Agency.

U.K. Hardcover: 978 1 408 49337 3 (Chivers Large Print)
U.K. Softcover: 978 1 408 49338 0 (Camden Large Print)

Printed in the United States of America
1 2 3 4 5 6 7 14 13 12 11 10

BULLET TRAIL

I. FEUD FLARE-UP

Determination, grim and inexorable, modeled a harsh mask on Clem Hayden's leathery old features as he turned his sweat-streaked horse into the main street of Godwin and slowed to a trot. Hayden's shrewd blue eyes glanced swiftly along the length of a slightly winding thoroughfare, taking in a few pedestrians sauntering on the plank walks, seeing the buildings of adobe and the high, false-fronted structures of commercial enterprise bordering both sides of the dusty, unpaved roadway.

Though Godwin was the county seat of Cougar County, on this sweltering day of mid-afternoon August it might have been the sleepiest of small Mexican villages for all the activity shown. Mostly, folks were enjoying their *siesta* hour; there weren't many people on the move. Loungers drowsed in front of stores in the shelter of wooden awnings that reached out almost to the long lines of hitchracks stretching on both sides of Main Street. Here and there could be seen a Mexican huddled in the shadows between buildings, drawing listlessly on a corn husk cigarette. Overhead, swinging somewhat to the west, a blistering sun beat down from the cloudless, blue sky.

It was only in the fall, when nearby ranchers were shipping beef stock from the cattle pens east of town, that Godwin really awakened and took on a definite semblance of life. Then things moved! From early morning until late at night the streets were lined with cowhands, cattle owners, Mexican *vaqueros* and the business men of Godwin. On the spur the T. N. & A. S. Railroad had run to the town, cattle cars were shunted back and forth, engines steamed and snorted, cattle inspectors toiled and perspired. Only when the last steer had been prodded reluctantly along the runway and the final train had pulled out, headed for the east, did Godwin relapse, once again, into drowsy complacence, and wish for something exciting to happen. And cursed with annoyance when it did.

Godwin, after all, wasn't much of a town. There was just a single, main thoroughfare and three or four cross streets. The main street contained the usual business shops,

8

saloons, restaurants. There was a ramshackle hotel known as the Godwin House. On the eastern outskirts of the town was a scattered collection of shabby Mexican dwellings equipped with the usual assortment of small, naked children, goats and chickens wandering aimlessly about. A daily stage coach reached Godwin from Rankintown, sixty miles to the east, but carried mostly newspapers and mail — and not a great deal of either.

Thus it was that old Clem Hayden's intrusion into the peaceful scene of the afternoon was viewed with a certain resentment by the scattering of men witnessing his arrival. A particularly keen eye wasn't necessary to see that Hayden was definitely "on the prod" as the saying is. He ignored greetings from two or three friends and rode grimly on, his eyes ever on the alert for —— Well, just what it was, or who it was, nobody knew, but the old cattleman's attitude seemed to spell trouble. A couple of pedestrians sauntering along the walk paused to wonder, upon noting the six-shooter slung at Hayden's right thigh.

That, in itself, was unusual. Clem Hayden hadn't been known to wear a gun for the past eighteen months. Hayden's temper was too "hair-triggered" the judge had main-

9

tained, and had issued certain orders relative to Hayden's disarming when coming to town. There hadn't been an arrest; Joe Frame, the surprised victim of Hayden's hot temper, had recovered. Besides, there were reputable witnesses who claimed Frame, as much as Hayden, was to blame. Be that as it may, the judge had issued his orders; until today Hayden had abided by those orders. Now, plainly, something serious was afoot.

Men lounging along the street sat straighter as their curious gazes followed Hayden's tall, gaunt figure as it dismounted before the office of the sheriff of Cougar County and tethered the horse at the tie rail. Giving his faded overalls a hitch at the waist, Hayden rocked stiff-legged (like a belligerent terrier dog trying to promote a fracas) toward the sheriff's open doorway. At the entrance he paused once more, glanced swiftly along the street, and disappeared inside the building. An almost audible sigh passed along the thoroughfare. There was a larger portion of the citizenry abroad now, mysteriously popped into view, it seemed, by Clem Hayden's arrival in Godwin.

Seated on the porch of the General Store was Zeke Cartwright, elderly proprietor of

10

the business, talking to one of his ancient, bewhiskered cronies. Zeke noted Hayden's disappearance in the sheriff's office, spat a long brown stream that scored a direct hit on a tiny horned toad basking in the dusty sunshine beyond the walk, and said to his companion seated on the edge of the porch: "Luke, Hayden had his gun." Luke nodded solemnly. Cartwright continued, "Do ye reckon Hayden's a-seekin' a rampage?"

Luke gave the question serious consideration and finally handed down his decision: "I wouldn't go so fur as to say thet, but I'm a-bettin' a pretty, Clem Hayden didn't buckle on thet hardware to swat hawss-flies."

Zeke Cartwright frowned gravely and pondered. "Hayden might," he spoke at last, "be tryin' to get Sheriff Cameron's permission to tote his iron again."

Luke shook his head. "Hayden won't get it," he stated definitely. "You know, Judge Thomas' orders ——"

"Luke Porter, ye know as well's I do, Jedge Thomas ain't in th' county no more — not since last 'lection."

Luke fingered his scrawny whiskers contemplatively. "I know thet — well's you do," he jerked out. "But ye can mark it down as Gawd's truth thet Hayden won't get permission to pack his iron from th' sheriff — not right away, leastwise."

"Ye're dang certain, ain't ye?" scornfully. "How-come you to know that Cameron won't give thet permission right to once?"

Luke's whiskers waggled with sudden merriment. " 'Cause Cameron ain't in his office. I seed him go down th' street, twenty minutes back," he cackled explanation. "Fooled ye thet time, Zeke."

Cartwright grunted disgustedly. "Ye got a queer sense o' humor," he said in injured tones. "Anyway, Cameron's deppity is there, I reckon."

Luke snorted scornfully. "You ain't sech a fool as to think Link Dexter would make a move 'thout Poddy Cameron's say-so?"

That ended the argument between the two ancients for the time being. Cartwright finally emerged from a sulky silence to concede reluctantly, "Reckon ye're c'rect. I wonder what's up. Hayden looked like he'd been chawin' a diet o' raw beef that hadn't digested proper."

"He looked plumb riled, thet's a fact," Luke nodded. "Mebbe we're due to see a flare-up of thet old feud with Joe Frame."

Cartwright looked startled. "Frame in town?"

"I seed him go in th' Faro Saloon 'bout

12

two hours back, while you was in th' store. He ain't come out. If Joe was drinkin' real hard we might see something happen ——"

Luke broke off suddenly and concentrated his gaze in the direction of the sheriff's office where Clem Hayden had reappeared at the hitchrack. Hayden glanced along the street, went out to his tethered horse, paused a moment as though in doubt as to the next move. He removed his battered old sombrero, drew out a bandanna, mopped his forehead, one gnarled hand passing the handkerchief back over his sparse white hair and around the back of his neck. Then he busied his fingers with the manufacture of a cigarette, searched his vest pockets for a match. A cloud of grey smoke issued from below his long mustaches as Hayden swung up to the saddle of his big, rawboned horse.

A tall, muscular man of thirty-five or -six appeared in the doorway of the Faro Saloon, diagonally across from the sheriff's office. He wore overalls, unbuttoned vest, roll brim sombrero, riding boots with big spurs. A holstered six-shooter hung low at his right hip. His hair and eyes were light — the eyes either pale brown or blue; they didn't remain motionless long enough for anyone to determine with certainty. He was smooth-shaven, his nose was wide-nostriled, with tight lips and a bulldog jaw, which at present was clamped hard on a long black cigar. He called across the dusty roadway, "Hey, Hayden!"

Hayden, backing his horse from the tie rail, paused, jerked his head around, snapped, "Sheridan, this time a showdown's due."

Quint Sheridan, owner of the Circle-Cross outfit, stepped quickly from the Faro Saloon porch and started across the street. He said, cold-voiced, "Hayden, Frame don't want any trouble with you. You'd better go home."

Hayden laughed. It wasn't a nice laugh, having nothing to do with his normally quiet blue eyes. Only his lips stretched in a sort of sneer as he said shortly, "You're damn right Frame don't want trouble with me — nor you either. But you're going to get it. I'm through palaverin' around. Just as soon as I can see Poddy Cameron. . . ."

By this time, Sheridan was standing near Hayden and what was next said is only a matter for conjecture. On the porch of the General Store, Zeke Cartwright and Luke Porter strained their ears to hear what followed, but Sheridan and Hayden had lowered their voices. Eyes all along the street followed the movements of the two ranch owners. Hayden was speaking more quietly

14

now, but hate, mingled with triumph, showed in every line of his leathery features. Twice the on-lookers saw Hayden pound home certain points in his argument, as one clenched fist smashed into his other, open, palm.

Sheridan seemed to be trying to calm the older man, but with no success. Finally, Sheridan appeared to lose his temper. He invited Hayden to go to hell, in louder tones, added further words of profanity, then swung abruptly around, crossed the street, and reentered the Faro Saloon, followed by Hayden's jeering laughter. Sheridan pushed through the swinging doors without making any further reply. Hayden swung his horse away from the tierail.

Zeke Cartwright turned to Luke Porter, said complainingly, "Dammity blazes! Luke, I couldn't make out what they was talkin' about, could you?"

Sadly, Luke shook his bewhiskered head. "Not a blasted syllable."

"Huh! Sell a what? What you talkin' about ——— ?"

Zeke broke off suddenly; Hayden was just riding past the General Store. Zeke called, "Howdy, Clem! Nice day."

Luke added hurriedly, "H'lo, Clem! Th' country needs rain bad, don't you think?

Whyn't ye come up an' rest your saddle a mite . . . ?"

The words trailed off into disgusted silence as Hayden nodded shortly to the speakers and kept on past, his horse's hoofs kicking up slow clouds in the thick dust of the street.

Zeke looked at Luke. Luke grunted disgustedly and the sound was echoed by Zeke. Zeke said, "I don't think he felt like talkin' to us."

Luke donated grave consideration to the comment, finally nodding slowly. "By Hanner! I think ye've hit it, Zeke. I knowed there must be some reason for him not stoppin' to visit."

Zeke said, "Hayden's pullin' up in front of the Gunsight Bar. Now, if he was th' type to get liquored up, we'd be shore to see trouble."

The gaze of the two men followed Hayden's movements as the cowman pulled his horse to a halt before a saloon on the next corner, on the same side of the street as the general store.

Hayden stepped down from his saddle, rounded the end of the tierail and walked stiffly through the swinging doors of the Gunsight Bar, the oldest drink emporium in Godwin.

The interior of the saloon was shadowed and cool after the brilliant sunlit glare of the dusty street. A long bar ran along the wall to the right, behind which was a shelf of bottles and glasses, a cash drawer and, a trifle higher up, a mounted deer's head, its points serving as a support for an ancient, muzzle-loading rifle.

Along the opposite wall were a half dozen wooden-topped tables and chairs, at one of which sat a tall red-haired man reading a paper and nursing along the contents of a bottle of beer. The red-haired man was a stranger in Godwin, having arrived only a short time before, but from the cut of his togs he was all cowman.

Light entered the Gunsight Bar through a window in the front wall, facing on Main Street, and another, smaller window, in the rear wall, just to the left of a back door, now closed against the heat of the day. A few framed pictures adorned the walls. The floor was swept clean, the bar polished from countless moppings.

At the far end of the bar, resting on its side, was a cylindrically-shaped fly trap manufactured of screening, from which rose the steady droning of thousands of captive flies. The inner side of the trap was black with the crawling, buzzing insects. The back of the fly trap was a circular, hooked door, which could be opened from time to time for purposes of emptying. The front of the contraption was funnel shaped, with a small hole in the center through which led a long strip of paper smeared with syrup. The luckless flies followed the paper through the small hole leading into the trap; once inside they seemed to have no conception of the route out. Nick Fitch, owner of the Gunsight, did his best to keep patrons free of the annoyance of pesky flies.

Aside from the red-haired cowman reading a newspaper at one of the tables, there was only a single customer in the Gunsight — an undersized, wiry looking individual with a cocky manner who had registered under the name of Callahan upon arriving, via the previous day's stage, at the desk of the Godwin House. Callahan was somewhere in the vicinity of twenty-eight years of age and, definitely, not a cow country product. He was dressed in a grey suit of "city clothes"; a black derby hat rested jauntily on a thick head of hair that could, by no stretch of the imagination, be termed anything except brick colored.

What Callahan's business was in Godwin, the clerk of the hotel, despite many roundabout questionings, had been unable to determine. All attempted "pumpings" had been neatly evaded by the pugnacious-featured Irishman with his freckles, snub nose and devil-may-care blue eyes. From other sources too Callahan had sidestepped all questions regarding his business. His white collar and shirt, black four-in-hand and silver watch chain stretched across his high-cut vest, bespoke respectability, but certain folks in Godwin wondered just how deep appearances went.

Like the other red-head engrossed in the newspaper, Callahan was drinking beer, while he talked to Nick Fitch, proprietor and barkeep of the Gunsight. Fitch was a dark complexioned man in his fifties, with a white apron tied about his middle. Callahan, having finished his beer, requested another of the same. Fitch set out a fresh bottle. Callahan dropped some money on the bar, poured his glass half full. Fitch dropped the coin in his cash drawer, turned back, saying carefully, "You expecting to stay in Godwin long, Mr. Callahan?"

If the undersized Callahan heard the question he gave no sign. Replacing his empty glass on the bar, he motioned toward the fly trap. "Say, don't you ever open that thing and clean it out, Nick?"

Fitch looked indignant. "I certainly do.

You ain't no idea how fast them dang flies collect in that thing."

"When'd you empty it last?" Callahan asked skeptically.

Fitch thought it over. "Reckon she ain't been emptied in a week or so," he admitted reluctantly. "Y'see, day times it's been so dang hot, I hate to stir. Nights I'm busier an' I sort of forget, when that dang buzzin' dies down —— "

At that moment Clem Hayden pushed through the swinging doors. He came up to the bar, his face hard.

Fitch said, "Howdy, Clem. What you takin'?" Fitch's eyes bulged in startled fashion as he noted the gun slung at Hayden's hip, but he didn't say anything.

Hayden said, rather hard voiced, "Let me have a touch," laying a dime on the bar.

Fitch set out bottle and small whisky glass. Hayden poured a neat "three fingers" and downed it at a gulp. He placed the glass on the bar and stood moodily gazing down on a small wet ring on the mahogany surface. He didn't say anything; just seemed to be pondering some weighty question in his mind.

"How's things at the 8-Bar?" Fitch tried to make conversation.

"So-so," Hayden replied, without looking

up. Then he laughed shortly. "I'm expectin' 'em to improve shortly, Nick."

"That's fine." Fitch hesitated, then, seemingly fascinated by the sight of a gun on Hayden, ventured, "I see you packin' your hardware again, Clem."

Hayden glanced down, half absentmindedly, at the gun. "I just rode in to speak to Poddy Cameron 'bout this gun," he said.

The red-haired cowman seated at the table glanced toward the bar, spoke quietly, "If you're lookin' to see Sheriff Cameron," he stated in an easy drawl, "maybe I can save you a few steps. He's down to the court house; won't be back for a spell. I just came from his office a short while back."

Hayden said, "Thanks, stranger. I just come from Poddy's office myself. His deppity told me."

The red-haired man nodded. "Come to think of it," he recollected, "I saw you ride past, in that direction, about the time I was 'lightin' out front." He resumed his newspaper.

Hayden nodded shortly, said "thanks" again, turned to the bar and reached for the bottle Fitch had left standing there.

Fitch laughed, a trifle nervously, as he took the second dime Hayden gave him, and said, "You figured you'd sooner wait here for Poddy, eh, Clem?"

Hayden said, "That dang deputy of Poddy's was plumb tongue-tied. Th' minute he saw me he acted like he'd seen a ghost."

"Hell! That Link Dexter is tongue-tied most of the time," Fitch chuckled. "He never does know what to say, 'bout anythin', unless Poddy Cameron says it first." Fitch added uncertainly, "Say, Clem, did you know Joe Frame is in town?"

Hayden's jaw hardened. "If he'll keep out of my way, there won't be any trouble," he said quietly.

Callahan put in, "Is this Frame you're talkin' about, a chunky-shouldered guy with a lantern-jaw?"

Hayden vouchsafed a "none of your business" look on Callahan and made no reply. Fitch shook his head slightly at the Irishman, then said, "That's Frame, I reckon."

Undaunted, Callahan went on, "I was in the Faro Saloon a while back. Frame acted like he was out to win a drinking championship."

"That," Hayden said coldly, "is no skin off my teeth."

Callahan shrugged his shoulders. "All right, all right," he said cheerfully. "You don't need to get mad. I'm just telling you. Because —" and here Callahan lowered his

22

voice, "— if it is any skin off of your teeth, here comes Frame now, and he don't look to me like he was bearing any olive branches."

At that instant, the swinging doors crashed against the walls on either side of the entrance, and a wide-shouldered individual with a long, unshaven jaw came barging up to the bar. His right hand was resting on his cartridge belt, not far from the butt of his holstered six-shooter, but he didn't look at Hayden as he staggered in.

Fitch said nervously, "Howdy, Joe. What'll it be?"

Frame clutched the edge of the bar with his left hand, swayed back, then forward again. He bent his bloodshot gaze on the bartender without replying.

Hayden took four quick steps that carried him farther into the room, away from Frame. At the far end of the bar, Hayden came to a stop, gaze concentrated on Frame. Frame glanced along the mahogany, looked at Hayden a moment, then laughed.

The very atmosphere seemed quivering with emotion. Nick Fitch had turned ashen. Frame suddenly broke the tension: he swayed back to the bar, saying, "Gimme a slug of whisky, Nick."

Tremblingly, the barkeep set out a bottle

and clean tumbler. The money Frame placed on the bar remained untouched.

II. Murder?

Joe Frame's right hand wavered a trifle as he slopped whisky over the rim of his glass, banged the bottle down on the bar. As though unaware of the other occupants of the room, he held the glass of amber liquid against the light from the front window, squinting through it meditatively, but made no attempt to drink.

Fitch, leaning both hands on the bar, looked worried. The fingers of one hand worked nervously at his bar towel. At the far end of the long counter, Hayden stood as before, gaze glued on Frame's swaying form. Frame, apparently, was unconcerned that he stood with his back to his old enemy. Callahan lounged at the bar, between Frame and Hayden, looking nonchalantly from one to the other, not realizing, or perhaps caring, that his position, between two prospective gun-slingers, was a precarious one.

The red-haired man at the table had put aside his newspaper, and shoving back the grey sombrero on his head, sat surveying the scene, sensing, probably, something of greater import than appeared on the surface. Slowly he rose to his full, lean height. A frown of annoyance creased his long bony face, drawing his normally tolerant grey eyes to thin slits of speculation. He said, abruptly, to Callahan, "Come here a minute, son."

Callahan looked puzzled, but left the bar and crossed the floor, his shrewd gaze taking in the sinewy, overalled form and woollen shirt, the twin forty-fives slung at thighs, the wide mouth and aquiline nose. Callahan realized suddenly he had seen a picture of this man someplace, and in the sudden realization overlooked the fact that the red-haired man had drawn him out of the range of fire.

Callahan said suddenly, low-voiced, "You're Tucson Smith."

Tucson Smith nodded shortly, his eyes watching Hayden and Joe Frame.

Callahan said, "Say, what are you —— ?"

Tucson cut short the eager tones, saying quietly, without looking at Callahan, "You better stay over here."

The others in the room didn't hear the remarks. They stood, tense, like statues graven from living granite. Frame lowered his glass from the light, gulped it down, refilled his glass.

Tucson's frown deepened. Something tragic was afoot. He wanted to interfere, but had no business to. Both Frame and Hayden were strangers to him. Any interference on Tucson's part would be, at least, an impertinence that might lead to worse trouble.

Again, Frame had lifted his glass of whisky to the light and was squinting through it meditatively. Here, Tucson considered, was a man who was trying to nerve himself for a killing. And yet, Hayden had shown no sign of fear. The elderly cowman appeared fully capable of looking out for himself; if anything, Hayden appeared to be a better man than Joe Frame.

Callahan looked from Tucson to the two men at the bar, his eyes curious. Nick Fitch was breathing heavily. The sounds of Fitch's breathing and the steady drone from the myriad flies in the trap were the only breaks in the tense silence.

Gradually the noise of voices from the street permeated the quiet of the barroom, indicating the presence of a gathering crowd. Frame suddenly turned back to the bar. His head went back as he tossed off the glass of whisky, sent it rolling along the counter to fall unnoticed back of the bar.

Suddenly a harsh laugh parted his lips. He turned, as though seeing Clem Hayden for the first time, and said, "Howdy, Hayden."

Hayden said coldly, "Howdy, Frame."

Hayden tensed a trifle, as Frame took a couple of steps along the bar, bringing him closer. The old cowman's right arm dangled at his side, his left hand rested on the bar.

Frame motioned toward the gun at Hayden's side. "Thought there was a law against you packin' a gun, Hayden."

Fitch came suddenly to life. "You look here, Joe Frame. I don't want any trouble in the Gunsight. You better leave ——"

Frame's jeering laugh cut the words short. "Who said anythin' about trouble, Nick?"

Hayden said heavily, "Let him stay, Nick. I'm not lookin' for trouble with Frame."

"You're damn right you're not," Frame sneered. He took another step toward the older man.

Hayden shook his head, "Mebbe you'd better leave, at that, Frame." Patience softened the hardness of the tones. "I don't want trouble with you. Let's forget that old business."

"Nope, I ain't forgettin' it," Frame said stubbornly. "You was lucky to beat me to the shot that time. You know it was luck. Now you're hopin' to potshot me from behind, I figure."

Hayden commenced to breathe heavily. His old eyes flashed angrily. Still he fought to control his temper. "Don't be a fool, Frame," he said slowly. "I don't want a fight with you. I'll get out to avoid one."

Hayden started toward the door. Frame waited until he was only six or seven feet away then called him a name. A hot flush of crimson suffused the old features. He swung suddenly around to face Frame, one hand starting toward the butt of his holstered gun. Midway in the draw his hand paused, as he refused to complete the draw.

Even while Hayden's gnarled fingers hesitated above the gun, Frame's right hand swooped to holster. A heavy, barking roar shook the barroom. Hayden put out one protesting hand, before his gaunt form went rigid.

"You — you know I — I ——" Hayden gasped.

What his words might have been, no one ever knew with certainty. Hayden's legs jack-knifed and he slipped sidewise to the floor to sprawl facedown. Frame fired twice more before the old man's form struck the planks.

From the street came sudden, startled yells. Frame cursed, moving backward toward the doorway. His gun swung in a half arc that covered the barroom.

"You — you all saw it," he rasped.

"We saw it," Tucson Smith said level-voiced.

"You know it wa'n't my fault," Frame insisted. "You saw him start for his gun — even before I did."

Tucson said reluctantly, "He started for his gun — even before you did."

"All right, then." Frame breathed easier, approached the dead man on the floor. "That clears me. You're all witnesses to what this gent said. Sorry it had to happen, but Hayden come ridin' in, totin' a gun. I just reckon I'll take that gun for a souvenir." He stooped down reaching toward holster.

Tucson said sharply, "Hold it, Frame!"

Frame growled, "What in hell's the matter with you?" He relinquished his hold on the dead Hayden's gun, swinging in his stooping position toward Tucson, his gun starting to bear on Tucson.

Quite suddenly, Frame noticed that one of Tucson's guns was out of its holster. Frame lowered his own weapon, rose to his feet.

"I don't get the idea," he said sullenly.

"That corpse ain't to be touched," Tucson ordered.

"But look here, feller, I just want his gun

for a souvenir. He shot me once. This time I won out — hell, there ain't no harm in ——"

"Don't touch that gun," Tucson said sternly.

There were faces peering above the swinging doors, now, excited voices outside. Frame commenced to back away from the dead man on the floor, saying, "Hell, you all saw it. Hayden went for his gun first."

"Hayden went for his gun first," Tucson nodded, "but there's somethin' funny about this. I'm not so sure you didn't commit murder ——"

"You're crazy!" Frame yelled.

"Maybe I am," Tucson conceded, "but you keep away from that body until the sheriff gets here."

Men were pouring into the saloon now. Tucson said, "Frame, you better put your gun away."

Angrily, Frame shoved the six-shooter into his holster. Tucson sheathed his own forty-five. Quint Sheridan, owner of the Circle-Cross, pushed through the knot of figures clustered at the bar, took one look at the dead man, then turned to Joe Frame.

"You had to do it, eh, Joe?" Sheridan said.

Frame nodded. "He went for his gun first. I got witnesses."

Sheridan said, "Where's his gun."

"In his holster," Frame replied angrily. "I wanted it for a souvenir, but this stranger wouldn't let me ——"

"I wouldn't let him take it," Tucson interrupted.

Sheridan eyed Tucson coldly. "What you got to do with it?" Sheridan demanded. "Hayden a friend of yours?"

"I never saw him before," Tucson admitted quietly. "I know the law. That corpse or nothin' on it will be touched until the sheriff gets here."

"Now, look here, Red-head ——" Sheridan commenced angrily.

"The name is Smith — Tucson Smith."

Callahan put in, "And he's known as a rip-snortin' terror on gun-wheels, in the Southwest, Sheridan. Ever hear of him?"

Sheridan looked slightly put out, but he shook his head. "There's a hell of a lot of hombres travelin' around under that Smith moniker," he sneered.

Tucson laughed easily, but refused to become angered. "Some hombres," he stated, "don't change their names as soon as they should."

Sheridan flushed. "Exactly what do you mean by that?"

"Just as much as was intended in your

remarks concernin' my name. Suit your-self."

Sheridan swore under his breath and turned away. He stood talking in undertones to Joe Frame. Callahan was bustling around the barroom asking questions relative to the dead man's history, family, and so on. In one hand he carried a few sheets of paper, folded lengthwise, on which he was busily engaged in jotting notes. Nick Fitch, still pale, was repeating over and over his impressions of the fight — if fight it might be called.

A middle-aged man with a bulky middle pushed through the crowd. He wore a close-cropped grey mustache and black Stetson sombrero. His corduroy trousers were tucked into knee boots and on his open vest was pinned a sheriff's badge. His eyes lighted when he saw Tucson. "Tucson Smith! You dang ol' rannyhan!"

The two men clasped hands, as Tucson said, "It's good to see you again, Poddy," then pointing toward the floor, "Business here for you."

Sheriff Poddy Cameron looked down at the dead man. "I'd just reached my office and my deputy was telling me you were in town when we heard the shots. I came as fast as I could." The sheriff was still panting heavily. "What's the story, Tucson?"

Here, Quint Sheridan intruded, "Look here, Sheriff, I figure you should get the story from local citizens — not from strangers that just arrived ——"

Cameron cut in, "Oh, you think so, do you, Sheridan?" belligerently. "Were you here when it happened?"

"No, but ——"

"Well, Tucson was, I figure ——"

Sheridan persisted, "This Smith hombre will tell you Hayden went for his gun first. Frame come in here mindin' his own business and Hayden went for his gun ——"

"That right, Tucson?" Poddy Cameron asked quickly. "Did you see it all?"

"I saw it all," Tucson nodded. "There's no doubt about it, Poddy. Hayden started to draw his iron. He didn't go through with his draw, but Frame was already pullin' his gun by that time. He fired three times ——"

"It was a clear case of self-defense," Sheridan insisted. "You figurin' to hold Joe, Sheriff?"

Callahan put in, "Self-defense it might have been. It looked that way, but Tucson said somethin' about murder."

"You did?" Cameron looked startled.

Tucson looked steadily at the sheriff, then, "I must have been excited, Poddy. I reckon

Frame shot in self-defense ——"

"Huh!" Cameron commenced scornfully, "*You* excited —— ?"

Tucson nodded. "I'd had a run in with Frame. You see, somethin' looked funny to me. Frame seemed mighty anxious to take Hayden's six-shooter ——"

"Cripes A'mighty!" Frame growled. "Ain't I told you I just wanted it for a souvenir?"

"— and I wondered," Tucson finished quietly, "if, maybe, the gun wasn't loaded and Frame was aware of the fact."

Frame and Sheridan looked startled. Callahan gave a sudden exclamation of surprise and reached down to get the dead man's weapon out of its holster. Poddy Cameron's arm darted out, jerked the gun from Callahan's hand. Men gathered closely around the sheriff as he spun the cylinder of the six-shooter, then announced, "It is loaded, all right. Five full shells and the hammer resting on an empty — like most of us carry 'em. The mechanism seems to be in working order, too."

"Can I have the gun for a souvenir, then?" Frame's voice was eager.

"No, you can't!" Cameron said testily. "You and your damn souvenirs!"

"Aw, you don't want that iron, Joe," Sheridan cut in suddenly. "Let Poddy keep the blasted thing."

Something in Sheridan's eyes made Tucson aware that the man knew Cameron wouldn't relinquish the six-shooter, and that Sheridan was facing the loss with as good grace as possible. But why should Sheridan care about the gun?

"In the first place," Cameron was saying, "this gun now belongs to Clem's daughter. In the second place, it will have to be produced at your hearing."

"You ain't holdin' me for this shootin', are you?" Frame looked alarmed. "It was a clear case of self-defense."

"I figure you're right," the sheriff said reluctantly, "but I'm aimin' to hold an investigation. No, I ain't puttin' you under arrest. But you stick around town, until we have a hearin' on this matter. Go on, clear out now. All you fellers clear out of here. I've sent my deputy for the coroner. He'll be here any minute. Excitement's all over. Go on, clear out."

The crowd started to move slowly toward the entrance, though Sheridan and Frame lost no time in leaving now. Callahan was busily putting down writing on the slips of paper he carried, listening intently to every word spoken.

"Look here, sheriff," he asked, "do you

think this is an out and out case of self-defense? I understand there was bad blood between Frame and Hayden. What was their other fight about? Is Frame known as a killer? Tucson, what's your opinion? What did you mean by saying it was murder? Do you think it really was? And if it was murder what was the motive? ——"

"Hey, hey!" Poddy Cameron protested. "What's the idea? I don't get you at all. You hit town yesterday. Nobody could find out your business. All of a sudden you turn into a human question mark. What's the idea?"

Callahan grinned insolently. "It's news, gentlemen, news. I want it for my paper. If this is a mystery killing I've scooped ——"

"It's a newspaper reporter!" Tucson laughed suddenly.

"The best in the business," Callahan admitted brazenly. "At present representing the *Los Angeles Clarion* ——"

"You mean," Cameron asked aghast, "that you come clean over here, from California, to report this killing? How in heck did you know it was going to take place?"

"That's the business of a good reporter," Callahan grinned.

"Well, I'll be damned!" Cameron grunted. "I never heard the like ——"

"Callahan," Tucson smiled, "what are you

doing over in this country? What brought you here? Not a killing like this, even if you did know it was going to happen — which you didn't."

"My paper sent me," Callahan said glibly. "It heard you were coming to Godwin. Where's your two pals — Lullaby Joslin and Stony Brooke?"

"They're due to hit town most any time," Tucson laughed. "I headed over this way to see my friend, Poddy Cameron. Lullaby and Stony had some pals down below the Mexican Border they wanted to visit. I'm goin' to meet 'em here."

"That's it," Callahan nodded enthusiastically. "There's a tradition that any place you Three Mesquiteers go, there's excitement. Excitement means news. That's what brought me here yesterday."

Tucson said good-naturedly, "Callahan, you're a liar by the clock. You got here yesterday, eh? Well, I didn't make up my mind until last night to come to Godwin. What do you say to that, Callahan?"

"Call me Micky," Callahan rushed on, scribbling notes. "Look, here's what I'm going to say, 'Famous Gunfighter Scents Mystery in Killing. Tucson Smith, of Mesquiteers Fame, States ——"

"Whoa! Back up!" Tucson laughed. "I'm

not stating anything. You leave me out of this. All I want to know is what really brought you here."

Callahan started to leave. "I got to wire a story to my paper telling about this killin' anyway. Sheriff, there's telegraph service in this town, isn't there?"

Cameron said, "Go over to the hotel. The clerk will tell you all about it — and give you any other gossip that's boomin' around."

Callahan darted through the doorway. By this time, only Tucson, the sheriff and Nick Fitch remained in the saloon. The body of Clem Hayden lay on the floor as it had fallen.

Cameron grunted, "That reporter hombre is batty, I reckon."

"Unless I miss my guess," Tucson contradicted, "he's one smart little Irishman. I'd like to know what he's doing here." The two men were standing by the bar. Nick Fitch was automatically engaged in polishing glasses. From time to time he cast a horrified glance at the dead man.

Tucson said, "Poddy, let me see that gun of Hayden's?"

Cameron removed the gun from the waistband of his trousers where he had thrust it and passed it over. Tucson examined the gun closely, drew back the hammer, watched the cylinder revolve, until the empty shell on which the hammer rested had again come around. Then he carefully lowered the hammer, handed it back to the sheriff.

"It was loaded, all right," he said with a sigh. "Now why in Hades didn't Hayden go through with his draw? The gun's in working order."

Only the steady droning of the flies in the trap made any reply.

III. CALLAHAN ON THE TRAIL

A man pushed hurriedly through the swinging doors of the saloon, followed at a more leisurely gait by a second man. The first man was about forty years of age with iron-grey hair and pleasant, smoothly shaven features. He was attired in dark clothing and carried a small black hand-bag. The second was about ten years younger with sleepy eyes and a slouching appearance. A holstered gun dangled loosely at his hip and on his vest he wore a deputy-sheriff's badge. This second individual was Link Dexter, Poddy Cameron's deputy. Dexter never had anything to say, unless Cameron said it first. The other man was Doctor Noah Perkins, who also filled the position of town coroner.

Cameron introduced the doctor and deputy to Tucson. The three men shook hands. Doctor Perkins said, "I came as soon as I could, Poddy. Link was waiting for me when I arrived home. I was down in the Mex section on a sick call."

"I sent Link to fetch you, the minute I heard the shots," Cameron said. "I knew a doctor or coroner would be needed, ten to one."

"Sure, sure," Link Dexter said, "we knowed a doctor or coroner would be needed." He looked at the dead man, heavy-eyed, with no trace of emotion on his sleepy features.

Perkins opened his bag, knelt at the side of the corpse. "Hmmm," after a minute. "Shot three times."

Cameron was relating the story as he'd had it from Tucson. The doctor listened in silence as he worked, then expressed an opinion, in technical terms, regarding the course taken by the leaden slugs. "Death came practically instantly," he finished. "Did he say anything before he died?"

"Not much," Tucson said, "that meant anything. Just 'You ― you know I ― I ____.' "

"There was no tellin' what he meant by that," Cameron said.

40

"Nope," Link Dexter echoed, "there's no tellin' what he meant by that."

"He'd been in my office before he come here," Cameron stated. "Wanted to see me about somethin'. I don't know what. He was wearin' his gun. From the way Link acted when he told me, I reckon he was plumb shocked at seeing Clem with a gun on."

Dexter nodded, "Yep, I was plumb shocked."

Perkins closed the black bag and got to his feet. "I guess that's all there is to it. The body can be moved to the undertaker's any time. You holding Joe Frame?"

"I'd like to," Cameron growled, "but I don't see how it can be done. Accordin' to the evidence he fired in self-defense. Clem went for his gun first."

"Sure, nothin' but self-defense," Dexter mumbled. "Clear case o' self-defense."

"And I can't see any reason for putting the county to the expense of a trial that would just bring in a verdict of 'Not Guilty.' "

"No use spendin' a lot of money on a trial," Dexter said gravely. "Th' verdict would just be 'Not Guilty.' "

Cameron glared at Link Dexter and received a sheepish look. The sheriff went on, "I sort of figure to question Frame some more, but I know I won't get any place. But just for the looks of things."

"Yeah, we'll have to question Frame some," Dexter nodded solemnly. "You know, it'll make it look better. But there's no use bringin' him to trial ——"

"Link," Cameron said testily, "you're repeatin' yourself. You drag your bones down to the undertaker's and tell him to come get this body. He's probably all ready, just waitin' to be sent ——"

"Yeah, he's probably waitin' for us to send for him ——" Dexter commenced and halted suddenly under the wrath burning in the sheriff's eye. Reluctantly, Dexter turned and shuffled out of the saloon.

"Damn parrot," Cameron swore under his breath.

The doctor was writing out some sort of report and asking questions of the sheriff. Tucson wandered outside and stood on the saloon porch. By this time the excitement had died down, though there were still a few knots of men standing here and there, gazing toward the saloon. Deputy Link Dexter was some distance down the street, but not moving in any particular hurry.

Nick Fitch came out of the barroom and stood at Tucson's side. "Sort of had to have a breath of air," he said apologetically.

"Seein' Clem layin' there, made me feel sort of squeamish. I been in the bar business a good many years now, but that's the first time a man was ever killed in a place o' mine."

"It hits a feller hard sometimes," Tucson nodded sympathetically. "By the way, how come that feller Dexter is Poddy's deputy?"

Fitch smiled. "Poddy married him."

"Married him!"

"Just about. Link is Missis Cameron's brother. He used to live in Oklahoma, but he lost his job there, and Link come to live with Poddy's chickens ——"

"*With* 'em?"

"Well, the idea bein' that Link was to take care of that little chicken farm that Poddy's tryin' to get started, so he'll have somethin' to retire on when he gets through sheriffin'. You knew about that?"

Tucson nodded. Fitch went on, "Dang nice little place the sheriff is fixin' up. 'Bout three miles out of town. Well, to make a long story short, Link didn't repair some busted fence he was supposed to. A coyote got in and nigh massacred the hens. Poddy was pretty peeved, and when he got another herd of leghorns, he wouldn't let Link go near 'em. Link was plumb broke up and, to save his feelin's, Poddy explained that he

43

was goin' to appoint him deputy. Which same went through as per schedule. Don't make any mistake about Link. He don't say much, but he's a whirlwind in a fight once he's started. He swears by Poddy, does all the office work the sheriff needs, runs errands and so on. Link earns his money all right. His big fault is that he thinks slow and never knows what to talk about, unless he hears Poddy say it first."

"I noticed that," Tucson said dryly.

Fitch nodded and returned to the barroom. Tucson glanced down the street. In front of the Faro Saloon, he saw Quint Sheridan talking earnestly to a man in cowhand clothing, who was just preparing to mount his horse. Sheridan seemed to be detaining the man for a few last words.

Located kitty-corner from the Gunsight Bar was the Godwin House. Tucson saw Micky Callahan emerge from the double-doored entrance on Main Street and step across the road. As he came up, Callahan was grinning widely. "That dang sheriff thinks he's smart, I bet."

"What's the matter?" Tucson asked.

Callahan explained, "Cameron told me to see the hotel clerk about the telegraph service in Godwin, that he'd tell me about it. That's all that clerk could do, tell me about the telegraph service — they hope to get."

"No telegraph here, eh?"

"Not a wire. I wrote out my story, slipped it into an envelope. It'll leave by stage tomorrow noon and be wired from Rankintown."

"What did you say in your story?"

Callahan grunted disgustedly. "Just wrote a short squib about the killing. Told my editor to watch for big developments."

"The same bein'?" Tucson queried.

"I'm looking to you to furnish them," Callahan grinned.

"Look here, Micky, you're on the wrong track. I haven't any story to give you ——"

"I'd like to believe you, Tucson, but that link of talk sounds like egg-hash to me. Every place you've gone the past few years you've made news — you and your pardners. There's you and your big 3-Bar-O cattle ranch and everything you do. You're a famous man. Any time you open your mouth you make news ——"

"That," Tucson grinned, "sounds like egg-hash to *me.*"

"All scrambled, eh?" Callahan chuckled.

"Like a bad yolk."

Callahan uttered a squawk of dismay. "My God! The man makes puns — bad ones."

The little reporter became serious. "Look, Tucson, a story means a lot to me. If you could only give me a hint of what brings you here — just advise me."

"I'll advise you," Tucson said. "Get rid of that derby hat. It'll only get you in trouble in this country."

Callahan nodded complacently. "Yes, I know. Some big cow farmer in the hotel asked where I got the hard-boiled Stetson ____"

"What did you tell him?" Tucson grinned.

"I didn't have any time to talk to him. I was busy trying to find out if I could send a telegram from this town. He kept on butting in. After he got up off the floor, he didn't ask again." Callahan gazed reminiscently at the skinned knuckles on his right hand. "I gave his gun to the hotel clerk and said to let the fellow have it, if he came back. No hard feelings, you understand."

"You're entitled to keep your hat," Tucson said gravely.

The rider Quint Sheridan had been talking to was just riding past the Gunsight. He was a hard looking individual, apparently a cowhand. One of Sheridan's Circle-Cross employees, undoubtedly.

". . . and look here, Tucson," Callahan was saying, "I'd like to be in on any job you're

46

working here. If you'll only tell me a few things. Who sent for you to come here in the first place? What's back of it all? Do you think there really was something queer about Hayden's death? Did Joe Frame have some sort of Indian sign on Hayden to keep him from drawing his gun? What do you think the real motive is? Or was it just a grudge fight? Do you think Frame should be brought to trial? When do you figure you'll have some evidence —— ?"

"Cripes!" Tucson laughed with good-natured exasperation. "What am I going to do to get rid of you? You're a pest ——"

"If I can be of any help in solving this business," Callahan rushed on, "just tell me what I can do ——"

Tucson threw up both hands in mock dismay. He said solemnly, "You see that rider just leavin' town?" gesturing toward the Circle-Cross man who was just disappearing around a bend in the road.

"What about him?" he said eagerly.

"Follow him. See where he goes."

"Follow him? How?" Callahan asked blankly.

"Can you ride a horse?"

Callahan said, "I never have, but I guess I can do it, all right. I've seen it done enough times."

"That's fine," Tucson said gravely. "A good half of the battle anyway." He pointed across the intersecting side street. "There's a livery. They'll rent you a horse there."

"By geez! I'll do it!" Callahan stepped from the porch and started across the street.

Tucson called after him, "You better get a young horse, one that ain't been rode much. That's the best way to get acquainted if you ain't done much riding."

Tucson chuckled as the reporter disappeared in the livery barn. "Well, I got rid of him for a spell anyway. He like to wear me down with those questions." Tucson sobered suddenly, thinking, "Wouldn't it be funny as hell if Micky did turn somethin' up. The laugh would be on me."

Five minutes later he saw Callahan emerge from the livery astride a pot-barreled old horse that couldn't move much faster than a jog, the reporter's derby hat still riding at a jaunty angle on the red hair.

Tucson laughed, "He ain't so dumb at that. He had sense enough to get him a steady-goin' animal, 'stead of a pitchin' bronc. That dang Irish kid has got somethin'."

Doctor Perkins appeared in the doorway, talking to the sheriff at his shoulder. "I guess that's all there is to it, then," Perkins was saying. "You can't jail a man on self-defense."

"That's the way it looks to me," Poddy Cameron nodded. "Well, I'll stick around until the undertaker comes after the body. I'll see you later."

The doctor said good-bye to Tucson and moved off down the street. Tucson and the sheriff settled in a couple of chairs on the Gunsight porch. In a few minutes the undertaker's wagon arrived, and the body of Clem Hayden was taken away.

The sun was sinking far to the west now, touching the higher peaks of the distant Santa Madraza Range. A few lights commenced to appear in windows along Main Street. Tucson said, "So there ain't any telegraph service in this town, Poddy?"

Cameron chuckled. "I had to get rid of that crazy Irishman someway."

"I just got rid of him in another." Tucson told what had happened.

Cameron said, "No, it's not likely to produce anythin', but wouldn't it be funny if Callahan did turn up somethin'?" He changed the subject, "Tucson, I'd like to have you come out and meet the missus, have supper with us tonight, but I got to go out to Hayden's 8-Bar and break the news to his daughter."

49

"Mind if I ride with you?"

"I'll be dang glad to have you. Look here, I'll drift down to the office and tell Link to ride out and tell Martha — that's my wife — I won't be home to supper. You and me can eat in town."

"That's fine. While we're eating you can give me a line on the history of folks and things hereabouts."

"You gettin' interested?"

"I'm still wonderin'," Tucson said slowly, "why Clem Hayden didn't go through with his draw. Yeah, I'm a heap interested."

IV. Planned for a Rub-Out

Only a few faint crimson streakings showed above the mountains to the west by the time Poddy Cameron returned to the Gunsight Bar, after attending to various small businesses relative to his office, and rejoined Tucson. The two men went diagonally across the roadway to the Godwin Hotel at Main and Santa Fe Streets, entered the hotel bar through the Santa Fe Street entrance, stopped for a drink and then went on into the restaurant, situated on the lower floor at the rear of the hostelry.

They found a seat in one corner, where a waitress took their orders, after lighting a

50

kerosene lamp suspended in a bracket above the table. "The hotel has the best chow," Poddy Cameron was saying, "though the service ain't so speedy as you'll find at some of the other restaurants around town. Howsomever, I ain't in any hurry. I don't relish the task of breakin' the bad news to Clem Hayden's daughter."

Tucson nodded sympathetically. "Also," he pointed out, "it'll give us a chance to talk a mite."

"What brings you to Godwin, anyway?" Cameron asked.

"Chickens." Tucson smiled.

"Chickens?" Cameron looked puzzled.

Tucson explained. "Two years ago when I ran across you at the Cattlemen's Convention, in Tucson, you mentioned you figured to make a good penny in your old age, raisin' chickens. Am I right?"

The sheriff nodded. "I got a nice little place right now. Martha — that's my wife — supplies the eggs and hens to the hotel right along. She's makin' money."

"Well," Tucson continued, "after this spring's round-up was finished, there wasn't a heap to do on the 3-Bar-O. We've got a good crew, and things roll along whether us owners are there or not. Lullaby and Stony, like always, got itchin' feet. They insisted on draggin' me along to visit some friends down below the Border. Once we got into this country, I got to thinkin' of you ——"

"And chickens," Cameron put in.

"Right. I got an idea it might be a good idea to have some hens and roosters on the ranch. That would give us a change of diet. So I let Lullaby and Stony go their way, and I come over here to order enough hens to keep us in eggs at the ranch. Poddy, it's up to you to ship 'em. I'll give you my check ——"

"But, hell, Tucson, you didn't have to come 'way down here. You could order chickens up in your own country ——"

"Don't you think I like to say 'hello' to my friends, every so often," Tucson smiled. " 'Sides, I wanted to give you the business."

"That's dang nice, but you shouldn't ——"

"Forget it, Poddy. Now you give me some information."

"What do you want to know?"

"I'm interested in this Hayden killing. What's the story? Hayden one of the old residents of Cougar County?"

Cameron shook his head. "I reckon I better go back to the beginning when the 8-Bar outfit was owned by Clem Hayden's brother. Clem comes from California, from up around 'Frisco way. He was just a button when him and his father went through the gold rush days of '49. The old man died, but him and Clem had struck it rich. Clem was plenty wealthy at one time, and staked a brother to enough money to set up in the cattle business ——"

"The same bein' the 8-Bar, I suppose."

"C'rect. Well, the brother died and willed the outfit to Clem. Clem wasn't interested in cattle. He disposed of the stock, but never came here. Meanwhile he had married and had one daughter. A few years back he sold out his minin' interests in California, and plunged the money into real estate. I got this story from Nancy, Clem's daughter, a mighty nice girl. "Well, to make a long story short, that panic we had about that time wiped out Clem flatter'n a pancake. On top of that his wife died."

"The consequence bein'," Tucson commented, "that Hayden was through with California and decided to bring his daughter here and make a fresh start. Is that it?"

"You hit th' nail on the head. They arrived at the 8-Bar and started in to fix up the buildin's. Clem had saved a little money from the panic wreckage, and bought a coupla hundred head of cattle. Neither him nor Nancy knew anythin' about raisin'

53

stock, but they was ready to learn. Clem picked up knowledge fast. At least he knew how to handle a gun and had fought his way through the wild days on the Coast. He had a temper hotter'n explodin' dynamite, but he got along all right with other men. Anyway, there he was. The 8-Bar wasn't much of a spread, but it was a start. Clem was getting a grip on the cow business, when the trouble with Sheridan come up."

"What trouble was that?"

"Two years ago come next month, Clem came to me and said he wanted to buy a coupla hundred more cows and did I know of any for sale reasonable. I didn't, but a coupla days after I mentioned the matter to Sheridan. Sheridan allowed as he could sell a coupla hundred head, and went to see Clem Hayden. I don't know how much Clem was to pay on delivery, but the deal was made. The steers were to be driven to the 8-Bar the following spring."

At this point the waitress arrived at the table bearing platters of steaming food and cups of coffee. Tucson and Cameron started to eat. After a few minutes, Cameron continued.

"The day after the deal was made, Hayden was in town and got into an argument with some stranger that had dropped in.

What the argument was about, I don't know. Anyway, they went for their guns. Clem killed the stranger, but was bad wounded himself. He was forced to stay at Doc Perkins' place for six weeks before he could be moved."

"Who ran the 8-Bar in his absence?"

"Nancy. There wasn't much running to be done. The cows could take care of themselves. Nancy lived at the house ——"

"Alone?"

"Alone. The girl had grit. There wasn't any money to hire hands. She came in frequently to see her dad. . . . Less than a week after the shooting, while Hayden was laid up in bed, Quint Sheridan and some of his hands arrived at the 8-Bar driving the two hundred head of cows that wa'n't supposed to be delivered until spring."

"What was the idea?"

"That's what Nancy wanted to know. Quint explained he'd heard about her father's accident and thought it would be a neighborly turn to deliver the cows right to once. Clem wouldn't have to pay for 'em until spring as the agreement had said. Nancy wondered who'd take care of the stock. Sheridan said they'd take care of themselves. The upshot of the matter was that Nancy agreed to the delivery. Then and there, Quint and his men vented their Circle-Cross brand and rebranded with an 8-Bar ——"

"And, I suppose, the rebranded animals eventually disappeared," Tucson frowned.

"How did you know that?"

"I've been expecting something of the sort. Mostly, because I don't trust Quint Sheridan. From what I saw of him, I didn't like his looks."

"Me, neither. At the same time I don't know anythin' definite against him. He's got a hard-bitten crew, but, so far as I know, they're all law-abidin'. Get in fights now and then, but nothin' serious."

"Any rustlin' around here?"

Cameron shook his head. "No more'n you'd find on any other open range."

Tucson asked shrewdly, "Any doubt about those Circle-Cross animals actually being re-branded?"

"Not the slightest. I know what you're thinkin' — that Nancy, bein' green to the cow business, might have had somethin' slipped over on her. I went into that, explained carefully just how critters were branded, and so on. Nancy was mounted, watchin' careful. She was on the job, countin' the cows as they were branded and shunted to one side. She swears she saw

Sheridan and his men burn those cows."

Tucson forked a piece of steak into his mouth, nodded. Cameron went on, "By the following February, Hayden was able to ride again, and he immediate started scourin' his range to look over those cattle. Well, come calf-roundup, he couldn't locate more'n thirty-five head of those rebranded Circle-Cross animals. He swore a trick had been put over on him. I rode over his range, but there was nothing I could do. Sheridan had Nancy's receipt for two hundred branded cows, with the Circle-Cross vented. Well, Hayden borrowed some money and hired two hands ———"

"Where'd he borrow the money?"

Cameron shrugged his shoulders. "I don't know for sure. At the Godwin Bank, I suppose. . . . Anyway, him and his hands searched the hills. All the stock they located had come through with a natural increase, but one hundred sixty-five of those critters bought from Sheridan had just plumb disappeared."

"Did Hayden pay Sheridan for the two hundred head?"

"He was forced to. He swore he wouldn't pay, said Sheridan had swindled him, somehow, but couldn't say how. Sheridan had Nancy's receipt, took the matter to court, which ruled that Hayden had to pay. But that didn't shut Clem up. He talked plenty, every opportunity, about Circle-Cross cow-thieves. That brought about his first fight with Frame. Frame figured himself good with a gun. Some folks think Sheridan put Frame up to finishing Hayden. They met on the street one day, had some words. Both went for their hardware."

"And Hayden beat him to the shot, eh?"

"Hell!" Cameron laughed shortly. "Clem pumped a slug into Frame before Frame's iron had cleared leather. Frame got a smashed shoulder. There was another sheriff in office then — friend of Sheridan's. He stopped the fight. Sheridan was helpin' to run politics in this county, and had a drag with Judge Thomas. Hayden was arrested. However, there was witnesses to prove that it was a fair fight, so they couldn't hold Hayden. Nevertheless, Judge Thomas raked Hayden over the coals, bawled him out somethin' fierce for havin' a hot temper, and concluded by orderin' that Hayden wa'n't never again to wear his gun into town. Hayden was right mad, but until today he never violated that order."

Cameron went back to eating. The waitress brought more coffee and dried apple pie to the table. There weren't many further words spoken until coffee cups were drained and cigarettes rolled and lighted. Tucson was frowning thoughtfully. Finally he asked, "Have you any idea what Hayden went to your office for today?"

"Not the slightest. Link Dexter — my deputy — can't never think to ask questions. When he saw Hayden totin' an iron, he figured somethin' was up, but we don't know what. After Hayden left the office he had an encounter with Quint Sheridan. They was both mad, but nobody knows what was said, aside from Sheridan warnin' Hayden that Frame didn't want any trouble. After that, Hayden pulled out for the Gunsight Bar. You know what happened."

Tucson nodded slowly, then shook his head. "It's got me stopped," he confessed. "Look at the picture. Hayden was known to be hot tempered. He was a better shot than Frame, had proved that in their first fight. And yet, Frame came to the Gunsight looking for trouble. He tried to pretend he was peaceful by twice turning his back on Hayden. I saw that. Unless he had something pretty definite in mind, he'd never have turned his back on an armed enemy."

"Maybe," Cameron speculated, "he was counting on Hayden remembering the judge's order. Perhaps Frame figured that

Hayden would refuse to fight in view of that order."

Tucson shrugged lean shoulders. "I can't believe that was it. A hot-tempered man would forget such an order. In fact, Hayden did, momentarily. Frame taunted him into a fight, called him a name no white man will take. I saw Hayden's face. He was wild with rage. For a moment he forgot himself and started to draw. That's what Frame had been waiting for. Frame *knew*, somehow, *that no matter what happened, Hayden wouldn't pull trigger on him.* That accounts for Frame's nerve."

"I wish we had proof of that," Cameron growled. "I'd charge Frame with murder."

"We haven't absolute proof."

"What you basin' it all on?"

Tucson explained, "Frame's sudden nerve in picking a fight with a better gun who had already downed him, for one thing. Hayden's words, just before he died, for another."

"All Hayden said was, 'You — you know I ——'. Something like that, anyway. How can you make anything out of that, Tucson?"

"I can't for certain. But supposin' I finish those words? Supposin' Hayden started to say, 'You know I won't shoot' or 'You know I won't fight you' or something of the kind?"

Cameron gave a low whistle of surprise. "By Cripes! That sounds sort of logical. I'm going to question Frame and Sheridan ——"

"Go ahead," Tucson said ruefully. "But I warn you you won't get any place. The best you could bring against Frame would be a charge of disturbing the peace or something like that. So long as Frame and Sheridan keep their mouths shut, you wouldn't get any place. Bring Frame to trial and he'll go scot-free. There's witnesses that Hayden started his draw first. You can't convict a murderer on what he knows and won't tell — not unless somebody else learns the secret."

"Look here, Tucson," Cameron said eagerly. "Will you take a hand and see what you can learn?"

"I'll try. This business has got me interested."

"Good!"

"First, I want a line on the outfits hereabouts. What are they? Where are they situated?"

"Well, I reckon the best holdin's is the Hayden 8-Bar. The buildin's are situated about fifteen miles due west of Godwin, in the foothills of the Santa Madraza Mountains. The 8-Bar south line runs right to the

Mex Border, parallels it. There's a four strand barb wire fence along that south line. You see, Clem's brother, when he was alive, had a heap of trouble with Mexican cattle thieves who used to come raidin' over the Border. 'Bout that time, barb wire come in and Clem's brother strung a fence. I don't know's it helped much. Wire's easy to cut. Anyway, when Clem came here he put that fence in good repair again."

"How about water on the 8-Bar?"

"Plenty of it. The Sereno River runs right through the holdin's, after headin' up in the Santa Madrazas, curves south when it nears Godwin, passes my chicken farm, then sort of peters out in the semi-desert country east of town. Even in the driest spells, the 8-Bar had plenty water for its stock."

"What sort of an outfit has Quint Sheridan got?"

"Sheridan's Circle-Cross is twenty miles north of here. It's a good spread. Sheridan makes a nice sum out of beef ——"

"How about his water?"

"You figurin' Sheridan is trying to ruin Hayden to get water?"

"I wouldn't say for sure, but I got a hunch that Sheridan has planned things for a rub-out of the 8-Bar. That's just hunch, though."

"Mebbe so. But it wouldn't be for water.

You see the White Snake River borders north on Sheridan's holdin's. He's got a couple of good water holes besides. The White Snake also supplies Heine Schultz' Bearpaw Ranch, to the east of the Circle-Cross and eighteen miles northeast of Godwin."

"What kind of a man is Schultz?"

"Old German. Bachelor. Sort of crusty, but honest, I figure."

"Big outfit?"

"Just so-so. The Circle-Cross is the biggest in point of stock; the 8-Bar the biggest accordin' to land holdin's, though the 8-Bar hasn't many cows. I'd say offhand, the 8-Bar has pro'bly six hundred head on the range at present. That takes in the first two hundred head Hayden bought, natural increases, and a few odd bunches he's purchased from time to time, includin' the thirty-five head left from the Sheridan buy. Hayden never sold more'n enough beef stock than he needed to get along, though I think he figured to do some shippin' this comin' fall."

"What other outfits are there?"

"Not many to speak of. Small timers just trying to get a start with a few head. They're scattered around northerly of here. There's the Rafter-K, the Rocking-N, the Slash-O-

Slash and two or three others that will pro'bly sell out and pass on before long. The ND-Connected is 'way east o' here; just another hide-in-a-pot outfit. And then —" pridefully, "— there's my chicken ranch and buildin's, three miles southeast of Godwin."

"What's your brand?" Tucson smiled.

"I been thinkin' of brandin' the Cacklin'-C," Cameron said solemnly, "but I ain't bought any stamp irons as yet. Martha — that's my wife — sort of objects to th' odor of burnin' feathers."

Tucson suggested gravely, "You'd better just ear-mark 'em, Poddy."

"I will if I can save any from some of them Mex kids that come hangin' around. They get to tellin' how hungry they get for hen flesh and Martha — that's my wife — she's so soft-hearted she's always givin' 'em away."

"Is there much of a Mexican settlement in Godwin?"

"Quite a few families livin' near the cattle pens. They get jobs sometimes, when the outfits farther north drive down at beef-shippin' time. You watch, if you're here, you'll see Godwin lookin' like a bustlin' metropolis in the fall."

"How do the Mexes live the rest of the year?"

Cameron shrugged. "Pro'bly off'n their relatives in Herrero."

"Herrero?"

"Mexican settlement," Cameron explained. "Eight miles due south of Godwin, just t'other side of the Border Line. It's supposed to be the port of entry for this neck of the woods, but I never see much come through. Sort of a tough town, with as many *Americanos* as Mexes livin' there. It's the *Americanos* that make it tough. Howsomever, I can't kick. They don't worry us none."

"No, I reckon we got other things to bother us, Poddy."

Cameron sighed. "Yep. We got to get movin' if I'm to break the sad news to Nancy Hayden tonight. Where's your hawss?"

"Across the street, in the livery. I left him there for a rubdown and a feed."

Cameron nodded. "I'll drift down the street to my office, and get right back. By the time you're saddled up, I'll be with you."

The two men rose, paid for the suppers, and left the hotel restaurant. It was nearly fifteen minutes later that Cameron found Tucson, mounted in front of the livery, waiting for him. The street was dark, but in the glow cast from lighted windows Tucson saw that the sheriff had buckled on a second belt and gun.

"No," Cameron explained, "I'm not expecting any trouble along the way. These are Hayden's things. I stopped at the undertaker's and got the belt and holster. Figured to leave 'em in my safe, then I got to thinking, if Nancy felt like talkin', I'd question her about 'em."

"How do you mean?"

"Find out if she knows of any reason for her father going to town armed, see if she knows why he wouldn't shoot ——

"I figured to ask her those questions myself, if possible."

"I reckon. Besides, the gun's her property now. I might just as well turn it over to her. She might even want to wear it; I doubt there's any extra weapons at the 8-Bar. She might need it."

The two men spoke to their horses and moved off in the darkness, heading their mounts on the rutted trail running due west from town.

V. A Head for Clouting

Meanwhile, the afternoon had brought adventures to Micky Callahan. The little Irish reporter had left town, riding a fat bay mare he'd procured at the livery, fully determined not to lose sight of the cowhand Tucson had pointed out for him to follow. Riding, at first, seemed to Micky to be a very simple matter. The livery man had shortened the stirrups to fit the reporter, and Micky was commencing to think he'd been cut out for a bronco-buster. The sole deterrent to that idea, Micky finally conceded, lay in the fact he couldn't even get any speed out of the old horse.

At regular intervals he doggedly jiggled the reins, at which time the mare would break into something that only vaguely resembled a gallop. At the western outskirts of the town he clattered across the plank bridge covering the Sereno River where it swung south of Godwin; but this time the indolent animal had dropped to a steady, jouncing jog, from which it was extremely difficult to rouse her.

Before he was five miles out of town, Micky had lost sight of the rider he was following. He became disgusted with himself, and tried to urge the horse into a faster gait.

He wished now he'd taken the pair of spurred boots the livery man had offered to lend him.

The sun was still hot, though swinging farther to the west. Perspiration ran in a steady stream from beneath the derby hat. Five miles more passed. He was following the beaten trail through rolling grass country. Here and there grew clumps of prickly pear and mesquite. Up hill and down hill, the bay mare plodded on. Once, topping a rise of ground, Micky caught sight of the man he was after, riding far to Micky's left.

"I guess he must have decided he didn't want to follow this road any more," Micky pondered. "Lucky I caught sight of him. Well, get along, Lightning, we got to catch up and interview that guy."

He turned the horse from the trail, dipped down into a hollow, then climbed the next slope, always trying to urge his mount to greater speed. It was abruptly borne in upon the Irishman that that portion of his anatomy upon which he sat had become rather stiff and sore. The inner side of his thighs felt chafed. Then his legs commenced to ache.

"I'll be damned if riding isn't tough on a geezer," he groaned. "Horse, I wish you were just about half the width you are."

The bay mare seemed to be getting broader every minute as Micky's legs grew stiffer and stiffer. A sudden thought struck him, "I wonder if Tucson was playing a joke on me. Come to think of it, I don't see any particular reason for following that cowboy. I wonder just where he is now."

Topping another rise of land, Micky again caught sight of his man. The rider had slowed down and seemed to be riding aimlessly about the range.

"Looks to me like he was looking for somebody," Micky mused. He pulled to a halt and waited. The rider had swung around and was coming toward Micky. Suddenly he turned his pony and swung off to the left, heading for a long, high ridge topped with thick brush. At the bottom of the ridge grew a thick clump of cottonwood trees. The cottonwoods seemed to be the rider's destination.

Aching muscles were forgotten now, as Micky became more interested. He started to head his horse toward the cottonwoods, then changed his mind. "I figure it might be a good idea to climb up the other side of that ridge. Once I reach the top, perhaps I could find a place where I could look down on that gazabo and see what he's up to."

The old mare must have figured she was

headed home, for once Micky had swung abruptly to the left, she broke into a fast lope, that jounced every nerve in the runty Irishman's body. Gamely he hung on, reached the lower end of the ridge. Here he dismounted, when the mare showed no inclination to make a climb.

For a moment Micky staggered and nearly fell. His legs were made of wood — very painful, aching wood. They were so stiff he could scarcely move at first. Finally the blood commenced to flow, and Micky started up the side of the ridge on foot, after tethering the bay mare to a mesquite bush.

Foot by foot he ascended to the top. Once, glancing off toward the mountains to the right, he saw a small cluster of buildings nestling among the foothills, probably six or seven miles distant. But houses had small place in Micky's mind now.

At the top of the ridge he paused in the brush. Below him stretched rolling, grass-covered hills. The rider he'd been following wasn't to be seen now, but a short distance to the left, and below, Micky caught a slight movement among a bunch of cottonwood trees. He heard a horse nicker.

Micky started to move rapidly along the top of the ridge, the thick brush tearing at his clothing and scratching his face and hands. Within five minutes he was at a point where he could see the foot of the ridge. He heard voices.

A man was saying, ". . . and, dammit, Tate, it's just luck I come over this way. All Hayden had said was that he left you roped and tied down out here some place. Lucky I spotted your bronc."

Only a confused, thick mumbling reached Micky's ears in reply. Then the words came a little clearer. "Can't make much noise with a gag in my jaws. Damn that ol' Hayden!"

"He's already damned. Frame killed him."

What followed next, Micky couldn't hear. He shifted position, and some hundred feet below he made out, through the brush, the form of a man stretched full length on the earth. The rider Micky had followed was busily engaged in cutting the loops of rope lariat with which the man on the ground had been bound.

"Cripes! He shore tied you up proper."

"God! I was helpless. He roped me outta my saddle. That knocked me cold for a minute. When I come to I was like this — hey, get them piggin' strings he put around my ankles, will you?"

It was commencing to grow dark now. Micky leaned closer to hear better. The movement started a small rock to rolling. It went tumbling down the side of the ridge. It wasn't a large rock, and it made very little noise, so Micky never dreamed that to the range-trained ear it would mean anything significant. There was a dead silence below for a few minutes, then the little Irish reporter heard one of the men say, "Must be a coyote nosin' around up there."

Silently, Micky congratulated himself on the fact that the men below had been deceived by the slight disturbance. However, from that point on, they talked in lowered tones. A short time later the last bonds were removed from the man on the earth and he rose to his feet and mounted stiffly behind the other cowpuncher. A minute later, Mickey saw the horse with its double burden emerge into open country and move in a southerly direction, flanking the ridge, for some quarter of a mile. Here, the man seated behind the saddle dismounted and caught a second horse Micky hadn't noticed before. The animal was grazing idly, with its reins dragging, and made no effort to get away.

Micky watched the two men turn their ponies and come back, riding past below him. In a short time they had passed out of sight around the end of the long ridge.

Micky pondered. "I guess I'll be wise and stay right here for a while, until those guys get some distance away. There's no use letting them know I was spying on 'em. Gosh! I guess Tucson Smith had the right hunch when he sent me to tail that cowboy. I'll have something to report when I get back to town, and darn Tucson if he doesn't give me a story on what it all means. . . . I wonder if Tucson came here on the same thing that brought me. . . ."

The reporter settled to a comfortable sitting position to wait a little while longer before descending the ridge. He was realizing now that it felt pretty good to stretch his legs and rest on soft earth rather than in a hard, leather saddle. Somehow, it never occurred to Micky that the riders he'd seen might notice his hired horse, tethered below, at the bottom of the ridge.

Nor did he hear the soft movements at his rear as the two men silently climbed the side of the ridge. If his ear did note a rasping through the brush now and then — a soft rasping that came ever nearer — Micky laid it to the movements of birds or ground squirrels or rabbits, of which he had noticed many. In fact, it never occurred to Micky that he was in any danger.

And then, abruptly, it happened. Micky

heard a soft step at his rear. Startled, he half turned but before he could prevent the catastrophe a crushing blow smashed through the derby hat and terminated with no little force against Micky's head. The undersized reporter groaned once, and wilted to the earth.

The two men Micky had been watching but a short time before, rose to full length in the brush. One of them said, laconically, "You got him, Butch."

"I got him plenty," Butch Grier nodded with satisfaction. He was a heavy shouldered man with brutal features and small, piggish eyes. He still held, in his right hand, the weapon whose heavy barrel had crashed the little reporter into insensibility. "Shall I finish him, Tate?"

Tate Scorpio frowned. He was lean and lithe, with swarthy features, beady eyes and long black mustaches. Like his companion, he wore cowman's overalls, riding boots, and a worn sombrero. He didn't have any cartridge belt or gun, though. Red weals on his wrists still attested the bonds that had held him captive until released by Butch Grier.

Scorpio speculatively fingered the crimson bandanna at his throat. "We ought to finish the spyin', son," he said at last, "but it might

74

not be good policy. You know who he is?"

"Name's Callahan. After Joe rubbed out Hayden, this Callahan admitted to bein' a newspaper reporter. He can ask questions faster'n you can thumb a gun."

"Wonder how come he was trailin' us."

"We ain't certain he was. Pro'bly, bein' nosey, he just happened to blunder out here. We don't know how much he saw, of course, but it might be safest to put him out of the way."

"I don't reckon so," Scorpio shook his head. "That was a hired, livery horse. If he don't show up, there's goin' to be a search made. Right now we don't want too much fuss stirred up. If he was some local cowhand, I'd say go ahead, but we don't want his newspaper nosin' around here — not right now. Newspapers are hell for snoopin' — and his bosses might stir up somethin' they didn't intend to. Best let him lay. We'll get out of here. I want to get after that gun. You say Poddy Cameron took charge of it?"

"Yes."

"What did Quint do when he heard the bad news from Hayden?"

"Hell! You know how Sheridan is. He won't be greetin' you with no anniversary cake and flowers."

"I expected that. But what did he do?"

75

"Sent Frame to rub-out Hayden — as I explained. Then he sent Gabby Emmett ridin' to Herrero ——"

"What for?"

"I dunno. You know how Sheridan is. He won't tell his plans. He was so mad I didn't feel like gettin' inquisitive. My guess is that Quint looks for trouble and sent Gabby to hire a coupla good gun-throwers. There's a feller named Tucson Smith in town ——"

Tate Scorpio said suddenly, "Cripes A'mighty!"

"You know this Smith?"

"I know of him. He's poison. What in time brings him here at a time like this?"

"You tell me and I'll tell you. He's a friend of Cameron's."

Scorpio swore long and bitterly.

Butch Grier went on. "Anyway, that's all I can tell you. Quint sent me out to look for you, told me not to come back until I'd found you. He said he'd be around town for a spell, but figured to leave for the Circle-Cross right after supper. You're to go right to the Circle-Cross."

"I ain't so sure that I will," Scorpio growled. "Quint won't be good-natured nohow. If I can return with that gun, he'll feel better. I got an idea I can get it. You're going to help."

"Me, how?"

"C'mon, let's get out of here. This hombre won't be out so much longer. We'll talk while we're headin' for town."

The two men cast a last look at the unconscious Callahan, then started to leave. The dying rays of the sun were casting a crimson light through the brush and reflecting redly on Micky's unconscious features. Scorpio's and Grier's movements died away. A short time later they reached the foot of the ridge, mounted and headed toward town.

The sun dropped behind the Santa Madraza Range. Dusk set in. It was almost dark when Micky Callahan moaned, then opened his eyes. For a moment he lay prone, staring, puzzledly, at the darkening sky above. Then recollection came back with a rush. He swore softly and came to a sitting position.

His lips felt dry and cracked, his mouth parched. His head ached as though a battery of cannon were being exploded nearby. His fingers felt tenderly of the lump on his head. It felt as though it had bled a trifle, the skin was broken slightly.

Micky groaned. "I always felt I had a nose for news — but this is the first time I ever figured I had a good head for cloutin'. The dirty spalpeens! Or was there more'n one? I been thinking it was those two I was watching, but how would they know I was up here? Whoever done it, he must have used a shillalah."

Micky looked around for his derby hat. It lay to one side, on the earth, with the top crushed in. Micky shook his head sadly. "Tucson told me I should get rid of that bonnet. Maybe, at that, it's a good thing I had it on. That wallop might have cracked my skull, otherwise. Well, it served its purpose, but it's no good any more. I'll let it lay."

Painfully, he staggered to his feet and descended the hill. It was pitch dark by the time he found his horse. Stiffly, reluctantly, he climbed into the saddle and started for Godwin. The old bay mare was willing to take him in the right direction, but feeling that the horse was headed wrong, Micky kept pulling it around. In a short time he was lost in the darkness, didn't know where he was.

For fifteen minutes more he wandered this way and that, always jerking the old mare off the course it wanted to take. Finally, as the mare wearily climbed a rise of land, Micky spotted a light in the distance.

"There," he growled at the mare, "I knew I had the right direction for Godwin. Get along now."

Horse and rider dipped down a long slope. The top of another hill brought the light closer. Micky worked the stiffness out of his legs sufficiently to kick the old mare in the ribs. The animal broke into a reluctant trot.

It wasn't until sometime later, when he had drawn closer, that Micky discovered he was approaching a group of ranch buildings, rather than the outskirts of Godwin.

"Oh, well," he growled philosophically, "there ought to be somebody can give me a drink and set me on the right road."

The mare, by this time sensing a stable and food, broke into a more spirited jog.

VI. GUN VALUE

Callahan pulled the mare to a walk as he passed a frame-and-adobe ranch house, surrounded by tall cottonwoods. At the back of the house was a light in what Callahan judged to be the kitchen. Through an open window he could hear a girl's voice, singing.

"Sure, and if she looks anything like her voice, she's a howlin' beauty," the reporter meditated, forgetting for a moment the throbbing of his bruised head. He started to turn the mare toward the back of the house, then, suddenly remembering his bedraggled appearance, kept on toward another light that shone farther on in what proved later to be the bunkhouse.

In the vicinity of the bunkhouse, Callahan saw corrals, a barn, horse shelter, a blacksmith shop. Somewhere out of the night, with each vagrant breeze, came the dolorous clanking of a windmill. The reporter pulled to a stop a short distance from the bunkhouse. When he dismounted, his legs were so stiff that he nearly fell.

A cowhand's form was silhouetted against the light from the open bunkhouse door, then a voice, "That you, Clem?"

Before Callahan could reply a second form joined the first, saying, "Nancy's been holdin' supper for you, Clem. What kept you?"

The reporter said, "No, this ain't Clem. The name's Callahan — Micky Callahan ____"

"Who?" came simultaneously from the two punchers.

Micky repeated his name, adding, "I'm lost. I'd like about a gallon of water and information that will get me to Godwin."

One of the cowpunchers muttered, "I thought it was Clem."

At the moment the name held no significance for Callahan. He was too engrossed in his own miseries.

The other puncher came striding out from the bunkhouse, saying genially, "Sure, stranger, we'll water you — and eat you, too. You're in time for chow. And we'll set you on the right road."

He was rejoined by his companion who said, "Huh, shorthorn," as Micky came half-staggering into the rectangle of light from the open doorway, leading his hired mare.

"Hey, what happened to you, tenderfoot?" the companion asked suddenly, taking in Micky's condition, clothing and manner.

"Damn near everything!" Micky exploded suddenly. He paused, deciding not to say too much. "I hired this horse for a ride, then the damn beast dumped me off on my head. On top of that I got lost."

The punchers chuckled sympathetically. One of them said, "Here, I'll unsaddle yore bronc. You go on in the bunkhouse with Pete."

At that moment a girl's voice hailed from the back door of the ranch house, "Is that you, Dad?"

The puncher known as Pete raised his voice in reply, "No, it ain't. It's a lost shorthorn that just wandered in. He looks

81

sort of tuckered."

"Oh, that's too bad," the girl called through the night. "Take care of him, boys. Put up his horse — or did he have a horse?"

"Stew is unsaddlin' it now," Pete answered.

"That's good," the girl's voice again. "Take care of him. I'll bring some food down in a few minutes."

The puncher known as Stew disappeared in the direction of the corrals with the horse. Pete took Micky's arm and escorted him into the bunkhouse where the little reporter dropped wearily on a chair. Pete brought a dipper of cool water. Micky gulped it down, asked for a second dipper, which was supplied to him. Micky's head was aching worse than ever now. He put one hand up to it. Pete insisted on having a look, then he gazed queerly at Micky, saying,

"All right, mister, mebbe bein' dumped by your horse done this, but it shore looks to me like somebody'd creased you with a forty-five barrel."

"It felt like a barrel when it landed," Micky stated with unconscious humor. "Like a barrel of coal."

"Oh, when it landed . . ." Pete didn't finish what he intended to say, but continued

82

to squint puzzledly at Micky. Micky closed his eyes and leaned back against the wall.

Stew returned from corraling the bay mare. Some low words passed between the two punchers, they exchanged perplexed glances. There was a sound at the door and a girl stepped inside bearing a bucket of coffee and various dishes stacked carefully in a basket.

"No use you boys waiting for Dad to get back," she said cheerfully, glancing at Callahan. "You go ahead and eat."

Callahan heard her voice and opened his eyes. He staggered to his feet and made a shaky bow. A look of pity swept across the girl's dark eyes.

Pete said, "He says his name is Callahan."

"Never mind his name," the girl said. "No use trying to talk now. You men eat first. I'll be back later."

She was a tall girl, unusually tall, with great ropes of heavy, cornsilk hair twisted in braids about her head. Her shoulders were broad. She looked strong, capable; her lips were full, the jaw firm. Despite his condition, Callahan decided then and there that she was the most beautiful thing he'd ever encountered. The girl's skin was a creamy tan, pulsating with the red blood of vigorous health.

Callahan never was sure what she wore that night. Some sort of gingham dress, with sleeves rolled to the elbows; an apron, a bit of white, low at the slender throat. And then, before he had time to say a word, she had departed. Micky dropped back into his chair.

Pete was distributing plates, cups and food on the table, pouring coffee. He drew up a chair for Micky, saying, "C'mon, Callahan, throw some of this hot Java into your breadbasket. It'll make you feel a heap better."

Micky walked stiffly to the chair, dropped into it. Eventually he commenced to eat. The hot coffee went a long way toward reviving his spirits. His head commenced to feel better. The two punchers ate in silence, waiting until their guest felt more like talking.

Finally, when Micky had had a second cup of coffee and drew out a package of *Sweet Caporal* cigarettes, which he offered to his hosts (and which were declined in favor of the Bull Durham variety) Micky asked, "Just where am I, anyway?"

Pete looked up with a quick smile, "Gettin' some of your pep back, eh, Callahan? . . . Why, you're in the bunkhouse of the 8-Bar Ranch. I'm Pete Blair. This ranny across from you is Stew Trumbull. That's an abbreviation for Stewart and has nothing to do with his alcoholic capacity."

"Who was that girl?" Micky asked next, after shaking hands with the two men and giving his own first name.

Pete's face stiffened as did Stew's. Pete said, a trifle stiffly, "That's Clem Hayden's daughter — Nancy."

Something clicked in Micky's mind. He looked from one to the other, seeing only the unsmiling faces of two lean, bronzed cowpunchers — typical, loyal sons of the range. Micky said slowly, "What — name — did — you — say?"

Pete said belligerently, "Nancy. What about it?"

Callahan shook his head. "No, I mean — well — did I understand you to say Clem Hayden?"

Stew Trumbull nodded. "You heard Pete correct." And a minute later, "Why? What's wrong?"

Callahan considered, then said quietly, "Any relation to the Hayden that was killed this afternoon?"

There ensued a moment's tense silence. Abruptly, supper utensils clattered to the table. Stew and Pete burst into excited exclamations, questions. They were both on their feet now. Both were shouting angrily

85

at Micky.

Micky said, "I'm telling you. I was there. Yes, the name was Hayden. Yes, Clem Hayden. Fellow by the name of Frame shot him ———"

"Joe Frame?" Stew snapped.

"That's the name," Micky nodded. The two punchers sank slowly to their chairs. Micky told the story from start to finish, describing the parties concerned to his unbelieving audience.

"This," Stew Trumbull exploded, "is one hell of a note."

"I don't see why nobody's been to bring the news."

Micky said, "Gosh, I never dreamed that Hayden's family wouldn't know about it. I heard the sheriff say he was going to ride out and break the news."

"He'll pro'bly be here this evenin' then," Trumbull said heavily. "You see, we're quite a way out from town. Nobody else would want the job. It probably took him some time to see the undertaker and coroner and ———"

"Say," Pete burst in, "how come Clem was carrying his gun? He hasn't carried it ———"

"That's right," excitedly from Stew. "None of us have. You see ———" to Callahan, "— this outfit is awful shy of money. We haven't had the price of cartridges. Even food's been shy. Pro'bly on your account Nancy cooked up better than usual tonight. It's been beans right along ——"

"Nancy!" Peter groaned suddenly.

He and Stew eyed each other aghast. Stew said at last, "Somebody's got to tell her. We can't wait until the sheriff gets here."

"I don't want the job," from Pete.

"Look here," Stew said almost savagely to Callahan. "You said you were in Godwin in your capacity as a reporter for a paper. Don't reporters sometimes have to break sad news and things like that?"

Micky nodded. He didn't want the job either. "All right," he consented, "I'll do it if you say so, but I'm tellin' you frankly it's your job. I'm a stranger to Nancy Hayden. You men are her friends. She looked true blue to me, like a thoroughbred. But you know her. I don't. Maybe she'll take it with a stiff upper lip. Maybe she'll break down. I don't know. I've seen all kinds go to pieces under such news. All right, if she does break down, who do you think she'd rather have there — me, or her friends?"

"By Cripes! You're right, Callahan," Pete said. "I don't reckon she'll break down — but, Stew, it's our job. We're pretty small sidewinders if we can't do a duty for a

friend. I'll go."

"I'll go with you," Stew said loyally.

"That's a good idea," Callahan nodded.

Reluctantly, the two men started for the door. Pete glanced back, over his shoulder. "Callahan," he said slowly, "I think you're all right, but I'm not taking any chances. You didn't get that bump on your head from bein' thrun off'n your hawss. It's your business if you don't want to throw a straight loop, but you be here when we come back or I'll think you know more about this business than you've put in words. Savvy?"

"I savvy," Micky nodded quietly. "I'll be here when you get back."

He heard their departing footsteps on the earth, heard them trying, futilely, to plan a way to "break it gently." The footsteps died away. He heard the back door of the house open, close. Then silence. . . .

Stew and Pete weren't gone more than fifteen minutes. They came back to the bunkhouse looking weary and drawn. Neither one said anything as he dropped despondently into a chair. An alarm clock ticked loudly in one corner.

Finally, Micky said, "It was a tough job."

"It was a tough job," Stew echoed.

"How'd she take it?" Micky asked.

"Right on the chin. It shook her up a

heap, but she didn't falter. There was nary a tear," Pete said.

"We told her," Stew put in, "that Poddy Cameron was on the way. We offered to stay until he came, but she wanted to be by herself. She left us to go into the bedroom. . . ." He swore low and steadily under his breath, then, "First thing Poddy gets here I'm goin' to borrow the price of a box of forty-fives."

"And then?" Micky asked.

"I'm figuring to get Joe Frame," Stew stated flatly.

Pete didn't say anything. None of the men talked for a long time. Later, they heard Tucson and the sheriff riding into the ranch yard. . . .

Two riders trotted their ponies along at a leisurely gait on the trail running from Godwin to the 8-Bar Ranch. They were known as Sheepface Bogart and Trace Manning. Both of them were unshaven individuals with filthy clothing, hard eyes, and holsters, equipped with six-shooters. They laid claim to being cowpunchers but no one had ever known them to work at that occupation. Robbery and killing — provided there wasn't too much risk involved — was more in their line.

The moon wasn't up yet; the stars gave faint light. Only the soft *clop-clopping* of hoofs on dusty earth broke the silence. Finally, Trace Manning spoke, peering ahead through the darkness, "Think we should slow down a mite, Sheepface? We don't want to get too close to the sheriff and that other hombre. They might hear us follerin' 'em."

The two slowed pace a trifle. Manning went on, "I'd like to know the inside of this job. Why don't you come across?"

Sheepface said irritatedly, "You know as much as I do. I ain't holdin' out on you. All's I know that Circle-Cross waddy, Gabby Emmett, come thunderin' into Herrero this afternoon. After seein' the big boss, he left as fast as he come. Later the boss sent for me and says Quint Sheridan has a job for me and another man. You bein' a pal, I picks you."

"Yeah, but what does Sheridan want us for?"

"Exactly what Emmett told us when we met him in Godwin."

"I wish we could have talked to Sheridan hisself."

"Sheridan had left for the Circle-Cross. Emmett left as soon as he talked to us. There's somethin' big afloat, but Sheridan

90

don't want himself or none of his hands to look like they had a hand in it. That's why we're hired."

"Sounds batty to me," Manning growled. "Sheridan payin' us a hundred bucks each just to shadow the sheriff and see what he does with that gun. That's two hundred dollars!"

"I been thinkin' of that."

"And we don't have to even swipe the gun?"

"Nope. Sheridan just wants to know what's done with it. He figured we'd do our shadowin' around town, but Emmett said he didn't plan on Poddy Cameron leavin' town with the gun in his possession."

"Why is the gun so dam' important?"

"I'd like to know that myself. You heard what Gabby Emmett said as well as I. The gun was took off'n that old Hayden hombre that Frame killed this afternoon. If you ask me it's some sort of evidence against Frame — but what that evidence is, I don't know. All's we got to do is tell Sheridan what becomes of the gun. Then Sheridan will get it himself when the right time comes."

"Two hundred bucks is a heap of *dinero* for tailin' a gun, Sheepface."

"I been thinkin' that."

"Look, Sheepface, if Sheridan will pay all

that money just to have a gun follered, what do you think he'd pay for the gun itself?"

"I been thinkin' of that too."

"You mean," eagerly, "that you and me get the gun and sell it to Sheridan?"

"That's what. At our own price."

"Sheepface, you got a head on you."

The two riders moved along, meditating on their own shrewdness. . . .

VII. BULLETS FOR SIDEWINDIN' BUCKAROOS

It must have been about nine o'clock when Tucson and Sheriff Cameron arrived at the 8-Bar Ranch. A hail greeted them from the bunkhouse. The two men tethered their ponies outside the door, and went inside to be greeted by Pete, Stew and, to their surprise, Micky Callahan. Cameron introduced Tucson to the two cowboys.

Tucson said, "Howcome you're here, Micky?"

Cameron was saying at the same time to Pete and Stew, "Cowboys, I've got some bad news for you."

"We already got it," from Pete.

Stew gestured moodily toward the battered Micky. "He told us."

Cameron gave vent to a long sigh of relief. "Thank God! I won't have that to go through with. . . . How'd she take it?"

"I never saw anythin' finer," Pete said earnestly. "That girl's got the steadiest nerves I ever see."

"You'll have to see her, though, Poddy," from Stew. "She asked particular for us to tell you to see her as soon as you arrived."

"I'll get right to it. I want to talk to her, of course. I'm figurin' to have her come back with me and stay with Martha — that's my wife — until after the funeral. I'm a mite late gettin' here, but I made all arrangements, tentative, with the undertaker, before we left. I thought I'd save her that much. She can make any changes tomorrow that she may think necessary."

"What I don't understand," Stew said, "is how he happened to be carryin' his gun — and why he didn't go through with his draw — anyway, that's the way we got the story from Callahan."

Tucson broke in, "I reckon Micky gave you the story. He saw as much as I did."

"I brought his gun and belt along with me," Cameron nodded. "They're hangin' on my saddle-horn, outside. Started out wearin' the belt, but I'm a heap stouter than Clem was. I had the buckle in the last

93

notch. 'Bout three miles out of town I commenced to feel like my middle was sawed in half, so I took it off ——"

He broke off, listening to Micky explaining things to Tucson. ". . . and I just wandered in here," the Irishman was saying. "Sure, and the way I was feeling, any place to get off that damn horse looked like home, sweet home to me."

"But what happened to you? You looked banged up. Where's that egg-shaped hat?"

"Tucson," Micky said ruefully, "when you sent me following that cowboy, you certainly sent me into something. How did you know —— ?"

"Huh?" Tucson looked startled. "How did I know what?"

"Aw, you know what I mean. That guy meant news."

"Well, *that's* news to *me!*" Tucson exclaimed.

"I suppose it's news to you that I got slammed over the head," Micky exclaimed irritatedly.

"It sure is." Tucson couldn't suppress a smile.

Callahan looked at Tucson as though he didn't believe him. "All right, I'll give you the story. If you already know it and are playing a joke on me, it may be funny to you, but it's dang serious to me. I told these fellows —" indicating Stew and Pete, "— that I'd fallen off of my horse, but I could see the story didn't go down. Here's what happened after you sent me to tailing that fellow, Tucson. . . ."

From that point on, Micky told everything that had happened, up to and including his arrival at the 8-Bar and the breaking of the news of Clem Hayden's death.

Tucson and the others looked serious when the reporter had finished his tale. Tucson said, "Are you sure the two fellows you saw are the ones that knocked you out?"

"Not at all," from Micky. "I can't even see why they should have a grudge against me."

"Would you know them again if you saw them?"

"I think so."

"And one of 'em was tied up, eh?" Tucson said.

"Like a mummy in a shroud," Micky nodded.

"There's somethin' funny afoot," Cameron growled. "We'll talk about it later. I got to go up and offer my condolences to Miss Nancy. Gosh, how I hate it. Tucson, come along with me, will you? It'll make an extra person to do the talking. Ten to one, seein' you saw her father die, she'll want to see you."

Tucson winced. "If that killing proves to be murder, I'll never forgive myself for not trying to stop it —"

"Shucks!" Pete said. "It wa'n't your fight. You're a stranger. Don't ever let that worry you, Tucson. Stew and me have heard a heap about you and your two pards, Stony and Lullaby. We know you're all right. If there is anything crooked about this business, we're mighty glad you're here. The 8-Bar has been bucking a stiff game from the start, and it's reached a point now where we're flat broke. Us cowhands can't even spare the cash for cartridges, if we did have somethin' definite to fight against."

"You can quit worrying about that," Tucson said grimly. "I've got a hunch this affair is going to develop into plenty of action, and I'm aimin' to see that there'll be enough ca'tridges for you cowhands. And men too. If needful I'm willin' to call the whole 3-Bar-O crew down here. Lullaby and Stony will be showin' up before long."

"Which same means," Poddy Cameron put in, "that there'll be plenty hot bullets headin' for any sidewindin' buckaroos with crooked ideas."

Tucson smiled slightly. "Mebbe we better not talk until there's somethin' to talk about. . . . C'mon, Poddy. Let's go see Miss Hayden."

Outside the bunkhouse, Cameron stopped only long enough to lift from his saddle Clem Hayden's belt and holstered gun, then the two men headed up toward the ranch house, arrived and knocked at the door. Nancy answered the door and invited the two men in. Cameron, gulping a good deal, introduced Tucson. Nancy led the men into the main room of the ranch house where a lamp burned.

It was a sparsely furnished room, but the chairs were comfortable. The embers of a dying fire glowed in the fireplace. Animal skins and Indian rugs adorned the walls and floor.

The first few minutes were awkward. Cameron seemed scarcely to know what to say. Tucson put in a few words at the right moments. He'd been watching the girl closely and Nancy Hayden was growing in his admiration. The girl was dry-eyed; there were no outward signs that she had given in to her grief. Now and then a trace of bitterness showed about her lips.

Tucson thought, Maybe she'll break later, but she's holding out on sheer nerve right now. The girl's no weakling. She's got strength of character, if I ever saw it.

"I been thinkin'," Cameron said, "that we better hitch up your wagon, Nancy. Until after the fune— until after things are sort of finished up — y'know what I mean — you better come home with me and let Martha — that's my wife — take care of you. We got an extra room."

The girl smiled wanly. "You never forget to add the *that's my wife,* do you, Sheriff Cameron?"

Cameron looked puzzled. "Well, she is my wife."

"And I'll be more than glad to go back and stay with Mrs. Cameron," the girl went on. "It's good of you ——"

"Aw, shucks, we're glad to have you. We want to help out. Tucson, here, wants to help too. . . . Well, I guess we'd better go, Nancy. We'll be down to the bunkhouse while you pick up your things and get ready. Don't hurry yourself. Oh, yes, I hung Clem's gun and belt on that chair —" gesturing across the room, "— when we come in. Sort of figured you might want it here. Well, Tucson and I will wait in the bunkhouse for you." The sheriff rose, followed by Tucson.

"Sit still a minute, if you can wait," Nancy said wistfully. "I want somebody to talk to for a few minutes. This whole thing is such a shock that . . ." Her voice trailed off into silence, then grew stronger as she continued in a more bitter strain, "I don't see why this had to happen to Dad. He never harmed anybody. But we've had bad luck almost from the start. It's not right ——" She paused suddenly, then, "Oh, don't pay any attention to me. I don't know what I'm saying."

"You go ahead and talk, Miss Hayden," Tucson put in, "if it will make you feel any better. We're in no hurry. Maybe it will do you good to talk a mite, if you feel that way." He and Cameron had resumed their chairs.

"Thank you, Mr. Smith," the girl said gratefully.

"My friends call me Tucson. I'm hopin' we'll be friends."

A slight smile broke across the girl's pale features. "I'm sure we will. And I'm called Nancy. . . . You probably don't know what the situation here has been ——"

"I know a good deal of it," Tucson broke in. "Poddy has given me a line on things. He was telling me about those cows you bought from Quint Sheridan — the ones you saw branded."

"And you're wondering," the girl said quickly, "if they were really branded in our iron. I know; Sheriff Cameron question me pretty closely about that. I may be only a greenhorn to this country, but I know enough for that. I was new to the business then, but the bawling of the cattle and the smell of burning hair made quite an impression on me. I counted those two hundred cattle, myself."

Tucson shrugged his lean shoulders and smiled, "I reckon that's all there is to it, then. . . . Look, Nancy, do you mind me asking you a few more questions about your father?"

"Not at all, Tucson. I'll be glad to answer anything that might clear up things."

"Did you know your father was going to town today?"

Nancy nodded. "He left this morning, saying he was going to ride down along our south line, then cut across the range and go to Godwin for the mail."

"Did he say anything about Sheridan — or any of the Circle-Cross crew? Did he appear angry?"

"On the contrary. He was in very good spirits. Didn't mention trouble of any sort."

"That means," Tucson said grimly, "that somethin' happened during the day to change his mind. He discovered something."

"Have you any idea what?" the girl asked.

Tucson shook his head. "I can only make

100

guesses. This Micky Callahan — the tender-foot that wandered in here — saw something this afternoon that seems queer. He's a reporter, you know ——"

"What's he doing in this country?" Nancy asked.

"You got me. He isn't saying. Anyway, today, after the shooting, I saw Quint Sheridan send a cowhand riding out of town. Callahan was gettin' right pesky with his questions. For a joke and to get rid of him I sent him trailin' the cowhand. The trail led to your holdin's."

"Quint Sheridan and all of his outfit were warned by Dad, sometime back, to stay off the 8-Bar," Nancy said quickly.

Tucson's eyes narrowed at the remark. "Maybe we're gettin' someplace," he commented.

Cameron said, "What you aimin' at?"

Tucson went on, "Callahan saw the cow-boy he'd been following ride out this way and release another cowhand who had been left tied up. Callahan watched the two from the top of a ridge. He didn't hear much but what he did hear led him to suppose Clem Hayden had roped this hombre out of his saddle and left him tied up."

Nancy asked, "Does Mr. Callahan know who the men were?"

Cameron said, "Bein' a stranger here, he wouldn't. One thing is certain, he shore got slammed on the conk."

"What do you mean?" from Nancy.

Tucson gave brief details, explaining what had happened. Nancy's eyes widened at the recital. "Why, that poor man," she said sympathetically. "Stew and Pete didn't tell me that."

"Stew and Pete didn't know it when they came up to break the ——" Cameron broke off, finished awkwardly, "when they talked to you last. Callahan isn't even sure who hit him on the head. It may have been the two punchers he saw; it may have been someone else."

"But does all this prove anything?" Nancy wanted to know.

"Nothing in particular," Tucson admitted. "We can do some guessing though. We'll say Clem Hayden was riding his range and ran across a Circle-Cross hand, saw him doing something that proved to Clem that he had been swindled out of those missing Circle-Cross cows he purchased ——"

"What could he see?" Cameron asked.

"We don't know," Tucson replied. "We're just pretending that Clem Hayden got the deadwood on the Circle-Cross man. All right, he ropes him out of his saddle and leaves him tied up for keeps until he — Clem — can get in and talk to Sheridan ——"

"Clem came to my office first," Cameron said.

"All right, put it that way," Tucson nodded. "Maybe he was bringing proof to you, Poddy. He didn't see you, so he mentions his business to Sheridan. And then ——" Tucson broke off, not wanting to go into further details. Nancy's eyes were moist. Tucson again got to his feet. "It's all speculation. We're not getting any place. C'mon, Poddy, we'll go to the bunkhouse and wait for Nancy to get ready."

Cameron started toward the door. Nancy said, "It won't take me more than a few minutes to pack what I'll need."

Tucson and the sheriff passed through the back door and stepped outside. On the way to the bunkhouse, Tucson continued, "I didn't want to say it in there — no use impressin' details on Nancy — but I think that after Clem Hayden talked to Sheridan, Sheridan saw he'd have to put Hayden out of the way *pronto*. He sent Frame to kill him."

"Looks that way," Cameron agreed. "But it still don't explain why Clem didn't go through with his draw and beat Frame to the shot, as he was capable of doing."

"Nor why," Tucson pointed out, "the man that Clem roped out of his saddle didn't jerk his gun and take a shot at Clem. Of course, mebbe he did. We don't know. But unless Hayden sneaked up on him and caught him unawares, he'd have had time for a shot or so. If he was a Circle-Cross man he'd be expecting trouble, after Hayden's warning against trespassin'."

Cameron sighed. "There just seems to be a terrible epidemic of reluctance hereabouts of late."

"Reluctance?"

"Regardin' the drawin' of shootin' irons."

Tucson and the sheriff were so engrossed in the problems enveloping their minds that they didn't notice the two dark forms hidden in the darkness near the house. Sheepface Bogart and Trace Manning had arrived at the 8-Bar in time to see Tucson and the sheriff go into the house, carrying the gun and belt worn by the late Clem Hayden. Bogart and Manning had watched through a side window the meeting with the girl, had seen Cameron hang the gun and belt on the back of a chair. Now the two had shrunk back into the darkness to plan further.

Tucson and Cameron entered the bunkhouse to talk to Callahan and the cowboys until Nancy was ready. The five men were seated, discussing the various aspects of the case, making futile speculations. Pete Blair had started to leave to hitch horses to the buckboard to drive Nancy into town, when Stew Trumbull had announced his intention of getting some cartridges and going after Joe Frame.

This idea, Tucson and the sheriff had quickly vetoed as being impracticable. An argument had followed, with Pete finally siding against his pardner. The talk had drifted to other phases of the shooting, and the harnessing of the wagon was neglected for the time being.

Nancy suddenly entered the bunkhouse, looking rather excited.

Cameron said, "My Gosh! Ready already?"

"Not quite," Nancy replied. "Look here — I thought you ought to know ——"

"Know what?" Tucson sensed something unusual in the girl's manner.

"That Dad didn't wear his gun today."

"But we saw him, Nancy ——" Cameron commenced.

"No, you didn't! It was somebody else's ——" Excitement gripped the girl's throat. For a moment she couldn't go on.

"Take it easy, Nancy," Tucson advised quietly. "Let's have the details. Remember, a great deal may depend on what you say."

"But it wasn't his gun and belt the sheriff left hanging on that chair," the girl continued swiftly. "I picked them up to carry to Dad's bedroom, intending to hang them on the peg where he always kept them. *His own gun was already hanging on the peg!* It is about the same in appearance as this other — you see, I should have thought of it before, should have told you he never wore his gun when he intended going to town — never ——"

"Whose gun did he have, then?" Cameron asked blankly.

Nancy shook her head. "I don't know. I carried the belt and gun back to the other room, examined them in the light. The gun had small initials stamped in the wooden handle, initials T. S."

Tucson said, "Poddy, anybody on the Circle-Cross with those initials?"

Cameron frowned thoughtfully. "Lemme see — Butch Grier, Joe Frame, Frenchy Duproix, Tate Scorpio, Gabby Emm——"

"Tate Scorpio!" Tucson exclaimed. "There's your T. S. initials."

"Let me see that gun?" Cameron sounded excited.

"Look here," Callahan burst in, "I just remembered that fellow that was tied up was called Tate. I heard the other man call him that. This Tate guy didn't have any gun or belt either ——"

Cameron cut in, "Was he lean and muscular, with a sort of a cat-like walk, dark like an Injun, with shoe-button eyes and a long black mustache ——"

"That's the man!" Callahan exclaimed. "The fellow with him was heavy shouldered with tiny eyes. Had a face like a professional hog butcher ——"

"Butch Grier!" Pete Blair exclaimed.

Tucson said quietly, "Now we're getting some place."

"I want to see that gun with the T. S. initials," Cameron was saying. "Where is it, Nancy?"

"I didn't bring it with me," Nancy said blankly. "What an idiot I am! I was so excited that I just dropped it and ran down here to tell you. I'll go get it, at once."

"I'll go for you, Nancy," Pete Blair offered.

The girl refused. "I know just where I left it. I can get it quicker."

She turned and hurried from the bunkhouse.

Tucson said, "It really looks as though we were getting some place. Hayden must have captured this Scorpio hombre and took his gun away from him. Then he went into Godwin ——"

"It still don't explain why he didn't go through with his draw against Frame," Cameron growled, "regardless who owned the gun. It was loaded. Scorpio considers himself somethin' of a gun fighter. There wouldn't be anythin' wrong with his gun ——"

"Apparently, there wasn't," Tucson said, "but we can't be sure. Just as soon as Nancy brings that gun back, I'm going to see if it will actually shoot. The gun looked like it was loaded, but now we're pretty sure that Scorpio didn't fire on Hayden. Hayden was an enemy, unarmed. And yet, Scorpio allowed himself to be captured and tied up. Figure that one out."

"Cripes!" Cameron said impatiently, "I wish Nancy would hurry back with that gun."

He didn't know that, no sooner had Nancy entered her house, than a gun-barrel had been jabbed against her spine and a coarse brutal voice had snarled in an undertone, "One squawk out of you, gal, and I'll blow you to hell!"

VIII. Fair Exchange

Nancy had stiffened, said coldly, "What do you want?"

The kitchen was dark, but from the lamp shining through from the main room of the ranch house, she saw a bulky figure at her right, and sensed that two men had been waiting for her. She repeated, "What do you want?"

"Keep your voice down," one of the men said savagely. "You do as we say and you won't be hurt. One yell out of your trap and I'll bore you with a forty-five slug. We want that gun of yore old man's."

Bravely, Nancy opened her mouth to cry for help, but before she could utter a sound, a heavy hand was clapped over her mouth; a second fist struck her brutally on the side of the head. For a moment she nearly fell but the man holding the gun on her spine, wrapped one arm about her, supporting her struggling weight. She was too dazed, now, to cry out or put up much of a fight.

"C'mon, with that dishtowel. Hurry!" the man with the gun said.

Nancy felt a twisted dish cloth forced between her jaws, and tied at the back of her head, effectively silencing any loud outcries.

"Now where's that gun, sister?" one of the men went on. He was standing in front of her, but a bandanna masked the lower half of his face. "Talk fast. We don't want to hurt you, but this is risky business. It's your life or ours."

Nancy's eyes gleamed defiantly. She refused to make a move to lead the two bandits to the gun in question. The man holding the gun-barrel to her back, cursed impatiently. "Watch her, Trace," he snapped, and brushed past to enter the main room of the ranch house. Almost immediately he spotted the holstered gun and belt where they had been dropped by Nancy on a chair, after carrying them from her father's bedroom to examine them in the flame of the oil lamp.

Nancy took a quick step toward the main room as the outlaw finding the gun gave a triumphant exclamation, thus proving by her very action the man had located the gun he sought. Her other captor jerked her savagely back, even as the outlaw in the main room called, "I've got the hardware, Trace. Bring her along."

Nancy was jostled roughly into the other room. Manning said complainingly, "Lay off usin' my name, will you?"

Bogart chuckled, "Don't let it worry you.

With what we make on this gun we'll have enough *dinero* to clear out of the country."

"I hope so," Manning growled. "What about this petticoat?"

Bogart jerked one thumb in the direction of Nancy's bedroom. "Take her in there. I'll bring the lamp. We got to tie her up. You go get more o' them dish towels. I'll watch her."

Again Nancy tried to escape. Bogart gave her a violent shove that sent her spinning through the bedroom door to fall sprawling on the bed. Manning came hurrying with several dish towels. Nancy struggled futilely, but the two men overpowered her. Sheets were jerked from the bed, ripped into lengths. A second towel was bound across her face. Her ankles and wrists were knotted securely with the lengths of torn sheet.

In almost less time than it takes to relate, Nancy was stretched out on the bed, bound hand and foot. Panting a little from their exertions, the two men started to leave the room.

"Damn if she ain't a cougar for scrappin'," Manning puffed. "How long do you think it'll be before they find her?"

Bogart chuckled wickedly. "Tomorrow mornin', come breakfast time, they'll be wonderin' why the gal ain't showed up with the chow. C'mon, let's drift. I got the gun.

Lock that back door. We'll go out the front way, lock the door and throw the key away. That'll hold 'em off a few minutes longer."

The two outlaws passed swiftly through the house, after bolting the kitchen door. At the front door they paused to turn the key in the lock, after stepping out to a wide gallery, fronted by several gigantic cottonwoods. Manning threw the key as far through the gloom as he could.

The two men stepped down from the gallery, walked quickly to a nearby mesquite bush where their horses were waiting. Once in the saddle, they turned the ponies toward the northeast, not daring to put them into a lope for fear the drumming hoof sounds might be heard by those in the bunkhouse.

The moon wasn't up yet; the stars gave only faint light. A mile from the ranch house, Manning and Bogart put their ponies into a faster gait.

Bogart laughed, said, "Well, Trace, we done it. We got the gun."

Manning nodded. "I wish we hadn't been forced to manhandle that female. That's goin' to make her friends peeved as hell."

"Was it our fault?" Sheepface Bogart said irritatedly. "When we saw her headin' for the bunkhouse, how was we to know she was comin' back so soon? I figured we'd just slip inside, look for the gun, grab it and drift. And then, she has to decide it's her bedtime and walks in on us. But we got it, that's the main thing. Now to see Sheridan and make him pay plenty for this iron — if he wants it real bad, and I reckon he does."

The horses drummed on. Manning called a trifle nervously, "How do you think Sheridan will like it — bein' held up for the evidence he seems to want so bad."

"Hell! He's got to have it, ain't he? If it's worth two hundred bucks just to follow the damned gun, it'll be worth a heap more to Sheridan to have it in hand."

"Suppose he gives you an argument."

"I got a fistfull of argument in my holster."

Manning shivered a little. "I don't just like that."

Bogart said confidently, "You just leave it to me, Trace. We're in a position to talk turkey to Quint Sheridan if we have to."

The horses increased their pace. A faint aura of silvery light was hovering above the peaks of the Santa Madraza Range now. The moon would be up before long.

A long line of tall cottonwoods loomed through the darkness ahead.

"Trees!" Manning said suddenly.

"Sereno River," Sheepface called back. "C'mon, I know this country. Them cottonwoods grow along both sides of this stream, almost all the way to town. C'mon, it ain't deep."

Sheepface took the lead, plunging his pony through low brushy growth, eyes peering ahead, trying to locate the bank of the river. Manning followed more cautiously.

Bogart's horse snorted with sudden fright. There came the sounds of brush tearing against clothing, a scattering of mud and gravel; Bogart gave one startled yell that ended in a loud splash of water!

Manning jerked his pony to a quick stop. He said, "What the hell!" and noticed he had stopped on the very edge of a cut bank that had recently broken away. It was growing lighter now.

A few feet below, Bogart was still in the saddle, trying to steady his floundering pony, at the same time changing the air, through his lurid cursing, to a definite indigo hue. After a few moments the horse quieted, but Bogart continued to curse.

"Wha— what happened?" Manning demanded, from above.

A steady volley of profanity was his only reply. Finally, Bogart quieted down. "Damn fool nag!" he growled. "C'mon, Trace."

"But what happened?"

"Aw, the edge of the bank caved with my

114

horse. I must have misjudged the crossin' point. C'mon, it's only belly deep to your horse."

"You get wet?"

"Did you ever hear of water bein' otherwise?" Sheepface snapped.

"I mean, did you fall in, over your head?"

"Naw, this damn bronc stumbled, went to its knees. My boots are full of water. Hell, yes, I'm wet nearly to the waist on my right side. I damn nigh went out of the saddle, but I caught myself in time. C'mon."

Cautiously, Manning guided his horse down the bank and into the water, drawing his feet out of stirrups and holding them high. He drew alongside the scowling Sheepface. Side by side the two outlaws waded their ponies across the stream. The water became but little deeper as they progressed. The bottom was firm, affording good footing for the horses. On the opposite bank they climbed out, emerging from the trees bordering the stream, just as the moon lifted above the mountains, flooding the range with light.

Manning was laughing now. Bogart snapped, "What's eatin' on you?"

"I thought you knew this country. Sure, you knew just where to cross this river."

Bogart growled, "Cripes! A accident might

happen to anybody."

"Yeah, it might, but — say, Sheepface, you didn't lose that gun of Hayden's, did you?"

"Not a chance. I had it stuck in the waistband of my pants. It didn't even get wet. The holster and belt are on my saddlehorn. Mebbe the bottom of the holster got damp, but I don't reckon so. My own gun got doused, though." Bogart pulled his pony to a halt.

Manning drew to a stop beside him. "What's the matter?"

"My boots are full of water. So's my holster. I want to wring out."

The two men dismounted. Sheepface removed his trousers and boots, wringing out one, pouring water from the other. He up-ended his holster, wiped his gun off on the bandanna at his throat. In a few moments he was again dressed, shivering a little in the night air.

Manning said, "After all our trouble it's a good thing you didn't lose that gun."

"C'rect, waddy. . . . I just reckon I'll give a look at this gun, see if I can see anythin' important about it."

Manning drew near. The two men examined the gun. Sheepface said, "I don't see anythin' unusual about it. Single action,

Colt forty-five. Same length barrel as my own gun. Fact, it's the same model. Can't hardly tell any difference in the two. . . . Scratch a match, will you? Mine's wet."

Manning lighted a match, shielding it with his cupped hands. Sheepface continued the examination, drawing back the hammer and revolving the cylinder: ". . . five loads, hammer restin' on empty shell. . . . The gun seems to be in workin' order. . . ." He carefully lowered the hammer on the empty shell again, then, "Look here, here's initials on the butt. T. S. Who in time is T. S.?"

"What difference does it make? We ought to be pushing on."

"Right, waddy. Mister Sheridan is about to pay good money for this gun."

"Suppose'n Sheridan gets proddy?"

"I can get proddy too."

"I was thinkin' of somethin', Sheepface ____"

"Spill it."

"*Your* gun got wet. I've heard of dampness forcin' its way into ca'tridges. Then when a feller goes to shoot, they miss fire. If Sheridan got mad you wouldn't want that to happen to you. Why don't you swap cartridges with the ones in that T. S. gun?"

"You gave me an idea, Trace. I ain't worried much about the dampness in my

117

ca'tridges, but one of them little ratchets on my cylinder is wore off a mite. When I draw back my hammer, it don't always revolve like it should. I just reckon I'll exchange cylinders with this T. S. gun. Sheridan won't never know the difference."

Suiting the action to the word he drew out the base pins of both six-shooters, and quickly made the exchange of cylinders. The pins were pushed back into their sockets. Now the T. S. six-shooter was equipped with the loaded cylinder from Sheepface's weapon. Sheepface's gun now held the cylinder from the T. S. weapon. There'd been no change made in the shells, but that action, slight as it was, sealed Sheepface Bogart's death warrant.

Sheepface grinned. "I reckon fair exchange is no robbery."

"And if it was robbery it wouldn't bother you none," Manning said impatiently. "Come on, Sheepface, let's get goin'. Supposin' them hombres at the 8-Bar would discover what happened to the gal. They might be on our trail right now."

"Quit your damn frettin'. They know the gal left to go to bed. Are they likely to wake her up?"

"How do we know she was headed for bed ____"

"What would she be leavin' the bunkhouse for at that time o' night. Cripes! Quit stewin'. There ain't anybody on our trail. All right, all right! We won't argue about it. We'll shove on for the Circle-Cross. C'mon."

The two outlaws mounted and headed across the range.

But Sheepface was too confident. Tucson Smith was already on his trail, riding hard.

Back in the 8-Bar bunkhouse, the men had continued their discussion while they awaited Nancy Hayden's return with the six-shooter bearing the T. S. initials. Ten minutes had passed swiftly, before Cameron had said, "It's takin' Nancy long enough to get that gun."

The others nodded and went on talking. Five minutes more passed. By this time, Tucson was taking small part in the conversation. He kept glancing toward the doorway, his ears strained for the girl's approaching footsteps. Once he turned and looked up toward the house. The light from the oil lamp in the main room could be seen faintly through the kitchen window. Another five minutes dragged past.

Tucson said abruptly, "Nancy should be back by this time. Reckon I'll just drift up toward the house and see if everything is all right."

"Why shouldn't it be?" Micky Callahan wanted to know.

"Why isn't she back with that gun?" Tucson countered.

He rose and started for the doorway. The others crowded through after him, a sudden, nameless fear clutching at their throats. The back door was reached. Tucson knocked loudly. Naturally, there was no reply. Tucson called out, "Nancy! Where are you?"

No reply. Tucson tried the door, found it bolted. "It doesn't look right to me," he stated grimly.

Pete Blair left the group, darted around to the front of the house. In an instant he was back, announcing, "The front door is locked."

Stew Trumbull said, "Try the windows."

Callahan and the sheriff dashed to the two rear windows, found them locked.

Tucson said quietly, "To hell with the windows," and hurled his hard, muscular body against the kitchen door. There was a sound of splintering wood. Again, Tucson crashed the door. This time the bolt gave. The door swung inward. Tucson stumbled into the kitchen calling, "Nancy!"

The other men flowed in behind him, all of them raising their voices by this time. Tucson snapped irritatedly, "Keep quiet! Listen!"

From one of the other rooms came the sounds of a body threshing about. Tucson rushed into the main room.

Pete Blair cried, "The bedroom! To the right there!"

Tucson seized the lamp, rushed through the doorway. Still fighting to loosen her bonds, Nancy lay on the bed, stretched out between twisted sheets which ran from her shoulders and feet to the head and foot of the bed.

Pete Blair swore. The others made similar angry remarks. Tucson whipped out his knife, cut the bonds. Stew ran for a dipper of water. By the time he was back, Nancy was sitting up, smiling rather sheepishly at Tucson and the rest.

"No, no, I'm not hurt," she insisted a bit weakly. Her jaws were sore from the gag. "I tried to call out through that towel they had stuck in my mouth, but I couldn't make enough noise for you to hear. What an idiot I am. I should have yelled as soon as I found them in the house, but I didn't have time. They had a gun on me, but I'm sure I could have done something ——"

"Don't you worry about that," Tucson said. "Who were they? What did they want?"

"That gun — that gun with the T. S. initials. They took it away. There were two of them. I don't know who they were. They wore masks. One of them was called Trace."

Tucson stated grimly, "The back door was bolted. They must have left by the front door. . . . Stew, get me a lantern, will you?"

"Sure thing!"

Tucson headed for the front of the house, carrying the lamp in one hand. The front door was locked, but the key was missing.

He called, "Where's the key to this front door?"

"It should be in the lock," Nancy replied.

Tucson didn't wait. He unlocked a window to the right of the door, shoved it open, stepped out on the long gallery that fronted the house. Stepping off the gallery he stooped down and scrutinized the earth with the aid of the oil lamp.

In a few moments he found what he sought: boot tracks were faintly defined in the hard earth. They bore off to the right. Stew came running with a lighted lantern.

"Find any sign?" he panted.

"Yeah," exchanging the lamp for the lantern, "two men."

The tracks disappeared after a moment,

but Tucson followed the direction in which they'd been heading. Stew Trumbull brought the lamp back to the house. In a minute he had returned.

Tucson said, "Nancy all right?"

"Shook up some," Stew said shortly, "but she's all right. They don't come any gamer than that girl."

"I noticed that."

With the aid of the lantern the two men searched the earth for further footprints. "Here's another," Tucson said suddenly.

"And two more," from Stew. "They're comin' plainer now. This is a cinch. God! I'd like to lay my hands on the dirty sons!"

"That idea ain't original with you," Tucson said grimly.

The footprints led the trackers to a mesquite bush growing not far from the house. "Horses!" Tucson said. "They mounted here. Let me see. . . . Then, they turned their broncs . . . here . . . see?" He moved rapidly over the hoof chopped earth, then suddenly straightened up. "When they left they were headin' toward the northeast. The Circle-Cross lies in that direction, don't it?"

"Right you are," angrily.

"Any other outfits lie that way?"

"You'd come to the Circle-Cross first. I'm bettin' you wouldn't have to go any farther to find the measly skunks that ——"

"Don't be too sure, Stew," Tucson warned. "This was a dumb stunt to turn. Quint Sheridan wants that gun, but I figure him too smart to send anybody here and over-power Nancy, then steal it. Sheridan's smoother than that."

"Gosh, I reckon you're right at that, Tucson. What's the next move?"

"I'm goin' to get my horse and drift across to the Circle-Cross."

"Good! I'm goin' with you ——"

"No, you're not. I'm just going to scout around a mite, without lettin' the Circle-Cross know I'm on their holdin's ——"

"You ain't goin' alone?"

"Yes I am. One man can slip around easier than many. I'll see if I can learn anythin', then go on into Godwin."

The two were walking toward the house now. They entered by the open window, closed it. Nancy and the others were in the main room of the ranch house. The color had flowed back to the girl's face by this time. They were all talking at once.

Cameron said, "What did you find?"

"Two men," Tucson said tersely. "When they left they were riding toward the Circle-Cross."

Peter Blair said grimly, "All right, we go

to the Circle-Cross. You fellers can lend Stew and me some forty-five slugs ——"

"Hold it, Pete," Tucson cut in. "I know how you feel, but I'm going alone. No, wait a minute ——" as a chorus of protests rose, "—— I'm not aimin' to sling any lead. I just want to scout around, see what I can learn. . . . Poddy, you can drive Nancy to your home. Stew and Pete better stay here — now, wait a minute, you two fightin' cocks. Use your heads. Suppose this was just a trick to draw us all off so the ranch house could be burned down ——"

Pete said, "Cripes! I never thought of that."

"All right, we stay," Stew said reluctantly. "I'll go saddle up for you, Tucson."

"Thanks, cowboy."

"Saddle my snorting steed, too, will you, Stew?" Micky Callahan requested hopefully. "I don't know as I could get that harness on right or not."

"What you aimin' to do?" Tucson asked.

"I'm going with you," Micky said stubbornly.

"No, you're not. I've seen you ride ——"

"I haven't been thinking about anything else but my ride," Micky said painfully.

"Micky," Tucson said quietly, "face the facts. You'd just slow me up."

"Tucson," Micky begged, "I won't get in your way. If you get ahead of me, I'll stay behind. But, look, I'm supposed to be a good reporter. You're making news. Let me go, will you?"

"After what you've been through today," Tucson warned, "a long ride won't be any picnic."

"I never did like picnics, anyway," Micky said. "The ants always get in your food."

"You'll be lucky if they don't get in your pants," Tucson growled, then relented, "All right, you can come. But remember you got to follow orders."

"Sure, thanks, Tucson."

"I'll saddle up for Micky," Pete said. "The horses have got to be put to the wagon too, for Poddy to drive Nancy to his place."

The two cowpunchers hurried out. Nancy said, "You'll be careful, won't you, Tucson? And you, Mr. Callahan?"

"We're just going to scout around some," Tucson nodded. "No risky business."

"Sure, and I'll watch out for Tucson too," Micky said seriously.

The horses were brought to the back door. Tucson swung up to his saddle. Micky mounted stiffly, and they were off.

Before the men had been headed five minutes across the range, it was apparent to

Tucson that Micky couldn't keep up. He drew close to the little Irishman. "You better go back, son."

"Aw, Tucson," Micky wailed.

Tucson's heart melted — and at the same time hardened. "All right," he said, "on your head — or sit-spot — be it. Those skunks got about three-quarters of an hour start on us. We got to *ride.* Give me those reins."

Puzzledly, Micky passed the reins across.

Tucson went on, "I'm aimin' to lead that fat mare of yours, run some of the tallow off of her. All you got to do is hang on to that saddlehorn — there, that's the saddlehorn. Now grip it tight!"

Tucson plunged in his spurs. Reluctantly, the mare followed. After a few minutes she realized it was no use stalling further and she gave the best she had. The horses drummed swiftly across the range, Micky bobbing behind like a cork in a rough sea. The moon was up now. Before long, Tucson saw it through the trees, glimmering on the cool waters of the Sereno River. They crossed the river and went on. Micky's face was white, but not a protest escaped his lips. . . .

IX. DOUBLE-CROSSERS

Quint Sheridan sat scowling, silently, in the Circle-Cross ranch house. The furniture in the room where he waited impatiently was scanty — several straight-backed wooden chairs, a board table upon which stood a lighted kerosene lamp, a pack of playing cards, a half filled bottle of whisky and some soiled glasses. Cigar and cigarette stubs littered the dusty, uncarpeted floor. On the walls were illustrations on pink paper, of burlesque actresses, torn from ancient copies of the *Police Gazette.*

Across the table from Sheridan sat Joe Frame and another Circle-Cross hand named Gabby Emmett. Emmett, as his nickname indicated, was inclined to talk too much, without saying anything of importance. He was dark complexioned with a wide mouth and sail-like ears.

Down in the Circle-Cross bunkhouse were three more of Sheridan's employees: Frenchy Duproix, a down-at-the-heels puncher who was a wizard at changing brands; Soapy Randle, a listless individual who served as horse wrangler and general swamper for the outfit and was addicted to narcotics to some small extent; and T-Bone Hinkle, the slovenly Circle-Cross cook.

Ordinarily, as it was well past midnight, these three would have been in blankets, but their curiosity was keeping them out of their bunks.

The very fact that Sheridan, Frame and Emmett were still awake in the ranch house, and that two of the crew, Scorpio and Grier, were missing, indicated that something unusual was afoot. Inasmuch as Sheridan had never given the three in the bunkhouse his full confidence, they were never sure just what their employer's plans might be. They accepted his money; carried out his orders. Beyond that point they weren't interested in the type of morals involved in any of various deals.

Up in the ranch house, Sheridan lighted another of his long black cigars, smoked moodily for a few minutes. He hitched his chair nearer to the table to pour himself a drink. When he started to recork the bottle, Gabby Emmett said, "Leave 'er open. I'm drinkin'."

Sheridan pushed the bottle across the table. Emmett poured a small tumbler full, passed the bottle to Joe Frame who followed suit. The liquor disappeared with considerable smacking of lips. Frame and Emmett rolled brown paper cigarettes.

Emmett said, "I wonder what's happened

to Butch and Tate?"

Sheridan's face reddened angrily. "Dang you, Gabby," he rasped, "if you say that once more, I'm aimin' to drill you. That's about the hundredth time you've ——"

"But they should've got here hours ago ——" Emmett commenced.

"You've told us that too," Frame snapped. "Sure, we're as bothered as you, Gabby, but we ain't talkin' 'bout it all the time. Let up, will you? You act like it fair pained you to keep quiet and let a man think in peace."

Emmett looked hurt. "I was just wonderin' ——" he ventured.

"Well, quit your wonderin' and close your trap," Sheridan growled. "I never see such a hombre for jaw-waggin'. Sometimes I think I didn't have good sense when I let you in on our plans."

"Aw, Quint," he said aggrievedly, "I never spilled anythin' important, yet, did I?"

Reluctantly, Sheridan admitted that Emmett hadn't, adding, "It's just our good luck that you haven't, though."

That started another argument that was short-lived: the drumming of horses' hoofs floated through a partly-opened window at Sheridan's rear.

"Mebbe that's them now," Emmett exclaimed.

Sheridan rose from his chair and went to the window, peering out toward the buildings and grounds, now bathed in moonlight. Two riders loped past the house, heading down toward the saddlers' corral.

Sudden relief showed in Sheridan's voice as he called through the open window, "Hey, Tate!"

"We'll be right with you, Quint," Tate Scorpio's voice floated back.

Sheridan straightened up from the window as he heard Scorpio and Butch Grier yelling for Soapy Randle, in the bunkhouse, to come out and care for the horses.

Gabby Emmett was starting for the door leading to the rear of the house. Sheridan said, "Where in hell you goin', Gabby?"

"Goin' to see Tate and Butch, find out where they been ——"

"Come on and sit down," Sheridan snapped. "Don't be so damn impatient. You'd talk an arm off'n 'em before they got here. Take it easy."

Sheepishly, Emmett returned to his chair. Sheridan sat down. Joe Frame rolled another cigarette with fingers that trembled.

A rear door opened and slammed shut again. Steps were heard from the rear, then Scorpio entered, followed by Butch Grier.

Sheridan snapped, "Where in hell you two been?"

"Yes, we've been wondering what happened," Emmett started in. "We've been sitting, worrying, perhaps that ——"

"Shut up, Gabby," Frame rasped.

Grier and Scorpio came to the table, poured two drinks of whisky, dragged chairs up and sat down. Scorpio downed his liquor. Perspiration glistened wetly on his forehead below the black, matted hair. He wiped his long mustaches with the back of his hand, saying, "We tried to get that damn gun, Quint. It wa'n't any use."

"Huh!" Sheridan straightened up in his chair, frowning. "What do you mean? I didn't tell Butch to ——"

"It was Tate's idea," Grier cut in. "It might have worked, only the gun wa'n't there. Ten to one we scared Link Dexter out of a year's old age, at that. That fool deputy ——"

"What in hell are you talking about?" Sheridan demanded. He turned to Scorpio. "I sent Butch out to release you. You should have been back before ——"

"All right, all right," Scorpio said testily, "if you keep still I'll tell you. Have you got that gun of mine?"

"No!" Sheridan snapped.

"We got to have it."

132

"You're trying to tell *me* that?" Sheridan looked ready to explode. "If we don't get that gun, it just means we're out the money I paid — my money and your money and your mon——"

"Look," Scorpio said angrily, "it ain't doing any good to fly off the handle yet. If you'll listen I'll tell you what happened."

"Get goin'," Sheridan snapped. "It better be good, that's all!"

"I left Herrero this mornin', about nine," Scorpio commenced, "and rode west along the border ——"

"Anybody spot you when you pulled out of Herrero?" Sheridan interrupted.

"Not that I know of. The town was still asleep mostly. You know how that Mex town is. . . . Anyway, I didn't see any strangers that looked suspicious to me. If I was spotted, I didn't know it. I don't think I was. I took the course you'd laid out, cut Hayden's fence and started for Godwin across the 8-Bar range. When I got over near Hogback Ridge I hears somebody hollerin' about trespassin'. I looks around and there come old man Hayden ridin' like a bat outta hell. He sure looked riled ——"

"What did you do?" Gabby Emmett said excitedly.

"I run for it," disgustedly. "What in hell

else could I do? If things had been different I'd plugged him, but I couldn't. So I put spurs to my bronc and split the wind. Well, Hayden's horse must have been faster'n mine, 'cause he gained rapid. Next thing I knowed, he'd unleashed his rope, made a lucky catch and roped me out of my saddle. I lit hard on one shoulder, hit my head against a chunk of loose rock. Mister, she ached plenty ——"

"You give us all a headache ——" Emmett commenced.

"Shut up, Gabby!" from Sheridan. "What next, Tate?"

Scorpio continued, "When I come to, Hayden had dragged me under some trees and left me hawg-tied proper. I couldn't mosey a muscle. I reckon it had struck him queer I hadn't pulled my gun, and while I was unconscious he'd done some inspectin'. He's one shrewd ol' coot ——"

"Hayden *was*, you mean," Joe Frame pointed out.

"For which you got my thanks, Joe," Scorpio nodded. "Anyway, when I come to, he was grinnin' like the cat that ate the canary and replacin' the shells as he'd found them. He questioned me some, but I refused to make any kind of an answer. That didn't bother him. He stated that he had the sort

134

of evidence that would make Quint Sheridan pay for those cows that disappeared and that he was goin' right in to lay said evidence before the sheriff. An' he rode away, leavin' me helpless as a roped yearlin'."

"And came in to town," Sheridan said, "lookin' for Poddy Cameron. Cameron wa'n't in. I saw Hayden wearin' a gun, didn't know it was your gun, Tate. I figured he was gunnin' for Joe Frame. I broached him on the subject and he told me what he had found. I'm tellin' you it shook me up some. He offered to turn that gun over to me if I'd pay him for those cows. I told him he was crazy."

Scorpio sighed, "Maybe you was the crazy one, Quint. It'd been cheaper to pay for those cows and get the gun."

"Hell!" Sheridan protested. "How was I to know how things would turn out? To me it just looked like a good chance for Joe to even the old score, put Hayden away for good. But when Joe tried to get your gun, some hombre by the name of Tucson Smith stepped in and wouldn't let him take it. You've maybe heard of this Smith hombre, Tate."

Scorpio cursed fervently. Sheridan nodded, "I know how you feel. I'm hopin' this ain't the same Smith we've heard of, but

I'm afraid it is. Only thing, the Smith we've read about always has two pals travelin' with him. This hombre is a lone wolf. Then a fool newspaper reporter he started to ask questions. Rather than arouse any suspicions I told Joe to forget the gun; we got out of the Gunsight Bar as soon as possible ——"

"Yeah, we run into that damn reporter," Butch Grier growled. "We caught him spyin' on us from the top of Hogback Ridge ——"

"Th' hell you say!" Sheridan looked startled.

Grier told what had happened. Sheridan frowned. "Maybe it would have been wiser to rub him out ——"

"And get his newspaper down here, snoopin' around?" Scorpio said scornfully.

Sheridan considered that and nodded slowly. "I reckon you handled it the best way, fellers."

Scorpio continued, "Well, after knockin' this reporter on the head, we started for Godwin. All I wanted was to get that gun. I figured that Poddy Cameron would pro'bly put it in his safe ——"

"So did I, but he didn't," Sheridan said bitterly.

"We found that out," Scorpio growled.

"Me'n Butch went into Godwin, had supper and pretended like we was goin' out of town. 'Bout eleven o'clock when the town was dark and closed up ——"

"It wa'n't more'n ten," Grier contradicted.

"What's the difference, get on with your yarn," Sheridan said impatiently.

"Don't rush me," Scorpio snapped. "I'm tellin' it as fast as I know how. When we first hit Godwin I got my gun from Barney, in the Faro Saloon. I ain't never goin' to just wear one gun again, Quint. Your plans was all wrong. If I'd only had another gun when I run into old Hayden ——"

"Yeah," scornfully from Sheridan. "In that case it would have been your luck to run into a hombre with the authority to examine both guns. In that case ——"

"I'd chance that ——" Scorpio commenced.

"Cripes!" Sheridan half shouted. "Will you stop your wranglin' and get on? All right! I'm tryin' to stay with you. You and Butch sneaked back to town about ten o'clock. Then what?"

Scorpio went on sullenly, "We busted in the back way into that blacksmith shop on Main, and got us a heavy sledge hammer. From there we went to the sheriff's office. Like always, the door was unlocked. Nobody was there but Link Dexter. We stuck him up and busted open the sheriff's safe. It's just made of cast iron and cracked at the first blow ——"

Sheridan's eyes were starting from his head. "You what!" he fairly yelled. "Have you gone crazy, Tate?"

Doggedly, Scorpio repeated the words. "Cripes! I figured we'd get that gun. It wa'n't there ——"

He was interrupted by a torrid blast of profane language. "You fools! You utter fools!" Sheridan cursed them. "Cameron knew I wanted that gun. Now, he'll tie that safe-crackin' to the Circle-Cross. Gawd! What a dumb thing to do! And Link Dexter will identify you two and — oh, Gawd! What a gang I picked!"

"It was Tate's idea," Grier growled. "It sounded all right at the time ——"

"And if the gun had been in the safe," Scorpio said hotly, "you'd thought it was a fine idea. And you needn't to worry about that dumb Link Dexter recognizin' us. He can't ever say anythin' unless he's got Cameron to prod him. Besides we had our bandannas tied across our faces. Dexter is too dumb to know who we were. Quint, you might just as well quit your stormin'. All we got to do is deny everythin'. How is Cameron goin' to prove that job on us? If we'd got the gun, everythin' would have been fine."

"All right," Sheridan nodded shortly; again his temper was under control. His eyes were like cold steel, his voice frigid. "What's done is done, but you shouldn't try to use your head, Tate, while I'm here to handle things. Look, I wanted to be able to prove an alibi, if necessary. We all returned to the ranch this afternoon, except you and Butch. You should have been here early — earlier than this by a long shot. If that reporter saw you, someone else may have seen you — late tonight. You and Butch are the holes in my alibi ——"

"What alibi you talkin' about?" Scorpio demanded.

Sheridan explained, "As soon as I see Cameron wouldn't give up that gun, I sent Gabby ridin' to Herrero to see about gettin' two hombres to crack that safe for us — tonight. Gabby couldn't get anybody that had worked for us before, but before he got back to Godwin, two hombres caught up to him, sayin' the Big Boss of Herrero had sent them. Their names are Bogart and Manning. They come on into town with Gabby. Gabby didn't feel like trustin' 'em all the way, and he stalled off for a spell. Me and the other boys had returned here, in the meantime. Gabby used his head, didn't say anythin' about crackin' the safe to Bogart and Manning ——"

"But what —— ?" Scorpio commenced.

"I'd told Gabby I'd pay two hundred dollars for the job. Gabby thought it over all through supper. Later, when he saw Cameron leaving town with that gun, he gave Bogart and Manning the job of following the sheriff to see just what happened to the gun. He told them distinctly not to do anythin' but spy out the sheriff's movements, and promised 'em two hundred dollars. That's a lot of money for a trailin' job, but Gabby didn't feel like trustin' 'em to try and get the gun while the sheriff had it on him."

"Where's these two hombres now?" Scorpio asked.

"Tailin' that gun, I hope," Sheridan replied. "After they tell me if the sheriff left the gun at the 8-Bar or brought it back to town I'll be able to make plans."

"Gabby should have told them hombres to go back to Herrero," Scorpio growled, "and done his own trailin'."

"Gabby was followin' my orders," Sheridan said tersely. "I don't want any of our regular hands any place near that gun. We're

140

under suspicion now. Soon's those two had left town, Gabby come direct here and joined us. I don't know what more he could have done."

"Talk about bein' dumb!" Scorpio exclaimed scornfully. "Payin' them hombres two hundred dollars just to trail a gun. Don't you suppose they'll do some thinkin'? They might be a pair of double-crossers. I don't trust that big boss in Herrero any too far. Mebbe he gave orders to those fellers to grab anythin' that came their way."

The room suddenly fell silent. Sheridan had taken on a sick, greenish hue. One shaky hand reached for the bottle. He gulped down a big drink, spilling it over his chin. The glass clattered back to the table.

Abruptly, the staccato pounding of hoofs was heard approaching the ranch. "Maybe," Sheridan said unsteadily, "that's Bogart and Manning now."

"If it is," Scorpio snapped, "I'll be plumb surprised."

The horses stopped near the bunkhouse. A few minutes later came a hail from Frenchy Duproix: "Quint! Hey, Quint!"

Sheridan went to the window, shoved it up. "What's up, Frenchy?"

The answer came, "There's a coupla hombres just rode in. Names o' Bogart and

Manning. They claim they got business with you."

"They have," Sheridan shouted back. "Tell 'em to come up here."

Some of the color had returned to his face by the time he returned to his chair. A long sigh of relief went through the room. Sheridan laughed shortly, "Double-crossers, eh, Tate?"

Scorpio growled. "You ain't got that gun yet. Two hundred bucks is a lot just for learnin' where it is."

Gabby Emmett went to the back of the house to show Manning and Bogart in. In a few minutes the three entered the room, Gabby talking feverishly. "Look, Quint," Emmett babbled, "they got the gun!"

Sheridan stiffened. Sheepface Bogart and Manning had stopped just inside the doorway. Sheepface carried a belt and holster in one hand; in the waistband of his trousers was stuck the gun with the T. S. on the butt.

Emmett went on, "This is Sheridan, Sheepface Bogart and Trace Manning. Fellers, shake hands with Tate Scorpio, Joe Frame —— "

"Shut up, Gabby!" Sheridan said. He looked at Bogart and Manning, eyes narrowing. Something in the uneasy manner displayed by the two men warned Sheridan that all was not well. Scorpio was eyeing the gun in Bogart's waistband. Sheridan decided to stall for a few minutes.

"You got the gun, too, eh?" Sheridan's geniality was assumed.

Bogart nodded. "Yeah, we got it. We been thinkin' ——"

"Never mind. We'll have a drink first. Gabby, pour your friends a coupla drinks. Pull up chairs."

Emmett approached the table, poured drinks which he passed to Bogart and Manning. The two reluctantly accepted the glasses, but held back, near the doorway. Joe Frame kicked a couple of chairs nearer the table, but the visitors made no move to sit down.

"Drink up, drink up," Sheridan urged.

Bogart shook his head, eyes wary on the other faces in the room. "We'll drink later, Sheridan. Business first." The T. S. six-shooter remained in his belt. "It's like this, Sheridan," he continued, "we figure this gun to be worth more'n two hundred ——"

Scorpio ripped out a curse, started to reach for his gun, but Bogart's right fist was already clamped on the butt of his holstered six-shooter. "Go on, jerk it!" he snarled.

Sheridan shouted, "Hold it, Tate!"

Scorpio flung his arms in the air, backed

away to the far wall, eyes glittering angrily. The other men backed across the room. Sheridan was on his feet now, a wave of sudden anger sweeping through him, but he held his voice steady, "Just a pair of double-crossers, eh?" he sneered.

Sheepface said heavily, "Have it that way if you want, Sheridan. Me'n Trace don't give a damn. We know what we want. You'll pay. And don't get any funny ideas. We're important to that man in Herrero; he wouldn't want us to have trouble. So — the next move is up to you!"

X. Hot Lead!

Slowly, Sheridan reseated himself. Gabby Emmett, Scorpio, Joe Frame and Butch Grier were cursing in steady monotones, waiting for a cue from Sheridan. Sheridan said, "Shut up, you hombres. We'll talk this over. Maybe these gents have a right to be heard. Let's all be friendly. No sense gettin' proddy. Sit down, gents."

"We feel more comfortable near the doorway," Manning said uneasily. "We ain't makin' trouble, and we ain't takin' chances ____"

"Gabby," Sheridan ordered, "shove chairs to these gentlemen. Bogart, you and Manning drink up. What you afraid of?"

Bogart and Manning still held their drinks, unwilling to take their eyes off the other men.

Sheridan went on, speaking easily, when Bogart and Manning had gingerly seated themselves. "So you got the gun, eh? That's fine. How'd you work it?"

Bogart gave brief details. A storm of anger welled up in Quint Sheridan, but he held his voice to normal. "I figure that was a fool move," he stated flatly. "Manhandlin' women doesn't set so well hereabouts. How-somever, what's done is done."

"That's how we figure," Bogart nodded. "You wanted the gun. We got it the best way we could. We figure you ought to pay enough for the extra work ———"

"Took you quite a bit of time to get here," Sheridan cut in smoothly. "Where you been?"

"We come straight here from the 8-Bar," Bogart said, by now thrown a trifle off guard. "We didn't see any reason for killin' our broncs. We took it easy. Besides, my horse stumbled, crossin' the Sereno River. I got pretty wet. Had to stop and wring out my pants, empty my boots and so on."

"I suppose, I suppose," Sheridan nodded. He forced a wide smile. "What makes you think that gun is worth more than two hundred to me? I'll pay that, of course."

"Listen, Sheridan," Bogart said, "you want this gun bad or you wouldn't pay two hundred just for trailin' it. If it's worth that for trailin', well, you'll pay a lot more to get your hands on it. That makes sense, don't it?"

"I reckon it does." Sheridan breathed a trifle easier. "Just how much do you figure it is worth to you boys?"

"One thousand dollars," Bogart said promptly. "That's five hundred each for me and Trace. After knockin' that gal around and tyin' her up — well, we'll have to get out of the country. We don't want to go with empty pockets."

Sheridan burst into sudden loud laughter. "One thousand dollars! Well, if this isn't funny!" He went off in another roar of mirth.

Scorpio, Emmett, Frame and Grier looked at their chief in astonishment. Sheridan was acting out a part, of that they were certain, but just what the plan was they couldn't see. However, they too commenced to chuckle.

"What's so damn funny?" Bogart snapped.

"The price you're asking," Sheridan chuckled. "Why, sure, I'll pay you a thousand. Boys, I swear I thought you were pulling a hold-up on me. I expected you to ask at least twenty thousand or so. Hell! You've earned one thousand. I'll pay it gladly. Let's have the gun, Bogart."

Bogart had commenced to wish he'd asked for five thousand. "You show me the thousand bucks; you get the gun," he smiled.

"Of course, of course," Sheridan laughed. "Gosh, that's funny. One thousand bucks. And I thought you'd be tryin' to make a hold-up out of it. Drink up, Bogart — Manning. Then I'll get your money. Here, I'll have one with you."

He poured himself a small drink, held it up, "Well, here's to good luck ——" he commenced.

Sheridan's treacherous intentions were now clear to the other Circle-Cross men. Momentarily thrown off guard, Bogart and Manning started to lift their glasses. Manning's drink was at his lips when a torrent of hot lead ripped through his middle from the six-shooters of Emmett and Grier.

Sheridan had dropped his glass, reached for his sixgun. Bogart caught the movement too late, flung his glass to one side, jerked at the gun in his holster. The weapon came out surprisingly fast, but his hammer only fell with a dull, clicking sound that was lost in the savage wave of gunfire flaming from the six-shooters of Sheridan, Scorpio and Frame. That Bogart's gun had missed firing was lost on Sheridan who took it for granted the report had been drowned in the sudden roaring of Circle-Cross guns. In the excitement of the moment, he gave the matter no thought.

Manning had crashed sidewise from his chair. Bogart had almost reached his feet when the Circle-Cross slugs slashed through bone and flesh and muscle. He spun half around, then pitched, headlong, at Sheridan's feet, his useless gun — the gun carrying the cylinder from the T. S. gun — clattering from his outstretched fingers, to lie unnoticed on the floor. The room was thick with swirling powder smoke. Bogart moaned a little and was quiet. Manning's six-shooter wasn't even out of holster. The two men sprawled as they had fallen.

The Circle-Cross men approached, guns at ready. Sheridan shoved his forty-five back into holster. The others followed suit. An ugly smile creased Sheridan's features. He said coldly, "The dirty, double-crossin' bastards. They must have thought I was a fool if they figured to get away with a play like that."

Scorpio said, "Do you reckon Bogart knew about that gun?"

"Do you think we'd ever put eyes on those two, if he had?" Sheridan demanded scornfully. "Or that they'd only asked us for a thousand bucks? Don't *you* be a fool, Tate."

"Reckon you're right," Scorpio conceded. "Well, that's my sixgun. I'm aimin' to get it right now." He crossed the room to Bogart's side, seized the unconscious man by one shoulder, employed a brutal boot toe to assist in turning over the body. Bogart was breathing with difficulty; crimson foam bubbled at his open mouth.

Scorpio reached to the six-shooter in Bogart's waistband, then stopped suddenly at the sound of footsteps near the doorway. The other Circle-Cross men shifted their gaze to see Tucson Smith framed in the doorway, a level forty-five in each hand.

"Up with 'em, hombres," Tucson smiled. "I'm sort of interested in that hardware myself."

Scorpio swore and backed away. Sheridan ripped out an oath. Obedient to the order, the Circle-Cross men raised their arms high.

"Back — away from these bodies," Tucson continued. "All of you move yonderly against that far wall." The order was obeyed with alacrity. Back of Tucson stood the grinning Micky Callahan.

"This," Callahan stated, "is news!"

"Look here, Smith," Sheridan found his tongue, "what business you got cuttin' in here? This is a private scrap. Them hombres pulled on us and we had to down 'em ——"

"Cut it short, Sheridan," Tucson rapped out. "We heard enough through your open window to learn these two are the skunks who came to the 8-Bar and roughed up Miss Hayden. Besides, I'm interested in that gun of Scorpio's ——"

Scorpio cursed loud and fluently, then abruptly fell silent.

Tucson nodded. "You with the foul mouth. I reckon you must be Scorpio. Don't stall. We know it was your gun Clem Hayden was packing, Scorpio. I aim to learn why that gun's so important. I just reckon I'll take it in to Sheriff Cameron. There's a good deal requires cleaning up in the Hayden killing. . . . Micky!"

"That's my name, Tucson."

"Go to that skunk on the floor. Get that gun out of his waistband. I'll keep these sidewinders covered. Then we'll be travelin'."

Micky had taken but one step toward Bogart's body when a voice at his rear snarled, "Stop right where you are, feller. Another step and I'll bore you." A second voice said, "Drop that iron, Smith. Reach high, both of you!"

Behind Micky and Tucson, in the doorway, stood Frenchy Duproix and Soapy Randle and T-Bone Hinkle. Duproix and Randle held Colt guns on Micky's and Tucson's backs. T-Bone backed up his companions with a double-barrelled shotgun. Tucson's forty-fives dropped to the floor. He and Micky put their arms in the air.

"Make one move," T-Bone rasped, "and I'll scatter your innards from hell to breakfast." The guns of the other Circle-Cross men were in sight by now, also covering Tucson and Micky.

Sheridan leaped forward, smiling exultantly. "Good work, boys. You arrived in the nick o' time. How'd you do it?"

Duproix explained, "Us three were sittin' in the bunkhouse when we heard shootin' up here. We grabbed our hardware an' come a-runnin'. Half way to the house we saw these two hombres sneakin' in the back door. We slowed up and waited to see what would happen. When it was time to arrive, Quint, we arrived."

"You sure did," Sheridan chuckled.

Scorpio was scowling at Tucson. "If you're supposed to be the great Tucson Smith, I'm plumb disappointed. You don't look tough."

Tucson said easily, "You've got me at a disadvantage, Scorpio. Maybe next time I'll show up better."

"There ain't no certainty there'll be a next time," Scorpio snapped.

Sheridan said, "Shut up, Tate." Then to Tucson, "Smith, you've barged into somethin' that isn't your business. There's a lot of things I could do, but I'm willing to let bygones be bygones. Those two hombres on the floor made a mistake ——"

"A damn bad one, I'd say," Tucson cut in.

"You don't think I'm fool enough to send them to the 8-Bar to mishandle that girl and steal the gun, do you?"

"Frankly, I don't," Tucson replied. "I give you credit for more sense than that, Sheridan. But to me you look crooked as hell ——"

"You tell it to him, Tucson," Micky exclaimed.

"—— and I figure you hired those hombres to get that gun somehow," Tucson finished.

"I tell you I didn't," Sheridan protested. "They must have been in town today when Joe Frame, thinkin' it was Hayden's gun, wanted to have it for a souvenir. They pro'bly thought I'd pay good money for the gun. They were mistaken. They went for

152

their guns when I refused and ——"

"It don't go down, Sheridan," Tucson interrupted. "I want to know why Hayden didn't draw that gun when he had the opportunity. There's something damnably crooked on the wing. I want to know what Scorpio was doing on 8-Bar property. I want an explanation of a lot of things. I'm figuring to examine that gun and ——"

"*You're* figurin' to examine the gun," Sheridan sneered. "Smith, you're in no position to state what you're going to do. The way I figure it, you and this runty Irishman ——"

Micky Callahan said belligerently, "The runty Irishman can knock your face from under your hat, if you'll call your gunmen off, Sheridan!"

Sheridan ignored that, continuing to Tucson, "You're both trespassin' on my property. The law says you can throw lead through a trespasser and ——"

"You don't dare, Sheridan!" Tucson said sternly. "Certain witnesses knew we were coming here. If anything happens ——"

"If," Sheridan blustered, "your witnesses can prove you ever came here, why that's different. But if your bodies were never found ——" He broke off, realizing that the less questions he had to answer, the better it would be, and went on in a quieter tone. "Look here, Smith, I don't want trouble with you. I'm willing to let you clear out. I'll report these shootings to Cameron and ——"

"Sure, we'll clear out," Tucson nodded promptly, "but I figure to take that gun with me."

"You ain't takin' my gun," Scorpio snarled.

"You're all wrong, Smith," Sheridan said, shaking his head. "You're only butting in where you ain't wanted. You'll find yourself in a pretty bad way unless you take a tip from me. You are not wanted in this country. You'll make enemies. I can't be responsible for what happens."

"Sheridan," Tucson snapped, "I'm holdin' you responsible for a lot. I won't get out of the country and ——"

At this point two new voices entered the conversation, the first saying in a sleepy drawl, "That's right, Tucson, stand up for your rights."

The second voice came crisp and determined: "There seems to be a heap of excited gun-slingers here. Unless their hard-war hits the floor *plumb sudden,* I aims to put on a thumbin' act that will bring on some *real* excitement!"

From the Circle-Cross men came sudden astonished gasps, startled oaths. Their guns clattered abruptly to the floor. Tucson smiled broadly as he swung around, facing Duproix, Randle and Hinkle who had gone ashen. Behind these three, gripping forty-five Colt guns in each hand, stood two men, Lullaby Joslin and Stony Brooke. That trio of valiant gun fighters, known as The Three Mesquiteers, was together once more!

XI. MESQUITEER ACTION

Tucson yelled, "Stony! Lullaby! You old gay-cats, you!"

Stony laughed cheerfully, "You ought to be ashamed of yourself, Tucson, lettin' anybody get the drop this-away." Stony was shorter than Tucson, with a stocky, barrel-like torso. His hair was dark; he had innocent blue eyes and a good-natured, cherubic grin. He wore overalls, woolen shirt, roll-brim sombrero.

"I never saw anythin' like Tucson for gettin' into trouble when we ain't here to mind him," Lullaby Joslin said sadly. He was nearly as tall as Tucson with dark eyes and hair like an Apache's. There was something reminiscent of the scarecrow about Lullaby: he was slouchy, indolent-looking, sleepy-eyed and soft-spoken. "What Tucson needs," Lullaby continued, "is a nursemaid." His features were long and dour with leathery skin. "An' maybe a perambulator," he added sorrowfully.

Micky Callahan had given one whoop of delight and stood looking at Lullaby and Stony. Here, at last, he had actually encountered the Three Mesquiteers in action, the three most-hated (by law-busters) and the best-liked trio in the length and breadth of the Southwest Country, the owners of the famous 3-Bar-O Ranch.

Tucson had scooped his forty-fives from the floor and started giving orders. "Micky, you gather up this armament, scattered around the floor, kick it to one side. Get that gun out of that hombre's waistband, put it with the belt and holster on the table ——"

A sudden howl of protest went up from Sheridan and Scorpio, Scorpio adding, "That's my gun and belt and ——"

"Shut up, you scuts!" Stony snapped. "You, Micky Whatever-Your-Name-Is — go ahead and follow Tucson's orders."

Sheridan was red-faced, swearing, perspiring. "Now, look here, Smith, this is an injustice ——"

"I reckon it is from your viewpoint,"

Tucson said cheerfully. "That's tough, Sheridan. Howsomever, I'm takin' Scorpio's iron in to the sheriff. You just stand near that wall where I sent you hombres once, and you won't be hurt. You three —" speaking to Frenchy Duproix, Soapy Randle and T-Bone Hinkle, "— get across the room with the rest of your pards."

The Circle-Cross men were again herded against one wall; this time they were without guns. Micky was busily engaged in piling the guns on the floor into one corner, after placing the T. S. gun from Bogart's waistband on the table with Scorpio's belt and holster. Tucson, a gun in each hand, was standing, talking to Lullaby and Stony now, and keeping one wary eye on their captives.

"Looks like," Micky muttered half to himself, "that a man should have a gun if he's going to buck the spalpeens in this cowboy country. I just guess I'll have to carry one. Might as well get one now as any time."

At the moment, he was picking up the weapon that had fallen from Bogart's nerveless fingers, which was equipped with the cylinder from Scorpio's gun. Micky looked it over a bit warily, then shrugged his narrow shoulders. "This," he decided, "looks as good as any." Shoving the weapon into the waistband of his trousers, he went on with his job.

Sheridan had again started a protest. Lullaby said softly, "Go on, scut, make yourself disagreeable. Or if you feel like makin' a fight of things, go get your gun that half-pint picked up. We can settle matters now. Any way at all suits me."

Sheridan fell silent. He and his men watched the Three Mesquiteers in a glowering, sullen quiet. Tucson had left his two companions and was bending over Trace Manning's body. After a moment he rose, shaking his head, "I reckon he died instanter."

Going over to Bogart he again knelt down. He looked up suddenly, "This hombre's still breathin'. Micky, forget those guns. See if you can rustle me something to use for a dressing. I'll want water too."

Sheridan was suddenly anxious to please. "You can find some water and towels at the back of the house, Callahan."

Stony asked, "You figurin' to save that hombre's life?"

"There's a chance," Tucson nodded.

Sheridan said, "I don't get the idea."

"You're not supposed to," Tucson replied, "but I don't mind explainin'. If we can get this hombre into Godwin, perhaps the doctor can pull him through. I aim to question him when he gets so he can *habla* a mite."

Sheridan sneered, "About me, I suppose."

"You suppose c'rect," Tucson answered tersely.

Sheridan laughed coolly. "How do you figure to get him to town? He can't ride and ——"

"That's where you come in."

"Me? What have I got to do with it?"

"You're goin' to send one of your men to hitch up your buckboard. We're goin' to pad it with blankets and see if we can't pull this hombre through ——"

"You ain't takin' my buckboard nor blankets either," Sheridan snapped.

Tucson shrugged his shoulders, then rose from Bogart's side and crossed the floor to Sheridan. "You can suit yourself, Sheridan," he said quietly. "With your permission or without it, I'm takin' your buckboard. A few minutes back you spoke about lettin' bygones be bygones. All right, I'm willin' to overlook certain things that happened here, tonight. I'm not even going to ask you any questions; I know you'd only lie to me. For the present I'm willing to let things ride as they are — providing you want to let us use your wagon. Otherwise, we take it anyway, and you and every one of your hands go to town with us. In that case, I figure to turn you over to Sheriff Cameron ——"

"But look here," Sheridan protested, suddenly frantic, "you can't do that. You're trespassin' on my holdin's. This is a hold-up. We shot these men in self-defense. We don't even know which of us did it. Everybody was shootin'. Hell! I'll tell Cameron about this shootin' myself when I see him. Smith, I won't do it!"

"Suit yourself," Tucson said quietly. "But you're comin' in with us."

Sheridan wilted suddenly. He turned to Randle. "Soapy, go out and hitch up. Get what blankets are needed."

Randle started toward the door. Tucson said, "Stony, you better trail along with this Soapy hombre and see that he don't get any queer ideas about bein' slippery."

Stony nodded, adding, "Lullaby and I spotted your horses, hid among the trees, just before we got here. At least one of 'em was your horse, Tucson. There was a fat mare that didn't look good for much except tallow."

"That's Micky's prancin' charger," Tucson said.

"We figured that," Stony nodded. "Soapy and I will get your prancin' chargers after we've hitched the wagon." Soapy slid

160

through the doorway with Stony on his heels.

By this time, Micky had returned with a basin of water and towels. Tucson, noticing the gun in the Irishman's waistband, said, "Have you decided to start packin' a gun, son?"

Micky grinned, "It don't look like a mousetrap, does it?"

While Lullaby kept the Circle-Cross men covered, Tucson knelt at Bogart's side, ripped open the man's shirt. As he saw the extent of the wounds, Tucson shook his head dubiously, then started to wash the bullet holes. Bogart's whole upper body was bathed in crimson. There didn't seem much chance for the man to recover, but, stubbornly, he continued to breathe, though with difficulty.

The Circle-Cross men looked on in sullen silence. The minutes passed while Tucson worked. Once, Tucson said to Lullaby, "How'd you know where we were, pard?"

Lullaby explained, "We were riding along, south of the Border, heading for Godwin. This side of the Santa Madrazas we come to a wire fence, stretched parallel to the Border Line. After a few miles we come to a spot that was cut. Looked like it had been done recent. Later we learned we were on

8-Bar Range."

Tucson turned his head, looking at Scorpio. "You cut that fence, Scorpio. Just a short time before Hayden found you on his holdin's."

Scorpio swore under his breath, then, "You can't prove that was me cut the fence," he challenged defiantly.

"That," Tucson said, "will come later."

Scorpio didn't reply. Tucson went on working.

Lullaby continued, "Cutting across the range we saw a light in a ranch house. Stopped to get a drink o' water. Met Sheriff Cameron, a girl named Nancy Hayden, two cowhands. Cameron said it was the 8-Bar. He was just startin' out in a wagon with the girl. We mentioned we was headin' to meet you in Godwin. Cameron said you and this Callahan hombre had pulled out only a short time before. Cameron gave us a brief story of what had happened. We got directions to the Circle-Cross and come on *pronto*. Ran into your broncs, hid among the brush and trees. We moved plumb cautious, then. When we got near the house we heard things through this open window. After that — well, we came in."

"And in time, too," Tucson nodded.

Another five minutes slipped past. Micky

had gone twice for fresh water. The water in the basin at Tucson's side was red. Tucson tied the bandages as tightly as possible, and rose to his feet.

"Maybe," he said dubiously, "that's wasted work, but I had to try ———"

"Wagon and horses are ready, pard," Stony's voice interrupted. He herded Soapy back into the room.

Tucson nodded, turned to Sheridan, "Sheridan, you and Scorpio carry this hombre out and put him in the wagon — and handle him as gently as possible ———"

"I won't do it!" Sheridan snapped angrily.

"Think twice, Sheridan, think twice," Tucson warned softly. "I don't want any more trouble tonight. Furthermore, we'll be holding our guns on you and your men. You're all going out to see us leave. After that, you can come back and get your guns that Micky piled in that corner so neat."

Sheridan gulped, "C'mon, Tate," he growled, then stopped suddenly and said, "How about Manning —" gesturing to the dead body on the floor, "— you ain't leavin' him here, are you?"

"Manning," Tucson said, "is beyond giving evidence. I'm not interested. You can bury him, or when you get your wagon back, take him to the undertaker's in Godwin. Come on, now, stir your stumps."

Swearing under their breath, Scorpio and Shreridan carried the unconscious Bogart out and placed him on the blankets in the wagon bed. Tucson, Lullaby and Stony herded the other Circle-Cross men out into the moonlight. Tucson's and Micky's horses were tethered to the rear of the wagon. He and Micky mounted to the driver's seat. Lullaby and Stony swung up to saddles, twisting around to keep their gaze on the Circle-Cross men.

Tucson spoke to the team, the animals threw themselves against the harness; the wagon wheels started to revolve. Tucson said quietly, "Sheridan, don't you or your men make a move until we're out on the road. My pards will plug you if you do. After that, if you're really itchin' for trouble, dash in and get your irons. We won't be drivin' fast. You can saddle up and catch us easy. If you want action, it's up to you — but I wouldn't advise it. Not if you want to stay healthy."

Sheridan made no reply. He and his men stood glaring at Tucson and his companions. Finally, Tate Scorpio raised one clenched fist, shook it in Tucson's direction. "You ain't heard the last of this, by a long shot," he threatened.

"I hope not," Tucson replied pleasantly.

"Just call on us sometime," Lullaby drawled sleepily. "Drop in any day you're lookin' for trouble. Nothin' formal, y'understand. Just a nice friendly call — you measly, snake-bit 'phobia skunks."

Stony said sweetly, "We'll do our best to show you some *real* excitement."

Sheridan and his men fell back as the wagon moved off, their faces contorted with helpless rage. The buckboard reached the trail running to town. The horses moved along at a faster clip. From time to time, Stony or Lullaby glanced back toward the ranch house lights receding at the rear, but no activity was to be seen.

A mile from the Circle-Cross, Lullaby said, "I don't hear, nor see, anybody following us."

"And you won't," Tucson laughed softly. "Sheridan and his coyotes have had all the action they want for one night. They'll have to plan out new moves, before we hear from 'em again. Right now, they don't know how they stand." Another thought struck Tucson: "Stony, you and Lullaby side your broncs over this way. You haven't had time yet to shake hands with Micky Callahan. He claims to be the best newspaper man east of the Pacific Ocean ——"

"Hey, Tucson," Micky protested cockily, "I don't remember putting any limitations on that statement."

"Regardless," Tucson chuckled, "I'm commencin' to think you're the toughest, anyway. Considerin' what you been through today, most shorthorns would be stretched out flat. Shake his paw, pards!"

XII. A DESTROYED THEORY

Stony said it was hopeless; Lullaby shook his head, but added something to the effect that he'd seen Tucson pull hopeless cases through on previous occasions. The men had stopped the buckboard and Tucson was examining the unconscious Sheepface Bogart beneath the white light of the moon. Tucson tightened certain bandages, looked dubiously at Bogart's pale, still features.

"If we only had a doctor here now," he muttered, "there might be a chance. Gosh! This hombre's pulse has gone plumb haywire. One minute I can't find it; the next, it's runnin' like a racehorse. We still got about ten miles to go before we reach Godwin too. Oh, well, we can't do any more than try."

He arranged the blankets beneath Bogart's body, then resumed his seat on the buckboard, and took up the reins. The wagon started to move again. Lullaby and Stony urged their ponies into action.

As Tucson had prophesied, there hadn't been any pursuit by the Circle-Cross men. Since leaving the Sheridan outfit he had been relating for the benefit of Stony and Lullaby the various events that had taken place since his arrival in Godwin. From time to time, Micky Callahan had put in a few words.

"If we can only bring Bogart back to consciousness," Tucson said, after a time, "maybe he'll do some talking. I figure Sheridan is too smart to hire Bogart and Manning to go to the 8-Bar and try to steal that gun of Scorpio's — especially since he wouldn't want 'em mishandlin' Nancy Hayden — but Sheridan gave those two some sort of instructions. If Bogart could talk we might learn a thing or two ——"

Lullaby shifted in his saddle a trifle, said to Tucson, "What I don't understand is why old Hayden didn't go through with his draw when Joe Frame started makin' wartalk ——"

"That's got us all knottin' our brains," Tucson replied. "I looked the gun over; apparently it's in good working order. It was loaded. I've looked at it since. Five car-

167

tridges and the hammer restin' on an empty shell. Well, right now I aims to see if it really will shoot."

He motioned to the belt and holstered gun with the T. S. on the butt, laying between him and Micky on the seat of the wagon. "Micky, I'll hang on to these reins. I don't know whether these horses will shy from gun shots or not. I don't figure to take chances of this team runnin' away and jostlin' Bogart. You take this gun, direct it off across the range, and pull trigger."

"Who, me?" Micky asked.

"What's the matter, Micky," Stony grinned, "ain't you ever fired a gun?" Stony was riding on Micky's side of the wagon.

Micky said solemnly, "Sure I've fired guns — on Fourth of July and such occasions. I never fired one of these big cowboy revolvers though. Once I shot off a shotgun. It kicked, gave me a lame shoulder. Do these cowboy revolvers kick?"

Stony said carelessly, "Not a bit. Fact is, they don't even kick as much as a small revolver shootin' twenty-two caliber ca'tridges."

Micky frowned. He had drawn the T. S. six-shooter from its holster and was examining it warily. "That's sort of funny," he said. "This is a .45 caliber. Seems to me the bigger the gun, the bigger the kick."

"You got it all wrong, Micky," Lullaby exclaimed glibly. "You see, it's the heavy load that holds the gun steady. It can't kick."

"Sure, that's it," Stony took up the story. "Now you spoke of that shotgun kicking. It was pro'bly loaded with little, tiny B-B shots in the shell, wasn't it?"

"Ye-es, I guess so," Micky said uncertainly.

"There, you see?" Stony's voice was confident. "Now, if that shotgun had been loaded with buckshot, fr'instance, you wouldn't have felt a mite of kick, would he, Lullaby?"

"Naw, nothin' to speak of," Lullaby replied, with a shrug. "Pro'bly about as much kick as you'd get from one of these slingshots, made o' rubber bands, that kids play with."

Tucson grinned silently. "Go on, shoot up the atmosphere, Micky," he urged.

Micky raised the gun, sighted it off across the landscape. He didn't notice that Stony jumped his horse quickly to the rear. Micky tugged at the trigger. Nothing happened.

Tucson said dryly, "You'll have to cock it first, son."

"Oh!" Micky looked a trifle foolish, then drew back the hammer. Again he leveled the gun, his trigger finger contracted.

169

Pow! A streak of flame flashed from the gun-barrel. The heavy report echoed and re-echoed across the range. Micky let out one startled exclamation and dropped the weapon as though it had been red-hot.

Stony and Lullaby let out whoops of delight. The horses hitched to the buckboard had paid no attention to the shot. Tucson was laughing at Micky. Stony leaned down from his saddle, retrieved the gun from the ground, reined close to the wagon and handed it to the dumbfounded reporter.

"You always have to hang on to 'em, Micky," Stony said gravely.

"Why — why," Micky stammered, "that — that damn gun jumped right out of my hand!"

Lullaby and Stony went off into fresh peals of merriment.

Tucson chuckled, "Yep, these forty-five Colts sure react when you pull trigger on 'em."

Micky looked sheepish. "Lullaby, you and Stony are just plain liars," he accused. "If I'd known that gun was going to jump like that I'd been ready and — —"

"It's just like I was sayin', Stony," Lullaby was stating solemnly, "the heavier the load, the less the kickback ——"

"Aw, you two can go to hell," Micky

grinned. "I just remembered that I saw a cannon shot off once. It jumped back a coupla feet."

"What were you aimin' at, Micky?" Stony asked.

"Why, er, nothin' in particular."

"I thought mebbe he was tryin' to hit the moon," Lullaby grinned. "I see the flash headin' that way."

Tucson said, "They're ribbin' you, son."

Micky nodded. "You see if I don't get even with 'em, too."

"Well," Tucson sighed, "that destroys one theory, anyway. We know the gun will shoot if you give it a chance. Now why in Hades didn't Hayden go through with his draw?"

"It not only destroyed a theory," Stony chuckled. "It damn nigh destroyed Micky."

Warily, Micky thrust the T. S. gun back into its holster. "Gosh, I don't see how you fellows ever hit anything you aim at, when your guns jump that way."

"You learn to judge your shots accordin'," Tucson said.

"I hope so," Micky said fervently. "I guess I'll require plenty practise before I get accurate with this gun —" patting the six-shooter stuck in his waistband, "that I took off of Bogart."

"We'll give you lessons in fast drawing,"

Stony offered.

"You and Lullaby will give me lessons in nothing," Micky retorted. "I don't quite trust you two eggs."

Stony said in hurt tones, "Now I don't take that kindly, Micky. Do you, Lullaby?"

"Not a-tall," Lullaby shook his head sadly. "And we might have taught him to shoot as well as old Lemen Sauer did ——"

Lemon Sour — ?" Micky commenced in surprise.

"Don't you try to get funny, Micky," Lullaby admonished. "The name is Lemen Sauer."

"Well, who was he, anyway?" Micky asked skeptically.

"Just about the fastest draw-and-shoot man that ever struck the Southwest," Stony said solemnly.

Micky appealed to Tucson: "Say, can I believe *anything* your two pards say?"

"Suit yourself," Tucson chuckled. "I never do."

The wagon rolled on, accompanied by the steady *clop-clopping* of horses' hoofs. Occasionally, from the bed of the wagon, came a rasping breath from Sheepface Bogart's tortured lungs. Micky repressed a shudder. Anything was better than that. He said to Lullaby, "All right, what about this fast gun artist? Where'd he learn to shoot?"

"Me and Stony gave him lessons," Lullaby responded promptly. "You pro'bly won't believe it ——"

"I don't expect to," Micky cut in.

"—— but when Lemen Sauer first come to this country," Lullaby ignored the interruption, "he didn't know one end of a forty-five from the other."

"And when *we* got through learnin' him," Stony said enthusiastically, "he certainly had something."

"I always did hear the hoof-and-mouth disease was contagious," Micky grinned.

Stony scowled. "I don't consider that genteel."

"Do you remember, Stony," Lullaby said hastily, "that trick with a deck of cards, Lemen used to do?"

"I suppose he'd shoot the pip out of the ace of hearts or something like that," Micky said scornfully. "Gosh, I saw that done on the stage in an opera house once ——"

"Shoot the pip out of the ace," Lullaby sneered. "That ain't any trick. Shucks! We'd throw the whole deck in the air. You'd see Leman go for his gun, you'd hear five shots so fast they sounded like one ——"

"And when the cards fell to the ground," Stony took up the story, "you'd see that Lemen had shot himself a poker hand, just nickin' the corners of the cards he wanted to hold! And he always shot himself a good hand."

"That's right," Lullaby nodded. "But that wa'n't much of a trick. Us three — me and Stony and Lemen — used to play poker by the hour that way."

"We sure did," Stony reminisced. "Fact of the matter was, Lemen got almost as good with his gun as me and Lullaby, after we'd given him a few lessons."

"What broke up the game," Lullaby said modestly, "was my shootin'. I don't like to boast but ——"

"What about *your* shootin'?" Stony sneered.

Lullaby explained, "It was my always shootin' myself a royal flush that sickened you and Lemen of playin' with me. Would you believe it, Micky, I kept Stony and Lemen flat busted all the time? While I was gettin' royal flushes they had to be content with pickin' straights and full houses and things like that ——"

"I taught Lullaby to shoot too," Stony put in. "He wa'n't worth a damn until I took him in hand. You see, Micky, it really ain't anythin' to shoot yourself a poker hand out of a deck of cards that somebody throws in the air. That's kid stuff. But it takes real shootin' to *plug the pips out of every card in the deck* ——"

"Shootin' off his mouth is what he means," Lullaby said to Micky. "He couldn't hit the broad side of a stable unless he was inside it. And then I wouldn't lay no money on his accuracy. Cripes! Shootin' *every pip* out of the whole deck. Stony, you don't expect Micky to believe *that,* do you?"

Stony nodded. " 'Course," he amended modestly, "I couldn't do it with one gun. I had to use both my Colts. And I wasn't one hundred percent accurate every time, nei-ther ——"

"I'll say you wa'n't," Lullaby agreed darkly.

"You see," Stony continued smoothly, "I fell into a bad habit on the king of clubs: I never could decide which eye, the right or the left, I wanted to shoot out. Once or twice I missed him altogether."

Lullaby swore under his breath. Micky said skeptically, "You better get back to Le-men. I refuse to believe such a story about *your* shooting, Stony. Hell! Most of the cards would fall to the ground before you had time to reload your gun after your first five shots had left both guns ——"

"Y'see, Stony," Lullaby put in, "Micky

ain't so green as you thought he was. He knew you'd have to reload. Five ca'tridges in each gun, only makes ten shots. There's fifty-two cards in a deck."

"That so?" Stony queried innocently. "Every time I played against you, Lullaby, there was fifty-five, at least, and the extra cards was all aces. How do you account for that?"

"Stony," Micky suggested, "mebbe you'd better not ask personal questions, and besides you're evading my question. As I was saying, you wouldn't have time to reload ——"

"Who said anythin' about reloading?" Stony said aggrievedly. "I suppose you never heard of a gun bein' invented that would take enough loads to take care of two or three decks of cards?"

Micky looked a trifle crestfallen. "We-ell," he conceded, "I hadn't thought of that. Maybe you're right ——"

" 'Course, I'm right," Stony snapped. "I invented the gun myself. It was a muzzle-loader. The barrels were made of rubber ——"

"What did you make 'em of rubber for?" asked the bewildered Micky.

"It's easy to see you don't know anything about guns," Stony explained. "The barrels had to be made of rubber so they'd stretch to accommodate as many loads as you figured to shoot. Now it wasn't no trick a-tall to stretch a barrel to take fifty-two bullets —— "

A howl of laughter went up from Lullaby. Micky turned to Tucson: "Are these pards of yours always like this?" he asked disgustedly.

Tucson nodded his head, chuckling, "And you'll need a rubber imagination, too, Micky, if you listen to 'em. Now, when they started talkin' about Lemen Sauer, that was all right. Lemen would have been the greatest shot in the world, if he had lived."

"Did he get killed?" Micky asked.

"He burned to death," Tucson said gravely.

"Burned to death? How?"

"It was right during his prime," Tucson explained. "The world had never seen faster drawing and shooting. One day Lemen was giving an exhibition when his holster caught fire —— "

"How'd his holster happen to catch fire?" Micky asked innocently.

Tucson said sadly, "The friction made the leather hot —— "

"What friction?" Micky was genuinely puzzled now.

"The fast draws Lemen was makin',"

Tucson explained, "heated the holster. It started to smoke, then it ignited. Lemen didn't notice it at first. He'd been pullin' trigger so fast, the lead couldn't get out of his barrel. The slugs crowded each other, flattened, busted the barrel. It was Lemen's pet six-shooter. He felt so bad about that busted gun that the fire gained headway that couldn't be stopped and before we knew it he was burned to a crisp!"

Micky's mouth fell open, his eyes bulged. Tucson's features were set in solemn lines. Micky eyed him steadily for a moment, then shook his head. "Tucson, I don't know who taught Lemen Sauer to shoot, but I know damn well who taught Stony and Lullaby to lie. By gosh! They're amateurs compared to you ——"

The remainder of his disgusted remarks was lost in the gale of laughter that rose. The moon was far to the west now, commencing its downward trend. The sky above the Santa Madraza Range was streaked with crimson. Dawn wasn't far off.

"All right, you guys," Micky said good-naturedly, at last. "You've had a fine time joshin' me. I'll get square if it takes me to my dying day — especially, if I ever catch you fellows in my town. I'm a stranger here; I've got to learn. I won't hold it against you."

There was more laughter. The wagon moved on. The morning light was grey when wagon, men and horses, entered the silent streets of Godwin.

At the first corner, Tucson turned the team into Main Street. There wasn't a man in sight. Shops and houses were closed, though here and there smoke could be seen ascending from a chimney.

As the wagon neared the sheriff's office, Poddy Cameron stepped into sight and hailed Tucson.

"Where in Cripe's name have you been?" he demanded irritatedly. "I been worried — hey, who's that?" catching sight of Bogart's unconscious form in the wagon bed.

"I'll tell it later, Poddy," Tucson said hastily. "I want to get this hombre to the doctor, see if I can save his life. His name's Bogart ——"

"Sure, sure, thought he looked familiar," the sheriff nodded. "Sheepface Bogart. He's no good. Be better if you let him croak. He hangs out in Herrero ——"

"Well, let's get him to the doctor's. You'll have to direct me, Poddy."

"I'll go along with you." The sheriff climbed to the rear end of the buckboard and gave directions.

A minute later, Tucson pulled the wagon

to a stop in front of Doctor Perkins' house on Longhorn Street. Cameron went to the door, knocked loudly. Perkins appeared, yawning sleepily, in his nightshirt. Cameron explained what was wanted. Bogart's unconscious form was carried inside the house and taken into what Perkins termed his operating room.

Tucson and the other men waited in the doctor's office while Perkins was examining the patient. Tucson told Cameron all that had taken place during the night.

". . . and we're pretty sure now it was Scorpio who cut the 8-Bar fence," he concluded. "But what he was doing on 8-Bar holdings is beyond me. His gun is on the seat of the wagon. You can have it now, to hold for evidence. It will shoot. We know that now." Tucson grinned, "Micky gave us a demonstration. What Bogart and Manning were doing at the 8-Bar, I don't know. I don't think Sheridan gave them instructions to do what they did. Nor do we know what the fight with Sheridan was about. By the time Micky and I got in there, Manning was dead and Bogart unconscious ——"

"Scorpio was there, eh?" Cameron could contain himself no longer.

Tucson nodded. "Why?"

"Somebody — two masked men — held

up my deputy last night. Held him captive while they took a sledge hammer and busted the door of my safe ——"

"What'd they steal?" Tucson asked quickly.

"Nothin'. There wa'n't nothin' in it, except some papers, records and sech."

Tucson's eyes narrowed. "You think mebbe it was Scorpio after his gun?"

"What thought occurred to me. I aim to question him."

"Let it slide," Tucson advised. "He wouldn't admit anything, anyway. We may learn more by keeping our mouths shut. Your deputy didn't recognize them, eh?"

"Naw," Cameron said disgustedly, "Link Dexter is too slow-witted to recognize his shadow. I asked him if it was Scorpio, but he said he hadn't noticed. He was plumb stirred up about it. Well, when I arrived with Nancy, Link give me the story. I sent Link with the wagon to take Nancy home to Martha ——"

"That's your wife," Callahan said quickly.

"—— yeah, that's my wife," Cameron went on. "When they'd left, I set out to investigate a mite. About all's I learned was that the robbers had busted in the back of the blacksmith shop and stole the sledge hammer there. Scorpio and Butch Grier were in town, earlier in the evening, but had left for the Circle-Cross, accordin' to Barney, the barkeep in the Faro Saloon ——"

At that moment, Doctor Perkins appeared in the office.

Tucson said, "Has Bogart regained consciousness?"

Perkins shook his head. "I doubt if he ever will. That man's a gone goose. He can't possibly live. He may hang on for a time. I'll do what I can for him, and let you know if he shows any signs of coming to. Meanwhile, you leave him here. If he's moved again, the least jar might finish him. I don't even dare probe for the bullets."

Tucson and the others got to their feet. There was some further, brief conversation, then they departed for the street. The early morning sun was shining now. Tucson reached to the seat of the buckboard, got the T. S. gun, belt and holster and passed them to Cameron.

"You hang on to these for a spell, Poddy," he advised. "Eventually, I suppose, they can be returned to Scorpio, but for the time being, keep 'em."

"What do we do next?" Cameron asked blankly.

"Nothing much to do. Maybe Sheridan will make the next move. If he does, we may get something to go on. Meanwhile I'll put this wagon and the horses up at the livery. Sheridan can have his team and buckboard when he calls for 'em. Right now, I'm aimin' to go to the hotel, get a room and hit the hay."

"Ain't we goin' to have breakfast first?" Lullaby demanded. "I'm hungry —"

"You always are," Stony snapped in pretended disgust. "Always thinkin' about your stomach."

"So would you, if it was yours," indignantly from Lullaby.

"Thank God it ain't."

"That works two ways."

Stony sneered, "If it was mine, I'd give it a dose of arsenic."

"If it was yours, it would deserve it," Lullaby retorted.

Tucson had climbed back to the seat of the wagon and turned the horses. "Scrap it out, hombres," he chuckled. "C'mon, Micky, if you're goin' with me, hop up here. I sort of feel like we've had a tough siege of it."

Micky sighed, as he climbed up. "I'm agreeing with you. But it's not my stomach *I'm* thinkin' about. Fights, stolen guns, killings, horses — especially horses. This is *news!* But I'm not so sure I ever want to ride a horse again. I repeat, it's not my stomach that's bothering me!"

XIII. Stony Wins a Bet

Two days passed with nothing untoward occurring. A thin thread of life still remained in Sheepface Bogart's bullet-riddled body; he hadn't yet regained consciousness, however. Doctor Noah Perkins was doing all in his power for the man, but predicted he would die without coming out of the coma in which he was submerged. None of the Circle-Cross outfit appeared in Godwin the day Tucson and his friends had brought Bogart to town. The following day, obeying orders from Sheriff Cameron, Sheridan and his men arrived to attend the inquest held over the body of Clem Hayden, at which time Joe Frame took an oath to the effect that Hayden had started to reach for his gun. As there was plenty of proof on this point, Frame was considered within his rights acting as he did.

Consequently, the coroner's jury discharged Frame and rendered a verdict to the effect that Hayden had met death "from gun wounds inflicted by one Joseph Frame durin' a fight in which the said Frame was forced to shoot in self-defense." Poddy Cameron swore long and bitterly at this verdict, but there was no basis upon which he could bring Frame to trial for the killing.

Prompted by Tucson, Cameron questioned and requestioned Frame and other members of the Circle-Cross outfit, but nothing new in the nature of evidence was produced. Scorpio denied he had been the one to cut the 8-Bar fence where it was strung along the Border, and maintained that he had been looking for strays when he had encountered old Clem Hayden.

Upon close questioning, Sheridan admitted that Hayden, upon coming to town, had told about roping and tying Scorpio. That was what the argument had been about, Sheridan claimed, and it had had nothing to do with Frame or Frame's fight with Hayden. Nor did Sheridan deny he had sent Grier to release Scorpio. Scorpio and Grier both swore fervently that they hadn't even seen Micky Callahan, let alone knocked him on the head. Nor could Cameron dig out any evidence regarding the masked men who had broken into his safe. When questioned on this point, the Circle-Cross crew asked Cameron if he had gone crazy. Why, they demanded, should they break into the sheriff's safe? Cameron had mentioned Scorpio's gun. Scorpio had laughed scornfully and admitted that he'd like to have his gun, but that it wasn't worth breaking a safe for.

Scorpio's assumed carelessness regarding the gun didn't deceive Tucson and the sheriff, and, later, when Scorpio became insistent that the gun be returned to him, Cameron flatly denied the request and refused absolutely to say where the gun had been placed for safekeeping.

The inquest had taken place in the morning. Shortly after noon Clem Hayden was buried in the little cemetery west of town, the funeral services being conducted by the local parson. Practically all of Godwin attended. After the ceremony, Nancy Hayden, dry-eyed and rigid, was driven back to the 8-Bar by her two punchers, Stew Trumbull and Pete Blair. To Nancy's surprise, when she arrived home, she was greeted by a Mexican woman who welcomed her at the door, this servant having been arranged for by Tucson. As Tucson had said to the sheriff, "It's not right for that girl to be living alone, Poddy. You scare up a good Mex woman, and send the bill to me."

The day was hot; it was but natural for men who had attended the funeral to seek shade and relief for parched throats when they returned from the cemetery. The larger portion of the town's thirsty citizens followed the Circle-Cross crew into the Faro Saloon. Tucson and his companions halted

186

their ponies before the hitchrack of the Gunsight Bar and trooped inside to the bar. A few customers already stood there, quaffing deeply from tall glasses of beer set out by Nick Fitch.

"Call your shots, gents," Fitch greeted.

"Glass of suds," Tucson said. His companions followed suit.

Micky Callahan wiped the foam from his upper lip, gestured toward the fly-trap at the far end of the bar, buzzing and black with movement. "Aren't you ever goin' to empty that thing, Nick?" he asked in aggrieved tones.

"By cripes!" Fitch exclaimed. "I plumb forgot. I was goin' to empty her this mornin'."

"You've been saying that ever since I've been in Godwin," Micky grinned. He had procured a stiff-brimmed Stetson now; a new pair of knee-length, laced boots, into which his trousers were tucked, adorned his feet. A woolen shirt was open at his throat. Beneath his coat, the butt of Sheepface Bogart's gun protruded from Micky's waistband. Micky was gradually assuming the costume appropriate to Godwin.

Tucson said, "You done any practising with that gun, yet, son?"

Micky shook his head. "I haven't had

time," he evaded.

"I saw Micky shoot a gun once," Lullaby drawled with a grin.

Micky got red. "And don't think I've forgotten that occurrence, Lullaby. I'll square matters with you fellows yet."

"I just wanted to tell you," Tucson continued seriously, "unless you intend to use that gun, I wouldn't wear it if I was you, Micky. So long as you're wearin' armament, the season is open for hombres that know a lot more about handling irons than you do."

"Uh-huh," Micky nodded. "Maybe you're right. I guess I better leave it in my hotel room."

"Or learn to use it," Tucson nodded. He lowered his voice, "Micky, what brings you to this section of the country anyway?"

Micky glanced narrowly at Tucson. "I'll swap news with you," he proposed. "You tell me what you're trailing and I'll come clean for you."

"I'm not trailing anything," Tucson replied. "I came here to see Poddy Cameron and get some chickens shipped to the 3-Bar-O. Then I got interested in this Hayden business. From that point on, you know as much as I do."

Micky grinned scornfully. "All right, all right. Suit yourself. You keep your secrets and I'll keep mine. If you don't want to come across for me, it's up to you. At the same time, it's news that every place you go there's something big stirring. Are you trying to tell me it's just luck that brought you into this business."

"Exactly," Tucson said truthfully.

Micky shook his head skeptically. "All right, all right. I can see we can't work together. But any time you have anything I can turn into news for my paper — well, maybe I'll swap with you. At the same time, I figure you know as much as I do about this."

"What do you know?" Tucson asked.

Micky grinned widely. "Not a damn thing, Tucson."

Tucson smiled and turned back to his glass on the bar. Stony returned from an examination of the flytrap.

"That thing looks plumb efficient," he commented. "It sure corrals the flies."

Lullaby grunted, "It's a wonder you'll admit it. Usually you try to make yourself out so damn smart, nobody can tell you anything."

"Well," Stony said modestly, "the only one I ever saw to beat it, was one I invented myself. Trouble with that one, it has to be emptied every so often."

"Nick don't think so," Micky snickered.

Nick glared at the reporter, turned to Stony. "Did you ever see one that didn't have to be emptied?" he challenged.

"The one I invented," Stony nodded. "On my trap I left one end open, with a fish hook hangin' in it."

"One end open?" Nick's eyes bulged. "Shucks! The flies would travel right through that kind and escape."

"Sure," Stony agreed, "that saved emptyin' it."

Nick looked groggy. "I don't see how you trapped 'em."

"I didn't. If I trapped 'em, they wouldn't have been flyin' around. If they wa'n't flyin' around what would have been the use of havin' a trap? Can't you understand that?"

"We-ell," Nick hesitated, choking a little. Then suddenly, "Say, you said somethin' about a fishhook?"

"That was to catch suckers on," Stony grinned. "I just caught me one."

A sudden gale of laughter rose. Nick's jaw dropped, then he laughed sheepishly and reached for a bottle. "All right, I bit hard, I admit. The drinks are on the house."

Lullaby said wistfully, "Nick, ain't you got any free lunch?"

Stony groaned, "Old stomach worshipper

190

is at it again."

Nick said apologetically, "I had to do away with my free lunch counter. Not enough business comes in. I couldn't afford it."

Tucson asked, "How come you don't get more business in here?"

"It's the Faro Saloon," Nick explained bitterly. "You see, Quint Sheridan is the real owner of the Faro. He just hires Barney, over there, to run it for him. Well, Sheridan is pretty well fixed, and he cuts prices somethin' fierce. I won't sell the rot-gut he does — which same he peddles for a nickel a glass. For good Bourbon, I have to get a dime for a whisky glass. Sheridan gives twice as much for the same money."

"I should think he'd lose money on a proposition like that," Callahan put in.

"Sure he will, for a while," Nick nodded. "But meantime I'll have to go out of business — me and two or three other bars in Godwin. I don't get enough customers to make it pay. There's a lot of hombres around town would like to give me their business, but Sheridan has given orders they're to drink at his place. Sheridan swings quite a bit of influence around Godwin."

Tucson said, "It's a dang shame. You run a clean, orderly bar here."

The others agreed it was a shame. The conversation switched to Sheridan and other subjects. Stony was looking thoughtful. Finally, he said to Nick: "Nick, you haven't gone at it right. If you used your head you could fill this place with customers in no time at all."

Nick sneered, "I suppose you could do it."

"Well, I could try," Stony said modestly, "providin' you made it worth while."

"What do you mean?"

"That was right good liquor you just set up. If you had another bottle, I'd be willin' to pay double for it if I couldn't fill the Gunsight with customers. If I make good, you give me a bottle free gratis. Is it a bet?"

"Dang right," Nick said earnestly. "How do you figure you can bring business in here?"

Stony refused to commit himself. "I've got to think matters over," he stated cryptically. "You've been buckin' head-on against this thing. Seems like to me it should be approached more from a rear door angle. I'm referrin' to the rear door of the Faro."

Nick frowned. "Dam'd if I know what you're gettin' at."

"That ain't any surprise to me," Stony drawled.

"Aw, you're just talkin' again," Nick said disgustedly, "tryin' to get me to bite on somethin'." He moved away, down the bar, where Tucson and the others were involved in an argument concerning the advantages and disadvantages of certain makes of guns.

So engrossed were the men in their dispute, that they failed to notice Stony's absence, when he slipped out through the rear door a few minutes later. He wasn't absent long. When he returned, he paused just a second or so at the rear end of the bar, then pushed up and took a spirited part in the discussion, though all the time he kept one expectant eye glued to the swinging-doored entrance of the Gunsight. Before long his vigilance was rewarded:

A man came walking briskly in, stepped to the bar and gave his order. Before Nick could serve the drink, two angry-looking individuals pushed into the room, calling loudly for whisky. A fourth man came in, almost at a run; three more were close on his heels. Slam! Bang! went the doors and a pair of cowhands rocked up to the bar. The swinging doors had scarcely come to rest when several more men entered. The doors closed and promptly flew open to admit a red-faced, gesticulating knot of heated citizens, all calling loudly for drinks. Nick's eyes bulged. Business had picked up with a rush!

The swinging doors were in continual motion. Nick commenced to perspire. The bar was crowded three deep by this time. Nick was racing back and forth along the counter, serving drinks, making change; money clinked regularly into his cash drawer.

Nick's eyes bulged at the unusual crowd. "By Cripes! If this keeps up ——" he commenced to himself, then, "Yessir! Be right with you, just as soon's I serve these gentlemen. Yep, be right there, sir. . . . Yeah, I know I ought to have another barkeep, but — yep, comin' as fast as I can. . . ."

Stony laughed softly, "Nick, do I win that bottle?"

Nick had no time to reply. Tucson was looking severely at Stony now, wondering just how his pardner had accomplished this feat of increased business. If the new customers knew the reason, they were all too busy drinking to do any explaining. Two or three of them acted rather sick to their stomach, but called for second and third drinks which they put down with rapidity. Nick was still working feverishly to keep up with the unusual demand.

"If you ask me," a man was saying angrily, "it's a damn shame the Faro can't make an effort ——"

"I never did like the place so well," another put in. "Only you know, the way Sheridan served drinks. A man would be a fool not to get as much as possible for his money ——"

"I'm through with the Faro!" a third stated definitely. "No wonder it gives such big glasses. Pro'bly a lot of their stuff is spoiled from the ——"

"That's it. Sheridan is just tryin' to get rid of it ——"

"Gawd knows what the bottles are filled from. I'd like to see inside the kegs he buys the stuff in ——"

"I'm dam'd if I would!" a man snapped. "Hey, Nick, fill 'em up again."

Micky Callahan had Stony off to one side. "Stony, how in Hades did you work it?"

"Work what?" Stony asked innocently.

"Aw, you know damn well ——"

At that moment an interruption put a stop to the words: the swinging doors flew apart with a bang to allow the precipitous entrance of a tall, skinny man with scanty hair and a long red nose, who was panting with mingled excitement and fright.

"Whisky, barkeep, whisky!" he squealed frantically, flinging a coin on the bar and coming to an abrupt, skidding stop at the long counter. Luckily, Nick happened to be at that point behind the bar and was in a position to take care of the frantic man's demands at once.

The man gulped down his drink, immediately ordered a second, put that away as fast as possible. Then he commenced to spit. His eyes bulged wildly.

Micky sidled up to him. "What's happened, Mister?"

"It's a jedgment on us, thet's whut it is," the man insisted. "It's th' plague of locusts it speaks of in the Bible!" His Adam's apple bobbed excitedly up and down. "Th' room was black with 'em ——"

"Blacker'n that," another customer insisted.

Everybody was talking at once, now that their first alcoholic demands had been taken care of. A babel of voices rose through the room, most of which seemed to be cursing the Faro Saloon.

Micky was insisting, "What was wrong over there?"

The man with the vibrant Adam's apple explained in gasps, "I'd fallen asleep over my drink, sittin' in one corner, comfortable I was. Somethin' tickled my face, woke me up. My Gawd! I was covered with 'em. I reached for my drink. They was swimmin' around in my liquor. I swallowed half the glass before I noticed. Then I leapt up. They was swarmin', buzzin', dronin'. Th' hull place had gone crazy. Th' barkeep was wavin' a towel but it didn't do no good. Everybody but him was gone. Th' hull top of th' bar was crawlin'. I don't see where they come from all to once ——"

"They pro'bly been there all the time," another man put in hotly. "They're pro'bly inside the casks and bottles. Do you know what draws 'em? Dirt, that's what! Barney pro'bly don't mop up clean and they crawl into everythin' ——"

"I dang nigh popped my cookies," from another man, "when I see 'em crawlin' an' crawlin' around the rim of my glass ——"

"By Gawd! I aim to speak to Sheridan ——"

"Sheridan and his crew was first to get out. They pro'bly didn't want to face us steady customers ——"

"I'll never go near that filthy hole again ——"

So ran the heated conversation of the men at the bar. Tucson and Lullaby were gazing puzzledly at Stony who was innocently listening to the various remarks, though a gleam of triumph glinted in his eyes.

Micky Callahan half shouted, "Will somebody please tell me what it was the Faro

Saloon was swarming with? Sounds like somethin' awful ——"

"Flies!" a dozen voices satisfied Micky's curiosity.

"Thousands of 'em!"

"Hundreds of thousands!"

"Millions!"

"The air was black ——"

"They was in our drinks —— !"

Stony said mildly, "The Faro should keep its back door closed. Flies is bound to get in when there's two entrances."

Nick glanced at his own back door, saw it was closed. As he last remembered it, it had stood open. His eyes went to his fly-trap on the far end of the bar. There wasn't a fly to be seen in it!

Tucson's eyes had followed Nick's, as had Micky's and Lullaby's. The three swung suddenly back to meet Stony's innocent, blue-eyed gaze. Stony was saying indignantly, "The Faro should keep a fly-trap and empty it every day, like Nick does. That's the only way to keep clean ——"

"The Faro can buy a dozen fly-traps and I won't go in there again," a man observed angrily. "I wouldn't trust what was in their containers!"

Tucson and his companions were shaking

198

with laughter now. Tucson tried to stand still, but it was impossible. He rocked, he roared and ended up by half-staggering to the outer air. Gales of laughter rose from Callahan and Lullaby, as they followed Tucson to the street. Stony rocked up to the bar, "If I ain't mistaken, Nick," he said gravely, "you got full pay for a bottle of prime bourbon. Are you too busy to let me have it now?"

Without a word, Nick reached back of the bar and handed Stony a bottle. The gaze that followed Stony through the swinging doors was still a trifle bewildered.

Outside, Tucson and the others were congratulating Stony and every so often going off into peals of merriment. "Damn if that isn't the neatest stunt I ever saw pulled," Lullaby grinned. "Pard, how'd you work it?"

"Wa'n't nothin' to it," Stony said modestly. "The back door of the Faro stood open. There was a gang in there. Nobody noticed me. I just opened Nick's fly-trap and set it down near the door. When the trap was empty I brought it back to await results. You hombres were so busy talkin' guns, you never even missed me."

"Cowboy," from Tucson, "you shore spoiled Quint Sheridan's saloon business from now on. The next thing is to spoil him complete."

XIV. SHERIDAN BACKS DOWN

The Three Mesquiteers and Micky Callahan were still laughing, lounging against the hitchrack before the Gunsight Bar, ten minutes later. From inside the saloon came loud indignant voices, clattering of bottles and glasses.

"Sounds like there was a boom in the liquor business," Tucson observed with a chuckle.

"Appears to be a lot of money bein' invested in reliable stock," Lullaby drawled. "Them customers in the Gunsight is what you might term as havin' been caught bad takin' a flyer in liquidated, unbonded securities ——"

Another howl of laughter burst from Micky Callahan. "Stony, I don't know how you ever thought up such a stunt."

"Somebody in this crowd has to show intelligence," Stony said modestly.

"Me, I've thought that for a long time —— " Lullaby commenced.

"*You* never done nothin' about it, though, did you?" Stony snapped.

"I never done anythin' about what?"

Lullaby demanded belligerently.

"About what you were sayin'," from Stony.

"Well, what was I sayin'?" Lullaby was beginning to be a trifle confused.

Stony laughed scornfully, "My gosh! Don't you know what you're talkin' about ____ ?"

"I answered you," Lullaby interrupted sharply.

"You answered what?" Stony wanted to know.

"Your question," Lullaby snapped.

Stony scratched his head. It was his turn to get mixed up in the swirl of words. Reluctantly he admitted, "I didn't know I asked any questions."

Lullaby heaved a deep sigh. "We started out," he explained patiently, "with intelligence as the subject, but we better pass over it and talk about somethin' simple ____ "

"Who in Hades wants to talk about *you?*" Stony sneered.

"By geez!" Micky grinned to Tucson, "I should think you'd go batty listening to a pair that talks like that all the time."

"They don't talk like that all the time ____ " Tucson commenced.

"Tucson's right," Lullaby nodded quickly. "Only when we're awake, and Stony's asleep on his feet twenty hours out of twenty-four. He's talkin' in his sleep now, though ——"

Lullaby paused suddenly. Quint Sheridan, accompanied by Joe Frame and Butch Grier, was rapidly approaching along the sidewalk. Tucson and his friends fell silent, waiting for them to pass. Sheridan and his companions glared at Tucson and the others but didn't speak. Turning, they started into the Gunsight Bar.

This was too much for Micky Callahan's sense of humor. The little Irish reporter gave vent to a sudden howl of laughter. "Sheridan — *haw-haw* — can't even — *haw-haw-haw!* — drink in his own place ——"

The words were just a trifle too loud. Sheridan whirled, one hand resting on the swinging doors, and surveyed the grinning Irishman. Then, his hand dropped. He came slowly back to the sidewalk, followed by Grier and Frame.

Ignoring the others, he fastened his gaze on Callahan. "You got anythin' to say to me, Irish?" he grated.

Micky sobered just a trifle. "We-ell," he chuckled, "I might ask how business is at the Faro. Understand you had an epidemic of insect life down there. Do you feel like making a statement for the press? I'll see that you get a good write-up. You know, something like this, 'Prominent Cattleman Fails to Shoo Horseflies. Pestilence Invades Circle-Cross Range. Business Ruined, Claims Barfly Sheridan, Owner of Faro Saloon. Liquor Draws Flies Better than Vinegar —— ' "

"You figure you're damn funny, don't you?" Sheridan snarled.

Micky grinned widely. "I leave it to you who'll get the most laughs from now on."

Sheridan's eyes narrowed. "Just what do you know about those flies, runt?" He hesitated, then, "I've thought right along there was somethin' damn queer about that business." He jerked his head toward Tucson, "You, Smith, what you smilin' about? By God! I believe you fellers are back of that business!"

"I bet they are too," Grier half-whispered to Frame.

Frame nodded, scowled, didn't say anything. He was waiting for Sheridan to make the first move.

Tucson said easily, "You hombres better take it easy, Sheridan. Don't make any accusations you can't back up ——"

"I'm askin'!" Sheridan was red with anger. "Somethin' tells me this damn reporter is responsible for the whole business, and you three put him up to it. I want an answer,

203

and I want it pronto!"

Tucson smiled, said softly, "Supposin' we don't feel like talkin', Sheridan. What you aimin' to do about it?"

"Plenty!" Sheridan snapped.

Tucson slowly straightened up. "There's three of you and three of us," he suggested. "Want to start that 'plenty' now?"

His eyes bored into Sheridan's. Sheridan tried to meet Tucson's steely gaze, but was finally forced to lower his eyes. "There's four of you," he pointed out. Though he couldn't see the gun, reposing in the waistband, under Micky's coat, didn't even know Micky was packing a gun, he seized upon the little reporter's presence as an excuse for avoiding a fight. "There's four of you," he repeated, red-faced.

Tucson laughed scornfully. "Does Micky look like a gun-slinger? Hell, Sheridan, go get some more of your crew, if you want action. We'll wait for you to come back — we'll wait gladly. It's up to you!"

Sheridan backed away a trifle. "This ain't the time for action, Smith. But don't get the idea I'm runnin' away. I've got a heap to square with you. I'm not forgettin'. But —" he continued doggedly, "— I'm still askin' how much you know about that fly business ——"

"Exactly as much," Tucson snapped, "as you know about the killing of Clem Hayden — the *murder* of Clem Hayden! You know why he didn't draw that gun. You know what became of those cows you sold Hayden. You know exactly what Tate Scorpio was doing on 8-Bar holdings the morning Clem Hayden caught him. You know, and I'm aimin' to know before I quit this neck of the range."

Sheridan had retreated step by step before the lash of Tucson's words. He opened his mouth to shout denials, but speech failed to come from his lips.

"That's how much we know about the fly business," Tucson continued sternly. "Just as much as you know about the things I mentioned. It's up to you, Sheridan. Do you want to swap stories now. We'll come clean if you will. The next move is yours. Talk, get out, or jerk your iron!"

For one brief moment Sheridan gazed wide-eyed at Tucson and his friends. His fingers itched for the feel of his gun-butt, but his courage failed. Abruptly, he swung around and started off down the street, flinging savagely over one shoulder to Grier and Frame, "C'mon, you hombres! You goin' to stand there talkin' all afternoon?"

Frame and Grier looked a trifle pale. Hastily they took steps to catch up with their chief, glancing nervously back over their shoulders as they beat a retreat.

The Three Mesquiteers and Callahan watched the receding backs of the Circle-Cross men as they proceeded along the plank walk. Micky heaved a long contented sigh, breaking the silence, "That," he stated with considerable finality, "is what is called talkin' turkey, Tucson."

Tucson nodded grimly. "Lord, I wish I could make Sheridan talk," he said. "He knows things, all right. I could see it in his face."

"I was sort of hoping," Micky said wistfully, "that him and his blackguard pals would start shooting."

Stony grinned, "Cripes! That's what I call bloodthirsty."

"Nice little pal we picked up," Lullaby drawled sarcastically. "Gentle, sweet disposition, kind to dumb animals. Just loves growing posies and little children ——"

"Aw, you don't understand," Micky protested. "I'm not worryin' about you three takin' care of yourselves. But if there'd been some shooting, I'd have had something to write up for my paper. I'll be catching merry hell from my editor. Last letter I sent in, I promised big developments. He'll be wantin' to know where in hell they are ——" He broke off, then, "By gosh! I know what I can do. I'll write up how those flies invaded the Faro. Gosh, I just got to get some sort of statement out of Sheridan ———"

"Shucks!" Lullaby grunted. "Them flies don't look like news to me ———"

"What?" Micky grinned. "They will when I get through writing 'em up. What was it that guy with the skinny neck called 'em? A plague of locusts, that was it. A 'jedgment' from the Bible. There's my lead! Boys, what a story I can make out of that. Gee, I got to give my editor something to fill space and keep him satisfied. He warned me about keeping down expenses before I started. But I got to get some sort of interview with Sheridan ———"

"Maybe it wouldn't be the sort you want, Micky," Tucson interrupted. "Sheridan is feeling right ugly just now."

"Just so he'll say something," Micky grinned, "I don't care what it is or how he says it. Hell! He wouldn't dare do anything to me. He'd have my paper on his neck quick as a wink."

And without further words the little reporter hurried off. Tucson frowned after him. "Somehow I just don't like it," he commented. "No tellin' what Sheridan might do in his present frame of mind."

"Micky's still carryin' Bogart's gun ——"
Lullaby commenced.

Stony groaned. Words weren't necessary.

"What I mean," Stony explained, "I'd feel better if he was unarmed. I'd hate to have those Circle-Cross skunks pull another of those 'self-defense' killings."

Stony and his companions would have felt a great deal worse had they known the truth about the gun Micky Callahan was carrying.

Tucson was still frowning as he gazed after the reporter. Ahead were Sheridan, Grier and Frame, rapidly being overtaken by Callahan. Lullaby and Stony were following Tucson's gaze.

"I don't like it," Tucson muttered slowly. "I sort of felt I should stop Micky, but, hell! he's of age. I haven't any authority over him. He knows his job and he's down here to do it. Just the same he don't know this cow-country — there! Sheridan and his skunks turned the corner, into Longhorn Street. They're out of sight. I noticed 'em look back once or twice. Mebbe they figure to draw Micky after them — get him out of our sight ——"

"Back of that courthouse on the corner of Main and Longhorn," Lullaby interrupted, "there's a vacant lot ——"

"I was thinkin' of that," Stony cut in. "If

Sheridan wanted to pull a shootin', out of folks' sight ——"

"C'mon," Tucson said abruptly, "I'm goin' to saunter down that way. If things turn out all right, we'll mind our own business. If they don't — well, we'll be on hand."

The Three Mesquiteers left the hitchrack and took up the course followed by Micky who, by this time, was out of sight, having turned the corner at Longhorn Street.

Meanwhile, Sheridan and his companions had turned the Main Street atmosphere an indigo hue in their vicinity as they strode along: Sheridan's cursing had been something to draw deep admiration from Grier and Joe Frame.

"By Gawd!" Frame muttered to Grier, "I'd give a pretty to be able to go on that way without ever repeating myself."

"He sure knows all the words," Grier nodded, gazing with a sort of awed envy on his chief.

"And so help me," Sheridan raged, a full step ahead of his companions, "if I ever get that Smith hombre where I want him, he won't never again be able to ——"

"That damn reporter is comin' after us," Frame broke in, glancing over his shoulder.

"How do you know he's comin' after us?"

Sheridan had stopped swearing momentarily.

"I don't, for sure," Frame replied. "He's comin' this way, walkin' fast. Maybe he craves to get some sort of news for his paper, Quint."

Quint swore. "He's another that wouldn't be so damn nosey, if I had him where I wanted him," he said savagely. "Him and his damn paper! I never knew anybody that could ask so many questions about things that's none of his damn business ——"

"He's comin', all right," Grier said, stealing a look back.

Sheridan was suddenly calm. "All right, let him come. We'll turn at Longhorn, give him a chance to come up, if he wants to talk to me. We'll wait in that vacant lot back of the courthouse. There aren't many folks pass that way ——"

"And then what?" Frame asked.

Sheridan's eyes gleamed wickedly. "I'll tell you what to do, if we get him within range. That damn undersized Irishman has got to be stopped!"

The three hurried on, turned the corner.

When Micky arrived at Longhorn Street he could see no sign of Sheridan and his two companions. Then, glancing obliquely across the street, Micky caught sight of the trio, just leaving the footpath to cross into the vacant lot at the rear of the two-story brick courthouse. There weren't any windows in the back wall of the building. Brush and a stunted mesquite grew in the vacant lot. Heaps of tincans and other rubbish dotted the ground at various points.

Micky hurried across the street. Longhorn was only sparsely built up. There weren't many houses on either side. The small house adjacent to the vacant lot was empty. Down the street, the distance of a city block, two small children were playing in the dust of the road. There weren't any other people in sight.

Micky found Sheridan and his henchmen standing idly against the rear wall of the courthouse. They glanced up in pretended surprise as Micky hurried up.

"Hello, runt," Sheridan forced his voice to be relatively pleasant for the moment. Grier and Frame didn't say anything.

"How-d'ye-do, Sheridan," Micky greeted pleasantly. "I'd like to have a few words from you for my paper. You're one of the biggest cattlemen around here. You own the Faro Saloon. I'd like to get some sort of statement from you regarding that swarm of flies that invaded your place. Do you think there was any natural cause to account for those flies, or was it just a phenomenon of nature? I'd like to have ——"

"How'd you like to have this?" Joe Frame grunted. While Micky had been talking, Frame and Grier had edged around to the side, away from the building wall. Joe Frame struck hard, his first landing against the side of Micky's head!

Micky staggered, nearly fell, managed to keep his feet until he crashed against the brick wall. There he slid to a sitting position.

Sheridan grinned nastily. "Let him have it again!" he ordered.

Butch Grier came in with a rush, swinging one clenched fist low. Micky, through dazed eyes, saw the blow coming, managed to jerk his head to one side.

Wham! Grier's fist struck the brick wall with considerable force. A howl of anguish split the air. Micky slipped quickly to one side, climbed to his feet. Grier was dancing around in agony, trying to get his bruised knuckles into his mouth.

"Feeling playful, eh?" Mickey said gamely. He made no attempt to escape.

"You'll see how playful we are," Sheridan snarled, lips drawn back from his teeth. "We don't like you, Callahan and ——"

Joe Frame had drawn his six-shooter.

"Shall I let him have it, Quint?"

"No, you fool. Put that gun away. A shot would bring people here. Grier, for geez' sake, shut up!"

Frame put his gun away and advanced toward Micky whose back was against the wall. Sheridan said cruelly, "So you want me to speak a few words, eh, you damn snoop! I'll speak 'em, but you won't like any of 'em. We're going to give you just about the neatest beating a man ever got. By the time we've bashed in your skull with a gun-barrel you'll lose all interest in reportin' news. Your body will be found under one of these heaps of rubbish one of these days, but nobody will recognize it."

Grier was still nursing his wounded hand at one side, taking no interest in the proceedings, as a steady flow of profanity issued from his wide lips. Frame and Sheridan commenced to close in, their hands clenching convulsively.

Micky gulped. "Just a little more," he said weakly, "I don't care what you say, but give me something I can write up." And at that moment he remembered the gun in his waistband, hidden by his coat. "If you'll just hold off a second until I can get my pencil ____"

His hand went inside his coat. Sheridan

and Frame were closer now, never dreaming that the reporter had a gun on him.

"You and your damn pencil," Sheridan grated. "I'll ——"

And then he stopped short, mouth dropping open in shocked surprise. Frame made a startled gurgling sound. Even Grier stopped short in amazement.

"By Gawd! He's got a gun!" Grier exclaimed.

"Stick your hands up!" Micky ordered coolly. "Quick! All three of you. I'm deadly with this revolver. I won't take any monkey business. And don't try to get your guns. I'll shoot at the first false move. Grier, get over there with your two pards. Keep well back, the three of you. And keep those hands up!"

Had any of the three realized Micky was packing a gun they could have drawn and fired while the reporter was thinking about drawing, but the surprise was so great that all three men threw their arms high above their heads. Their faces were crimson, a choked volume of choice curses drifted from their mouths.

"That's fine," Micky grinned, surveying the three enraged men. "So you were going to beat me up, eh?"

"Look here, Callahan," Sheridan protested, "we were just fooling. We didn't mean anything ——"

"Sure, sure, I understand," Micky chuckled. His gun swung in a short arc that covered all three of the men, as he continued, "Now that we're all good friends again, we'll go on with the statement I requested from Mister Sheridan. You remember the one, Sheridan? About the flies in the Faro Saloon? Do you really think that incident will permanently ruin your trade? Do you feel that there was anything unusual in such a —— ?"

But Sheridan had held in as long as possible. Now, he fairly exploded in a burst of profanity that seemingly shriveled the earth. He choked, he cursed, his features became apoplectic with rage. In short, he nearly strangled on the venom of his own remarks. And that was the moment in which Tucson and Lullaby and Stony rounded the corner of the building at a run. They took one look, stopped short, and started to laugh.

"Looks like," Lullaby drawled, "the runt is gettin' an interview of some sort."

"What kind of a statement did Sheridan make, Micky?" Stony chuckled.

"Even you would blush," Micky grinned, glancing sidewise. "I can't use any of the words in my paper."

Sheridan and his companions suddenly

fell silent and glowered sullenly at Tucson and his pardners.

Tucson said gravely, "Micky, it might have been a good idea to cock that gun. Otherwise it won't shoot if you pull trigger."

Micky gulped, went white. "My gosh!" he gasped, "I just plain forgot that part!"

XV. A Clean Knockout

That statement by Micky brought a fresh flow of profanity from Sheridan and his henchmen. In their surprise at seeing a gun in the little reporter's fist, they had entirely overlooked the fact that it wasn't cocked for action. In the Southwest cow country of that day it was taken for granted that no man was so insane as to point an uncocked gun at another man; the thumbing back of the hammer was a part of the draw; that much at least was thoroughly acknowledged by all gunfighters.

"Quiet down, you three," Tucson snapped. "A shorthorn has made fools of you. The more you talk, the more foolish you look. And don't get any ideas at this late date about pullin' your irons. On the other hand, suit yourselves. Either way suits us. But make up your minds — plumb *pronto!*"

"Aw, shucks!" Sheridan growled. "We

didn't mean the tenderfoot any harm. We were only joshin' him a mite. Hell! Do you think if we'd been serious, he could have got the draw on us?"

"You were sure usin' serious language when I first saw you," Tucson said whimsically. "Micky, how about it? What happened?"

"Nothin' much," Micky shrugged. "We all got sort of playful for a minute. Grier hurt his hand, somehow. Sheridan talked a lot, but I did some talking too. Oh, yes, I sort of remember that Frame took a punch at me when I wasn't looking." The little red-haired reporter grinned suddenly, glanced at the sky. The sun was dropping below the Santa Madraza Range. Micky went on, "I just happened to remember some unfinished business."

Sticking the six-shooter back in his trousers' waistband, Micky stepped up to face Frame, who started to back away a little from the gleam in Micky's eyes. "So you'd hit a man when he isn't looking, eh?" Micky said gently. "That doesn't show good manners, Frame. Now, you thick-skulled, lice-crawling gutter-spawn, you'd better put up your dukes. I'm just about due to devastate one filthy-moraled spalpeen."

"Now, look here ——" Frame commenced. He backed a step, but his guard came up. He didn't have an opportunity to say more:

Micky's left fist shot out like a battering ram and appeared to sink inches into Frame's middle. Frame grunted painfully, bent forward, his guard coming down for just an instant. And as his jaw came within easy striking distance, Micky's right swished through the air!

Frame grunted stupidly. The force of the blow lifted him from his feet. He landed heavily on his back, rolled over on his face and lay still. Sheridan and Grier gazed down in amazement at their fallen pardner.

"Clean knockout!" Tucson chuckled.

Lullaby and Stony didn't say anything. They just looked at Micky.

Micky dusted off his hands, strode cockily across to the Three Mesquiteers. "All business cleaned up," he smiled. "Let's go eat supper."

"Cripes!" Stony burst out. "Where'd you learn to hit like that, Irish?"

"In the bantamweight division," Micky said modestly. "I held the championship in my section for three years. Then I got overweight and decided to lend my talents to the uplift of journalism ——"

"You sure uplifted Frame," Lullaby

drawled. "Stony, maybe we better quit ribbin' this Irish hombre. He looks like dynamite to me."

Tucson and his friends glanced at Sheridan and Grier, still gazing dumbly at Frame's inert form.

"Yes," Tucson chuckled, "I reckon supper is next on the program."

Sheridan and Grier didn't even look up as Tucson and his friends headed for Main Street.

"Look," Micky proposed, "I've got to go over to the hotel and write some stuff about the plague of flies that descended on Godwin. The editor of the *Los Angeles Clarion* will be jumping down my throat if I don't give him something ——"

"Shucks," Tucson said, "today's stage is gone. You won't be able to send your letter until tomorrow."

"If I put it off until tomorrow something else might happen to keep me from writing it," Micky explained. "What I was going to say, you fellows wait for me in the Gunsight. I'll get my stuff written up, then we'll all eat supper together."

"All right," Tucson nodded good-naturedly. "We can wait a half hour or so, I reckon."

Micky hurried on to the hotel. Tucson and

his two pardners entered the Gunsight Bar to wait. The crowd in the bar had thinned out to a small extent, but Nick Fitch's business was still above its normal activity. The bar was lined with men.

"You hombres thirsty?" Stony asked.

"I ain't," from Lullaby. Tucson said, "Let's sit down at one of those tables and wait for Micky."

Two of the tables lined against the wall across the room from the bar were unoccupied. Tucson and his companions found chairs, started to manufacture brown paper cigarettes. Matches were scratched. Smoke spiraled about the heads of the three.

Tucson said reminiscently, "That runt packs a punch."

Lullaby nodded, "I'll bet Frame is still groggy."

"We'll have to sort of keep an eye out for Micky," Tucson said quietly. "If Sheridan and his skunks caught him alone, again, I don't think they'd stop at a beating."

"Bet they wouldn't either," Stony agreed. "We'll have to look out for him. I wonder just what happened before Micky got the drop on 'em — with his uncocked gun."

"Cripes!" Lullaby grinned. "Wasn't that funny? Leave it to the Irish for luck."

The heat of the day still blanketed the

town. Perspiring humanity in the Gunsight added to the thick, smoky atmosphere. Lullaby and Stony shoved their hats farther back on their heads. Tucson removed his sombrero, placed it on the table before him, mopped his brow.

"It's sure been a busy day," Lullaby commented. "An inquest, a funeral, a deluge of flies and a knockout. All this activity sure gives me an appetite. I wish Micky would hurry up. I'm hungry."

"I never saw you when you weren't hungry," Stony commented in a challenging tone of voice. "The way you eat, it's a plumb wonder to me you don't get hawg-fat."

"Is that so?" Lullaby grunted. "That theory don't work out in your case."

"I don't gluttonize the way you do ——"

"Gluttonize?" Lullaby's eyes opened wider. "What do you —— ?"

"Stow away grub," Stony explained. "Get a bait, go for chow, put on the feed-bag. In short, Stupid, eat! Is that plain enough?"

"I wasn't referrin' to eatin' ——" Lullaby commenced.

"By Cripes! That *is* a surprise. For once you opened your mouth and didn't mention food."

"What I'm tryin' to explain to your dull

mentality," Lullaby observed loftily, "is this: you say, because I eat regularly, I should be hawg-fat. For your enlightenment, I point out that you travel around with Tucson and me a heap ——"

"What's that got to do with it?" Stony said cautiously.

"If you had brains you'd know," Lullaby sneered. "I'll explain — you're in a position to pick up a lot of knowledge, but your intelligence don't seem to get any better. Matter of fact, it grows worse."

"You can't prove that," Stony snapped.

"*I* don't have to. You prove it yourself every time you open your mouth. I can't prove it! Cripes A'mighty!" Lullaby made a quick gesture of disgust with the hand holding his cigarette.

Unnoticed by the three men, the glowing tip of the cigarette dropped off and landed on the brim of Tucson's sombrero, placed on the table in front of its owner.

"Aw, you're just tryin' to change the subject," Stony protested.

"Yeah, and you're one of these old-fashioned fossils that objects to change!"

The wrangling continued to Tucson's amusement, getting a little more insulting with every word spoken. Tucson laughed softly as he listened to the verbal barrage passing heatedly across the table.

". . . and furthermore," Stony was saying, "I'm gettin' plumb weary of holdin' everythin' I say down to your one-syllable vocabulary. If dumbness was water you'd be the Pacific Ocean."

That, for the moment, stopped Lullaby. To cover his confusion, he lifted his dead cigarette to his lips, while he did some fast thinking. Then he looked at the end of the cigarette in some surprise.

"That proves what I been saying," Stony exclaimed, quickly. "You ain't even got sense enough to keep your cigarette lit. You let it go out ——"

"Aw, I did not," Lullaby grunted. "The end must've fell off."

At the same instant, Tucson sniffed the air. "I smell cloth burnin'," he announced.

"Nick must've sold one of his cigars to somebody at the bar," Stony snickered.

A thin spiral of smoke ascended from the surface of Tucson's hat brim. "There's your dang cigarette end," Tucson said, lifting the hat and brushing the tiny coal of fire to the floor.

"Gosh, I'm plumb regretful, pard," Lullaby said. "It must've fell off while I was talkin' to Stony."

"Not much harm done, I reckon," Tucson

commented. He blew away the ashes where they'd rested on the felt brim, rubbed the spot with his finger, scratched at it with his finger nail. Only a faint scorched spot showed in the thin nap of the felt surface. He replaced the hat on his head, repeating, "Not much harm done. But I reckon I better get my Stet out of your way."

"Yeah, he burns me up too," Stony sneered.

"Dry rubbish catches flame plumb easy," Lullaby said quickly.

Stony snapped, "Hear what he said about your hat, Tucson?"

"I wasn't referrin' to Tucson's hat," Lullaby chuckled.

Stony reddened, then started to grin. Tucson's eyes had suddenly narrowed. For an instant an angry look crossed his features. He said, "By cripes! By cripes!"

"What's up, pard?" Stony sobered suddenly.

Tucson, instead of replying, snatched the sombrero from his head and again examined the faint scorched spot in the felt surface of the brim. "I'll bet that's what happened," he muttered, half to himself.

Lullaby looked puzzled, "Gosh, pard, I'll buy you a new hat ——" he commenced.

"To hell with the hat," Tucson said shortly.

"You didn't hurt it any."

"Well, what —— ?"

"Keep still a second. I'm trying to think. I've got an idea."

Lullaby and Stony eyed Tucson soberly. They could almost picture the wheels going around in the lean redhead's brain. Finally, Stony could retain silence no longer. "What's up?"

Tucson looked up a bit blankly from his examination of the hat-brim. "Huh? What did you say?"

Stony repeated his question.

There was a certain satisfaction in Tucson's short laugh now. He pushed his hat toward Stony. "Look at it, you hombres. Does that burn tell you anything?"

Lullaby and Stony surveyed the hat. Finally they looked up, puzzled.

"Doesn't mean anything to me," Lullaby shook his head.

"All I see is a faint yellow spot where Lullaby's carelessness with a cigarette ——" Stony commenced.

"It's just the fact that it's faint, makes it important," Tucson insisted. "No damage done at all, to speak of."

"And you think that's important?" Lullaby frowned.

"Don't you?" Tucson asked.

Lullaby's brow creased deeper. "Danged if I see why," he admitted at last, "except that I don't have to buy you a new bonnet."

Tucson turned to Stony. "Doesn't that scorched mark give you any ideas, either?"

Stony said, "You mean regardin' the trouble with Sheridan?"

"You get the idea."

Stony pondered, but finally shook his head. "I don't get it. What do you see that we don't?"

Tucson sighed deeply. "All right, let it pass. Maybe I'm wrong."

"What you got on your mind, pard?" Lullaby queried.

Tucson shook his head. "Let it ride for a spell, until I've thought this matter over. I want to do some checking up. If things work out, I'll tell you ——"

"Ready to eat, gentlemen?"

Micky's cheerful voice broke in on the conversation, as he came swinging through the entrance.

Tucson looked up, smiling. "Ready, Micky."

Stony said, "We're more'n ready. Especially Lullaby. Like always, he's plumb famished. Fact is, he had thoughts of eatin' Tucson's Stet hat. If he hadn't stopped to cook it first ——"

"Aw, you know where you can go," Lullaby growled good-naturedly.

The Three Mesquiteers got to their feet. Tucson asked Micky, "Get your story done for your paper?"

"Sealed and in an envelope," Micky replied. "I played it up from the humorous angle. Sheridan will be fit to be tied if he ever sees it. Anyway, it'll help fill space, show my editor I'm on the job ——"

"That's what I'm interested in," Lullaby interrupted. "Fillin' space is the most important thing on my mind now ——"

"On your what?" Stony asked incredulously.

Before Lullaby could reply, the swinging doors opened, and an elderly man in cattleman's togs entered, followed by Tate Scorpio. The elderly man was red-faced, with long grey mustaches. He was slightly drunk and staggered as he walked. He seemed angry about something.

"I can't see why Sheridan won't talk to me," he growled to Scorpio. "After what he said last year, he ought to keep his word ——"

"Quint didn't have time, Kellogg," Scorpio was saying placatingly. "Like he told you, he had to get out to the ranch. Just as soon as we have anything you can use, we'll drive 'em over. But right now ——"

"Right now, you want me to get out of Godwin for some reason," Kellogg growled. "Dam'd if I understand it. I got orders to fill and you won't do as you promised. I don't think Sheridan left town at all. I figure he put it up to you to get rid of me ——"

"Looky here, Kellogg," Scorpio commenced patiently, "I can see your angle but ——" Scorpio stopped short upon noticing Tucson and his friends approaching the door, then abruptly changed the subject, "C'mon, I'll buy a drink. We'll talk it over."

The two pushed up to the bar. Scorpio glanced hard-eyed at Tucson, but said nothing. Tucson stepped to the street, followed by his friends.

No one said anything for a few minutes. Lullaby and Stony were waiting for Tucson to speak. Tucson finally said, "I wish we could talk to that Kellogg."

"What's he got to do with us?" Callahan wanted to know.

"It sounded to me like Sheridan wants to get him out of town," Tucson said. "Right now there's so much stirring, Sheridan has got to walk plumb easy. It might not be important. On the other hand it may have some bearin' on the things we're interested in."

"Scorpio dropped somethin' about drivin' somethin' over to Kellogg's place ——" Lullaby commenced.

"Cattle or horses," Stony said.

"And he shut Kellogg up with the offer to buy a drink," Tucson pointed out, "just as soon as he noticed us."

"Well, does all this mean anything to you, fellows?" Micky asked.

"Mebbe yes, mebbe no," Tucson replied cryptically. "C'mon, we'll go eat."

It was dark on the street by this time. Rectangles of light from doors and windows threw yellow patches along the sidewalk.

"We goin' to the hotel dinin' room?" Lullaby asked.

Tucson shook his head. "They got the best food there, but the service is sort of slow. Let's line out for the Chink's restaurant, down the street. His stuff is clean if he does need lessons in cookin'."

"And Micky hasn't told us yet," Stony put in, "just what happened with Sheridan and his plug-uglies, before he got the drop on 'em — with that uncocked gun."

"Aw, quit joshin' me about that and I'll give you the story while we eat," Micky grinned.

Two by two, the four men walked along the plank sidewalk, until they'd arrived at the restaurant. Tucson was deep in thought, but didn't put his thoughts into words for the benefit of his companions. And Stony and Lullaby knew full well that until he had the problem worked out to his own satisfaction, they'd receive no concrete knowledge of what was in his mind.

XVI. "What Reward Money?"

Supper was nearly finished. The four men sat at a long counter presided over by a grinning Oriental, who had served ham and eggs, coffee and dried apple pie to Tucson and his three companions. There were a few other men in the restaurant, seated at tables placed across the room from the counter.

Stony drained his coffee cup and reached for Durham and cigarette papers. "So Sheridan and his skunks were all set to beat you up, eh?" he said angrily.

Micky nodded. "They would have too, only I got that gun out in time."

Lullaby shook his head. "You don't know how lucky you were, boy. If they'd noticed that gun wasn't cocked, they'd have bored you prompt and plenty. Well, you gave 'em more than they bargained for. I guess you're square in that direction. Only you'd better keep out of Sheridan's way, unless you're with us."

"That's good advice, Micky," Tucson said seriously.

The restaurant door banged open. The man known as Kellogg entered. Scorpio was still with him.

"What in hell you taggin' me for?" Kellogg was demanding loudly. "I'll be leavin' town shortly, but I ain't aimin' to go until I've had my supper."

Scorpio caught sight of Tucson and his companions. His face darkened, and he said something in an undertone to Kellogg. Kellogg shook his head violently, saying, "No, I ain't goin' no place else. This joint looks all right to me. If you don't like it, go away. I can get along by myself."

Without arguing further, he steered a wavering course to one of the tables and sat down heavily in a chair. Reluctantly, Scorpio followed and took the chair opposite Kellogg. The Chinese came to take their order.

"And hurry it up," Scorpio snapped at the Chinese.

"You take your time, Chink," Kellogg bellowed belligerently. "I ain't in no hurry. I want that steak done through, understand, you yeller imp o' Satan?"

Grinningly, the Chinese nodded his head and headed for his kitchen. Tucson called him back and laid some money on the counter.

The Chinese returned, picked up the money. "You' suppe' all light?" he asked.

"Plumb elegant, Confucius," Tucson nodded. Then to the others, "C'mon, let's get going."

The four left the restaurant, followed by Scorpio's eyes.

Outside, on the darkened street, Tucson said, "Lullaby, you and Stony ride herd on that Kellogg hombre. For some reason he's not popular in this town with Sheridan. Scorpio is tryin' to get rid of him ——"

"Scorpio didn't even want to eat there when he saw us," Stony put in.

"I noticed that," from Lullaby, "which same leads me to believe that Scorpio is afraid Kellogg might drop somethin' that Scorpio wouldn't want us to hear."

"Exactly the way it looks to me," Tucson said. "Anyway, you keep tabs on him. If you get an opportunity to talk to Kellogg without Scorpio knowing it, see what you can find out."

"We'll do that," Lullaby nodded.

"What you aimin' to do, pard?" Stony asked.

Tucson said, "I'm going to saddle up and ride out to the 8-Bar."

"Any particular reason?" Micky Callahan said quickly.

"I want to talk to Nancy Hayden."

"What about?" Micky asked.

"Oh, one thing and another."

Micky scratched his head. "I sort of wanted to pay her a call myself."

"What for?" Tucson asked.

"Oh," Micky smiled, "one thing and another. Nothing important, from your point of view. I just didn't feel I should be calling on her, though, so soon after her father was buried."

"There are some things that can't stand on ceremony," Tucson said.

"What are you going to the 8-Bar for?" Lullaby asked curiously.

"I'll tell you later," Tucson replied. "I've been thinking about scorched hats — one scorched hat, to be exact."

Lullaby and Stony looked blank and said together, "Scorched hats?"

Micky repeated, "Scorched hats?"

Tucson nodded, "You wouldn't understand, Micky. Lullaby and Stony know what I'm talkin' about, but they don't get the connection. I figure to let 'em use their brains a mite."

"Look, Tucson," Micky said wistfully, "can I go with you?"

"Figured you'd had enough of forkin' a horse for a spell."

Micky winced. He was still walking a trifle stiffly. He grinned, speaking Tucson's words of a few moments before, "There are some things that can't stand on ceremony." Then, "Can I go?"

"I don't know how I can stop you," Tucson smiled. "I was figurin' to ask you anyway."

"Gee, that's fine."

"I'll tell you what you do," Tucson continued. "I'll go to the livery for my horse. I'll get one for you at the same time. Meanwhile, you drift down to Doc Perkins', will you? Ask him if there's any chance of Bogart regainin' consciousness tonight. I'd hate to be away, if Bogart should come to enough to talk."

"I'll do that."

Micky hastened off down the street. Lullaby and Stony said *"Adiós"* and took up a position across the roadway where they could keep an eye on the doorway of the Chinese restaurant and see Kellogg and Scorpio when the men emerged. Tucson walked off in the direction of the livery stable.

With the horses saddled and standing

before the livery, Tucson had only a few minutes to wait before Callahan returned.

"No chance tonight, doc says," Micky stated, as he climbed awkwardly into the saddle. "Bogart's just a little weaker than before. That's the only change. Doc says he don't see how he keeps alive. 'Course, Bogart might come to, just before he dies, but Doc doesn't think there's any use you waiting around if you've got anything else that's important." Mickey paused, then, "This isn't the same horse I had before."

"I got one that would make better time," Tucson said, swinging up to his own saddle. "No, don't you go to frettin'. That little bay is gentle as a kitten and won't act up none. I figure she'll be easier for you to sit, too."

They started out at an easy lope, Micky bouncing loosely in the saddle, but gradually getting accustomed to the feel of a horse between his legs. The moon wouldn't be up for some time yet, but the trail to the 8-Bar was easy to follow, especially with Tucson to lead the way.

Micky didn't say anything for some time, then he timidly broke the silence, "It's darn nice of you to let me come with you, Tucson."

"Forget it. Only I don't figure you'll get any news for your paper."

"I wasn't thinking about the paper. The *Clarion* gets a fair return for the money it pays. Er — uh — that Nancy Hayden girl is real nice, isn't she?"

Tucson smiled in the darkness, said gravely, "She seems like a mighty fine girl. It's a shame she's had all this trouble."

"That damn Sheridan and his skunks ——" Micky commenced angrily.

"You find yourself likin' Nancy?" Tucson said.

"Plenty." Micky's voice sounded a bit uncomfortable. "I sort of jumped off the edge the minute I laid eyes on her. I fall hard for her kind, anyway. You know, tall and capable-looking and yellow hair. What was it that poet said about her kind?" Micky quoted solemnly,

". . . a glorious Viking goddess
With tawny skin and hair pale gold
Like silk upon the ripening corn,
And eyes so deeply violet . . ."

Micky broke off and said awkwardly, "Something like that, anyway."

Tucson said quietly, "Your poet must have known Nancy Hayden. That sure sounds like her."

Silence for a few moments broken only by

236

the steady drumming of horses' hoofs. Then Micky said, a trifle sadly, "Trouble is, her kind never look at an undersized half-pint like me."

"You can't never tell, son," Tucson said sympathetically. "Of course, your rearin' has all been in the city. Nancy's got a spread to run now. It takes money and a lot of knowledge to run a cow ranch, until it gets on a payin' basis."

"Trying to let me down easy, eh?" Micky didn't resent Tucson's words. "Sure, I know what you mean. Me, with a reporter's salary, lookin' up to a girl with a cattle ranch to operate. And where would I fit in?"

"Somethin' like that, son."

"Do you know what I'd do?" Micky said enthusiastically. "If the girl liked me and I had the money, I'd start a newspaper in Godwin. The town's wide open for a paper. It's growing fast ——" He paused hopelessly, "Oh, well, what's the use of talking about it? First thing you know I'll be sloppin' over and crying on your shoulder."

"Girl or no girl," Tucson said quietly, "Godwin is big enough to stand a weekly paper. Of course, whoever run it would have to have a liking for the country and understand cow folks ——"

"Like it?" Micky exclaimed. "Tucson, I'm

plain batty about it — all the mountains and the desert stuff. I don't ever want to go back to Los Angeles. There's nothing I'd like better than to tell that slave-driving editor of mine to go snap at himself."

"How much would it cost to set up a paper?" Tucson asked.

Micky had figures at his finger tips and gave them.

Tucson nodded. "I know a hombre that has money to lend mighty reasonable sometimes. If you get an idea you'd like to go through with your idea, I might take it up with him."

"Say, Tucson! That's great! You're white. Of course, if I could collect that reward money ——" Micky halted himself abruptly.

Tucson waited for him to go on. Micky remained silent. Tucson asked, "What reward money you referrin' to, Micky?"

"That statement," Micky confessed disgruntedly, "was a slip. I can't say more now. For a minute I forgot I was a newspaper man, on the trail of a story. 'Course, if you want to swap yarns and tell me what you're doing around here, I might ——"

"I've already told you," Tucson insisted. "I've nothing to hide."

"By gosh! Sometimes I almost believe you."

"The reward you mentioned got anything to do with your editor sending you here?"

Micky changed the subject: "Come on, let's make some speed."

Tucson didn't press matters. He touched spur lightly to his pony. The two animals drummed steadily through the night.

XVII. Ambush!

It was shortly after eight-thirty when they pulled rein in the 8-Bar ranch yard. Stew Trumbull and Pete Blair came to the doorway of the bunkhouse and hailed them, then stepped out to shake hands. The four men chatted idly for a few minutes, the 8-Bar punchers asking Micky if he had "his riding legs yet?" The Tucson explained the reason for the visit, "I'd like to talk to Nancy a mite. Think she'll feel like having visitors?"

"I know dang well she'll be glad to see you," Pete said earnestly, "and thank you. That load of supplies you sent out came in right handy ——"

"I appreciated those forty-five ca'tridges plenty," Stew Trumbull put in. "Now we'll be ready for any skunks that might come smellin' up our vicinity."

"Aw, forget it," Tucson said.

"Go on up to the house," Pete went on.

"We'll take care of your broncs. Micky, you want to wait in the bunkhouse with us?"

Micky hesitated. Stew said, "We might play a three-handed game of —"

"I'd sort of like to have Micky with me," Tucson cut in, and received an appreciative glance from the reporter. "He's after news, you know, and may want to get some details I'd miss."

The door at the back of the ranch house was answered by a middle-aged Mexican woman named Berta, who escorted Tucson and Micky into the main room of the house, where they were greeted warmly by Nancy Hayden. Chairs were pushed up before the fireplace, then the Mexican woman left in the direction of the kitchen.

"I hope you don't mind us coming out to visit, tonight," Tucson was saying.

"Mind it," Nancy smiled. "I'm mighty glad to see you." Tucson thought the girl looked troubled about something, but he didn't interrupt as she continued, "It's — it's been so lonely. I'm going to miss Dad. And — and Tucson, I want you to know I appreciate what you've done —"

"Forget it," Tucson commenced.

"I can't forget things like this — sending Berta out here — buying those supplies and having them delivered. They arrived in good time. We were pretty close to hardpan. Pete and Stew have been unusually kind in staying on when we haven't been able to ——"

"Let's take all of that for granted," Tucson interrupted. "No — we *won't* speak about the money. It just happens that I and my partners are making a pretty good thing of the 3-Bar-O outfit we own. We can spare a few dollars, I guess. . . . By the way, do you mind answering a few questions regarding those cattle of yours that disappeared — I mean the ones you bought from Sheridan. One hundred sixty-five head vanished, wasn't it?"

"That's correct," Nancy nodded.

"You're absolutely sure you saw those cattle branded?"

"Absolutely." Nancy smiled a little at Tucson's insistence on this point. "They even vented the Circle-Cross brand."

Tucson considered a minute. "How long did it take? How many men did Sheridan put on the job?"

"A little over two days," Nancy said promptly. "There were ten men."

"Hmm! I didn't know Sheridan employed that many."

"I remember him mentioning that he hired some extra help for the job. He had men at each fire."

"More than one brand fire was employed, then?"

"Two."

Tucson pondered a few moments. "Two and a half days is longer than it should take ten men, to my way of thinkin'. I'd say they must have worked awful careful. Still, with Sheridan hirin' extra men he must've wanted to clear the job up as soon as possible."

"Why, I suppose so." Nancy seemed uncertain. "I didn't know much about branding cattle those days. It seemed all pretty nasty with that smell of burned hair ——"

"And you were watching all the time?"

"If I wasn't at one fire or the other, I was riding between the two. Tucson, I know positively that I counted two hundred animals with our 8-Bar brand burned on them."

"How about the knife-work — I mean the ear-marking? The Circle-Cross cuts a double-under-bit, right and left. I understand you split both ears. Sheridan's markin' couldn't very well be changed to yours, of course ——"

"I remember Sheridan saying," Nancy cut in, "that we wouldn't need to bother with ear-markings. On a friendly range it wasn't necessary, and the bill of sale and the vent took care of everything. I'd asked him about that. I was rather vague on the subject, but I knew ear-markings were registered, and I wanted to know all about it."

Tucson nodded. "Yeah, I suppose that was all right as far as it goes. Only I figure Sheridan went a little too far."

"What do you mean, Tucson?" Micky got into the conversation. He'd been sitting in silence, feasting his eyes on the girl's face.

"Are you hinting," Nancy asked quickly, "that you know where our cows went to, Tucson?"

"Where they eventually ended up, I'm not sure," Tucson replied. "But I've got a hunch I know what happened."

"What?" Nancy and Micky speaking together.

Tucson shook his head. "I'm not ready to commit myself, yet. I may be all wrong. Until I'm certain in my own mind, I'd rather not talk about it for a spell. If things break right, I'll get your cows back — that is, the same number that disappeared, or their equivalent in cash. Meanwhile you go on running your ranch and leave matters to me and my pardners."

A frown clouded Nancy's face. "It doesn't look as though I'd have the ranch to run, much longer," she said bitterly.

"How come," Tucson asked quickly.

"Fulton Hodge drove out here to see me, this afternoon; he arrived just a short time after I got home from the funeral."

"Who is Fulton Hodge?"

Micky Callahan supplied the answer to that: "Owner of the Godwin Savings Bank. I never spoke to him, but if he isn't a dirty skinflint, I never saw one."

"I've heard that about him," Nancy nodded. "Anyway, the interest on father's note ——" The girl broke off, started to explain, "You see, Father borrowed five hundred dollars, eighteen months back to ——"

"Poddy Cameron told me about that," Tucson cut in.

"He gave the 8-Bar as security ——"

"That's a lot of security on five hundred," Tucson pointed out.

"Dad thought so at the time he borrowed the money, but he didn't think he'd have any trouble paying it back. He paid the interest every six months. Interest was due the day he was killed ——"

"Now, look here, Nancy," Tucson interrupted kindly. "Don't you let it bother you. The interest on five hundred isn't enough to worry about. I'll take care of that. I'll see this Hodge hombre in the mornin'. I'll ——"

"I'm afraid it won't do any good," Nancy said hopelessly. "You see. Hodge claims that Father borrowed five thousand ——"

"What?" Tucson exclaimed.

"Five *thousand!*" from Micky.

Nancy's shoulders drooped. "That's what Hodge claimed. I'd always understood it was five hundred — that's what Dad always said, when he mentioned the matter. But Hodge had the note with him and showed it to me. It was for five thousand."

"I don't like this," Tucson said slowly. "You're sure somebody didn't forge your father's signature?"

"It was father's handwriting," the girl stated positively.

Micky was muttering angrily under his breath.

"Hodge said," Nancy went on, "that business had been bad, and that if the note, plus interest, wasn't paid by the end of the month, I'd have to let the ranch go."

Tucson smiled a confidence he didn't feel. "Now, don't you go worrying about that, either, Nancy. Five thousand isn't an unheard of sum. I'll see this Hodge hombre tomorrow. I think the whole matter can be straightened out."

Micky said, "He's a great little straightener, Nancy."

"Tell you what you do," Tucson continued to the girl, "you ride into Godwin in the morning and go to the bank with me. We'll talk to Hodge. Maybe I can take the note off his hands, if he gets hard. If you weren't with me, he might make some statements I wouldn't know how to answer."

"Gee, Tucson," the girl exclaimed, her eyes shining, "I don't know how I can ever thank you ——"

Tucson chuckled, "Forget that and just keep smiling. All this bad business is likely to be cleared up a heap quicker than you look for. . . . Well, I'd better be getting back to town. You meet me in the morning, about the time the bank opens."

"Tucson, why don't you stay the night? There's plenty of room in the bunkhouse."

"Thanks just the same," shaking his head. "Lullaby and Stony are working on a little job I left 'em on, and I'm curious to see how they come out."

Tucson and Micky rose to their feet — Micky reluctantly — and started to take their leave. Noticing Micky's hesitation, Tucson suggested, "Look here, Micky, too much ridin' is tough on a beginner. Why don't you sleep down in the bunkhouse tonight, and ride into Godwin with Nancy in the morning? That'll give her an escort

and leave Stew and Pete free for ranch work
——"

"Gosh, Tucson," Micky burst out, "that'd be great ——" He stopped short, in sudden confusion, and waited to see what Nancy would say.

"I think that's a good idea, myself," Nancy nodded sincerely. Her eyes met Micky's; her cheeks colored slightly. "I'll be mighty glad to have company on that ride to town."

Saying "good-night," the two men left the house and, arriving at the bunkhouse, told what had been arranged. Tucson mentioned to Pete and Stew the matter regarding Clem Hayden's note at the bank.

Both cowboys immediately "went hot into the air," as the saying is. "Why, I know damn well, Clem only borrowed five hundred," Pete exclaimed. "He told me so."

"I heard him say that once, too," from Stew. "We saw Hodge arrive at the house today, but as Nancy didn't say what he came for, we didn't think anything about it. I'll bet that skunk is cookin' up some sort of game."

"We'll see, tomorrow," Tucson nodded. "It looks crooked. If I find out it is — well, Mister Fulton Hodge is likely to find himself in hot water."

Ten minutes later, Tucson had saddled up

and was on his way back to town. The moon wasn't yet up, but the sky was bright with stars. The trail twisted a winding course between low hills for the first few miles, the dusty roadway flowing smoothly to the rear beneath the hoofs of Tucson's horse.

After a time the country flattened out. The pony drummed steadily on. The way ran straighter now over gradually rolling hill lands. Here and there a huge upthrust of granite reared a blocky black mass at various points along the trail. Tucson dipped down into a long hollow, then, slowed pace to ascend the next slope.

Once more, reaching the top, his figure was silhouetted against the sky line. To the right, just ahead, was a queerly-shaped jumble of boulders as high as a house.

"Behind them rocks," Tucson commented idly, "would make a dang good place for a dry-gulcher to wait for a victim."

Even as the thought ran through his mind, some sense of impending disaster flashed a warning signal to his brain. He was just passing the big pile of jumbled granite, when a slight noise reached his ears. Then it happened!

The night gloom was stabbed twice with streaks of orange flame. Two heavy caliber six-shooters roared viciously. Tucson's pony

248

whirled half round as its rider flung his arms in the air and pitched heavily to the earth!

XVIII. Lullaby Thinks Fast

Meanwhile, earlier in the evening, Lullaby and Stony had kept a faithful watch across the street from the restaurant operated by the Chinese. An hour passed. Evidently, Kellogg was taking his time eating supper. Slouched against the supporting uprights of a store porch shelter, the two pardners stirred impatiently. The store was closed, dark. Stony dropped a cigarette butt under his heel, commenced to roll a second smoke.

"By gosh," he said moodily, "that Kellogg hombre sure don't hurry any."

"He looked like the stubborn type to me," Lullaby grunted. "Put yourself in his place. If Scorpio was tryin' to hurry you out of town, wouldn't you take your time?"

"I reckon. But why is Sheridan, Scorpio, so anxious to get rid of him?"

"I can't answer that one. Tucson had some sort of hunch on the proposition, but what it was he didn't say, even if he knew. You know how Tucson is. He won't open his mouth until he's got everythin' straight in his mind ——"

"Say, Lullaby," Stony broke in suddenly,

"you don't suppose Scorpio has taken Kellogg and given us the slip, do you?"

"How do you mean? Scorpio doesn't know we're tailin' 'em."

"He might have had a hunch. Suppose there was a back door in that restaurant — and there probably is. They could have left by the back door and ——"

Lullaby swore softly under his breath. "You wait here, I'm aimin' to slip across the street and see."

Stony slouched back in the shadow. Lullaby walked swiftly across the street, peered through the window of the restaurant, then quickly returned.

"They there?" Stony asked.

Lullaby nodded. "Still there. From the looks of the dishes piled in front of Kellogg he must've sampled everythin' in the place. He looks pretty soused. They got a bottle on the table. Scorpio's pullin' on his arm, tryin' to make him leave."

A minute later, Stony said, "There they are now."

The restaurant door had opened to allow the egress of Scorpio and Kellogg. Kellogg staggered, as Scorpio seized his arm and guided him out to a waiting horse standing at the hitchrack.

". . . sure, sure," Scorpio was saying

impatiently, "we've had a good time, but there has to come an end to everything. You fork your horse and head home."

Kellogg suddenly jerked free of Scorpio's restraining hand and said angrily, "Always tryin' to — hic — hurry me off, ain't you? Whash th' idea? Thish — hic — free country. Ain't leavin' till I'm ready. Goin' to th' Gunsight, get a drink firsh."

Only a few pedestrians sauntered along the street. There weren't so many lights now. Shops and stores had closed. A few cowponies waited before saloons and faro houses. For the most part the citizens of Godwin were in their homes, though the Gunsight Bar was still doing a good business.

From across the street, Kellogg's drunken remarks, mingled with Scorpio's profanity, reached Lullaby's and Stony's listening ears. "All right," Scorpio conceded reluctantly at last, "we'll go to the Gunsight and have one more drink."

The two proceeded back to the plank walk and headed east along Main Street in the direction of the Gunsight Bar. Stony and Lullaby trailed along, walking on the opposite side. From their position, a trifle to the rear, they saw Kellogg and Scorpio cross Santa Fe Street and enter the swinging-doored entrance of the Gunsight, at the corner of Main.

Lullaby swore softly. Stony said, "What's the matter?"

"This," Lullaby replied, "is li'ble to keep up all night. We're losin' precious time. The way things are going, if we ever do get a chance to talk to Kellogg, he won't be able to talk. He's gettin' drunker every minute. First thing you know, he'll be passin' out ____"

"You aimin' to talk to Kellogg?"

"One of us is. We got to get him away from Scorpio."

"I suppose that's my job, eh?" Stony grunted. "Handlin' Scorpio? Nice easy job you pick out for me. Just a pal, that's what you are."

"Shut up! I got to do some fast thinkin'."

"Do you know how?" Stony sneered.

Lullaby didn't reply. This was serious, Lullaby not taking up such a challenge. Stony remained silent.

"Look," Lullaby said at last, "if I take care of Scorpio, will you get hold of Kellogg and pump him?"

"I'll do that. But how you aimin' to get rid of Scorpio?"

"That's my job. You and I are going in the Gunsight. Scorpio wasn't comfortable before, bein' near us, with Kellogg talkin' loud. I don't reckon Scorpio has changed any. I'll bet a peso to a plugged two-bit piece the minute he sees us enter the Gunsight, Scorpio will haul Kellogg outside."

"That's a safe bet. Then what?"

"Ten to one, Scorpio will head Kellogg back toward the Chink's restaurant. Kellogg's horse is waiting there. Scorpio will try to get him to leave."

"That sounds plausible too. But how you —— ?"

Lullaby scratched his head. "Seems like that hardware and undertakin' store is just this side of the Chink's, isn't it?"

"Uh-huh. I noticed it was closed, though. I can't see what that has to do with ——"

"C'mon," Lullaby broke in, "we're headin' for the Gunsight."

The two rapidly crossed the street, pushed into the saloon. Several men stood at the bar. The room was grey with tobacco smoke and the smell of liquor. Poddy Cameron stood at the bar talking to a couple of men. He nodded to Stony and Lullaby when they entered, then went on with his conversation.

Lullaby and Stony found a place at the bar, farther down, right next to Tate Scorpio. Scorpio and Kellogg had just been served drinks. Kellogg drained his glass at a gulp. Scorpio started to lift his glass, turned and saw Lullaby standing next to him.

Lullaby said, "Howdy, Scorpio. Flies still messin' up the Faro Saloon?"

Scorpio grunted something unintelligible, and set down his glass untasted. Turning to Kellogg, Stony heard him say something about going to a better bar. To that proposition, Kellogg was agreeable. The two turned and headed toward the entrance.

Lullaby said low-voiced to Stony, "Follow 'em, pard, as soon as they get outside. You get Kellogg; I'll take care of Scorpio."

Without waiting for a reply, Lullaby slipped toward the rear door of the Gunsight. Nick was busily engaged serving drinks. The men at the bar were deep in various discussion. No one saw Lullaby as he quickly opened the door, stepped outside, and softly closed it at his back.

Here, Lullaby found himself in an alley that ran parallel to Main Street. Lullaby turned west, crossed Santa Fe Street, entered the alley on the opposite side and broke into a fast sprint. A half a minute later he stood at the rear of a large, flat-roofed building, built of timber and adobe, in which was housed Regan's Hardware & Undertaking Establishment. The building was of one story construction. Two windows and a door showed in the back wall. The windows were dark.

Next door to the Undertaking Establishment was the restaurant operated by the Chinese. Between the two buildings ran a narrow passage to the street. Lullaby darted along the passage, crossed the sidewalk. There was scarcely anyone abroad now; no one in Lullaby's immediate vicinity. Farther down Main, Lullaby caught sight of two dark figures whom he took to be Scorpio and Kellogg.

They had stopped for a moment; Kellogg was arguing in drunken tones; Scorpio swearing.

Lullaby didn't hesitate; he had to think — and act — fast. Going to Kellogg's horse, waiting before the restaurant, which now had only one dim light burning inside, Lullaby looked at Kellogg's saddle, found what he had hoped to see there: a coiled lariat.

Seizing the lariat, Lullaby retraced his steps swiftly back to the passageway between the two buildings. An instant later, he stood, once more, at the rear of the hardware and undertaking store. Now, to mount to the roof. Luckily, a large packing case stood against the rear wall. Lullaby got to the top of this, stood upright. Above his head, several roof beams extended beyond the limits of the wall. Placing the coiled lariat around his neck, Lullaby jumped, fingers reaching for the nearest roof-beam end.

An instant later, his muscular arms had drawn him to the roof, and he climbed over the edge. Stepping lightly, he moved swiftly toward the front of the building, dropped to his stomach and peered over the edge, along the thoroughfare.

Far down the street, Lullaby caught sight of a dark form that looked like Stony's. Nearer, Kellogg staggered along the sidewalk, trying to break loose from Scorpio's restraining hand.

"You — hic! — lied to me," Kellogg was accusing thickly. "You said we'd — hic! — go to a better — hic! — bar. Now, you're tryin' to — hic! — put me on my — hic! — horse again ——"

"Now, look here, Kellogg," Scorpio commenced, "you got me all wrong ——"

"Only — hic! — way anybody could get you. Sheridan — hic! — lied to me, too. You're all a bunch of — hic! — liars."

Scorpio suddenly released Kellogg's arm. "You be careful who you call a liar, Kellogg. You been a nuisance tonight. I know one way to stop that."

Scorpio's hand had gone to his gun butt, but Kellogg paid no attention to him and kept on going, his feet unsteady on the plank walk. Evidently Scorpio thought better of the murderous plan that had entered his head, for he started after the intoxicated man.

Lullaby lifted to his knees, took the lariat in his hands and commenced to spin a loop, which he dropped over the edge of the building. Kellogg and Scorpio were almost below him now. Stony was coming along at the rear. It was probably the sounds of Stony's footsteps that had changed Scorpio's intentions of shooting Kellogg.

"Now, wait a minute, Kellogg," Scorpio commenced.

Kellogg had broken into a sort of staggering run, flinging back over his shoulder: "I ain't — hic! — waitin' for anybody. I know another — hic! — bar, down the — hic! — street."

"Kellogg ——" Scorpio commenced, and stopped short.

Too late the soft *swish* of a flying lariat had reached his ears. He felt a hempen noose drop over his head. He tried to throw it off, but it tightened savagely, pinning his arms to his sides.

Then, abruptly, Tate Scorpio felt his feet

leave the sidewalk, sensed himself being pulled quickly upward. His sombrero fell off.

"Kellogg!" Scorpio bawled frantically. "Look —— !"

Kellogg continued his staggering run, refused to look back. "I ain't — hic! — goin' to listen," he giggled foolishly. "It won't do — hic! — any good to talk!"

Scorpio struggled and kicked. He was rapidly nearing the edge of the roof as Lullaby pulled hand-over-hand on the rope. Even as he panted and sweated over the job, Lullaby saw Stony dash past below, in pursuit of Kellogg. Stony was laughing joyously as he ran.

Scorpio was nearly to the top now. Suddenly he let out a lusty call for help: "Help!" he yelled at the top of his voice, "Help! Hel-l-l-lppp!"

"By Cripes!" Lullaby grunted. "I got to stop that." He stopped pulling for an instant, reached for his six-shooter. Tightening the grip on the rope with his left hand, Lullaby lifted, bringing Scorpio's head just above the edge of the roof.

Scorpio's back was to Lullaby as he appeared above the edge.

"Help!" Scorpio bawled again. "Hel—— !"

The word ended suddenly as Lullaby brought the barrel of his heavy forty-five down on Scorpio's head. Scorpio went limp, as Lullaby finished hauling him to the rooftop and out of sight of the street.

Scorpio's cries had brought a few men running into the street. Doors and windows had banged open. But by this time there was nothing out of the ordinary to be seen. Stealing a quick glance through the gloom, Lullaby saw that Stony had caught up with Kellogg and was talking to him. He caught a glimpse of light on Stony's face as he and Kellogg passed into a small bar farther along on Main Street.

Below, Poddy Cameron came dashing along, gun in hand, followed by a small knot of men. Peering over the roof-edge, Lullaby heard Cameron say, "Dam'd if I see anything. It sounded like those yells come from up this way. The street's all clear though."

"Mebbe those cries came from back in the alley," a man suggested.

"We'll go see," the sheriff replied.

Lullaby gazed down on the face of the unconscious Scorpio. Scorpio was breathing easily, but he'd be "out" for some time.

"Those forty-five barrels sure land hard when they strike," Lullaby mused. He heard men stirring around in the alley back of the building. A short time later they returned to the street. There was some further conversation, suggestions, then the sheriff and his crowd of followers went off in the opposite direction.

Gradually, the street grew quiet again. Lullaby rose to his feet, listened. There wasn't anyone in sight. Then, stooping, he lifted Scorpio and carried him to the rear of the roof, lowered the man's limp form to the earth. Then he dropped the rope and climbed down beside him.

"Damn' if I know what to do with you now," Lullaby muttered. "It'll probably be close to an hour before you get your senses back. Mebbe more. Reckon I just better leave you here ——"

He stopped abruptly, struck with a sudden idea. Then, laughing softly, he went to the rear door of the building and tried the knob. The door was bolted. Next, Lullaby tried one of the windows. The window slid open easily under his touch. Lullaby climbed through, struck a match, gazed around. As he had expected, the rear of the building was partitioned off to accommodate the undertaking half of Regan's Hardware & Undertaking Establishment.

There were two or three miscellaneous benches in the room, some paraphernalia and other objects pertaining to the funeral business. Lullaby found what he was looking for. At one side of the room, resting on wooden horses, was a black casket with bright metal handles. Lullaby's match burned to his fingers. He dropped it on the floor, and crossed, chuckling, to the casket. The casket was uncovered. Lullaby struck a second match and discovered it to be lined with white satin. This, probably, was Regan's sample piece, the advertising he employed to promote his business.

"I reckon it'll do," Lullaby grinned, "I just hope it fits."

He put out the match, strode to the door, unbolted it. Stepping outside, he removed the rope from Scorpio's body, then lifted the limp form in his arms, carried it back to the coffin.

A moment later, Scorpio was resting peacefully on the white satin lining of the casket. Panting heavily, Lullaby stepped back, reached for another match. He stood looking down on the unconscious man. "Damn' if that thing don't look like it was made to your measure," Lullaby chuckled. "Gosh, if we only had some flowers now — wait!"

Looking quickly around the room he found a wreath of artificial roses hanging on the wall. This he lifted from the peg that supported it. The roses were pink and white and somewhat soiled. Lullaby placed the wreath across Scorpio's breast, took one look, and bent double with laughter. The laughter stopped suddenly when the match burned down to his fingers.

"Gosh, I better be gettin' out of here," Lullaby grinned in the darkness.

He closed and rebolted the back door, slipped through the open window to the outside, closed the window again, then picked up the rope. He coiled it as he passed through to the street, carefully hung it on the saddle of Kellogg's waiting horse. There was no one in sight. Even the restaurant was closed by this time.

Lullaby heaved a long sigh. "I'd call that a nice evenin's work," he chuckled. "Reckon I better go see what Stony's doin' with Kellogg. Gosh, I wish I could be there when Scorpio wakes up. He'll be fit to be tied!"

Cutting diagonally across the street, Lullaby headed for the small saloon which he had last seen Stony entering with Kellogg.

XIX. Roaring Forty-Fives

The echoes of the shots died away across the range. Tucson lay as he had fallen, facedown; his head was twisted queerly to one side. His horse, reins dangling on the earth, stood uneasily waiting between the silent form of its rider and the jumbled pile of black rock. Overhead, the stars gleamed brightly; a soft breeze lifted across the hills, carrying the pungent scent of sage. Somewhere, back of the rock, a horse whinnied.

A booted foot scraped on rock. Silence again. Then, cautious whisperings from around the corner of the rock pile.

There came another footstep. A man's sombrero pushed slowly around the rock and was silhouetted against the sky.

"By Gawd!" a voice said. "We got him!" It was Joe Frame's voice.

"There's the end of Tucson Smith, damn his hide!" came Butch Grier's reply. "Cripes! That was easy. We must have got him with our first shots. The way that hombre's rated, I figured mebbe there'd be a lot of lead slung before we downed him."

Joe Frame laughed nastily, "One slug in the right place does the trick. It was worth while trailin' him and that damn Callahan when they left ——"

"It's just too bad Callahan wa'n't with Smith. He must've stayed at the 8-Bar."

"Cripes! We can get him anytime. Sheridan will sure be pleased about this."

"Do you reckon Smith is dead yet?"

"Hell, yes. He didn't move a muscle after he fell. There was just that one groan."

"What I'm aimin' to do now," Grier growled triumphantly, "is empty my iron into his carcass. We'll leave it where it will be found as a warnin' to folks who snoop and ask too many questions."

"Yeah, and we'll get them other two, Brooke and Joslin, just as easy. C'mon, we'll go through Smith's pockets. He might have a roll on him."

"I dunno about that," Grier protested. "Some of the money might be recognized, in town, and then this would be pinned on us. You know, he might have certain bills, with ink blots on 'em, or somethin' ——"

"Aw, don't be so skeery," Frame laughed harshly. "Money's meant to be spent, ain't it? We'd be fools to leave any in Smith's pocket. Another thing, I crave to give his carcass a couple of good kicks, damn him! Butch, there's a heap of hombres in the Southwest will thank their stars when they hear Tucson Smith has gone to Boot Hill. I hate hombres like him, always pretendin' to be so law-abidin'. C'mon, I crave to empty my gun into him, even if he can't feel it."

Tucson's horse shied nervously away as the two men stepped boldly out from the rock and approached the silent form on the earth. They were only a few yards away from Tucson's sprawled body now. Frame lifted his gun.

And then things happened all at once: Tucson stirred, rolled over, coming cat-like to his feet. Butch Grier let out a frightened yell of dismay. Streaks of crimson fire were darting from the vicinity of Tucson's hips.

Grier fired once, turned to run. A hot leaden slug caught him in mid-stride. He stumbled and pitched to the earth. Frame had fired twice. A savage curse was suddenly torn from Frame's lips. He flung his arms wide, the gun spinning from his nerveless fingers.

Again, Tucson fired. Frame's body stiffened, his legs buckled at the knees. Sobbing convulsively, he fell forward and lay still.

The noise of the shooting died away. Tucson peered grimly through the night, then crossed to Frame's body. Frame had died almost instantly. Tucson proceeded on to examine Grier. Grier breathed his last as Tucson turned the dying man on his back.

Methodically, Tucson plugged out his

empty shells, shoved fresh cartridges into his cylinders. Then he spoke, "Just two bushwackin' skunks," he said, half to himself, "that didn't have sense enough to know I was playin' possum on 'em. They're better off dead, but I wish I wasn't the one to have done it. Howsomever, it was their lives or mine."

Shoving six-shooters back into his holsters, he walked around behind the jumble of rock, found the horses of the two would-be murderers waiting there. "Anyway," Tucson mused, "Frame's death avenges Clem Hayden's. I wish Frame had lived a mite longer; he might have told me the reason for Hayden not drawing that day. Oh, well, mebbe we'll all know in time. Right now, I'd better lash those bodies on their horses and lead 'em into Godwin. . . ."

There were ropes on both saddles. Tucson led the ponies around to where their dead owners lay on the earth. Lifting them across the saddles and lashing them in place took but a short time. Then, Tucson mounted his own pony and, taking the reins of the other horses in his hand, once more started for Godwin. . . .

It was nearly midnight by the time Tucson rode along the main street of the town, leading behind him the two horses with their grisly burdens. Only a few lights shone along the thoroughfare now.

Two men came sauntering along the sidewalk: Sheriff Cameron and his deputy, Link Dexter.

Tucson hailed, "Hey, Poddy. What you doin' out so late?"

"That you, Tucson? . . . Somebody did a lot of yellin' for help a coupla hours back, but I couldn't find anythin' wrong. We're just takin' a last look around to see —— Great Jehoshaphat! What you leadin' behind?"

The sheriff and his deputy came hurrying out to the middle of the road.

Tucson said grimly, "Just a couple of hombres that tried to bushwhack me from behind a pile of rock. I heard a noise and, suspectin' somethin' of the kind, threw myself off'n the horse just a split instant before they shook the lead out of their Colt barrels. It was close. One slug just about scorched my face ——"

"Judas priest!" Cameron gasped.

"Judas priest!" Link Dexter echoed.

"—— I stayed quiet," Tucson went on, "until they come out from behind their rock shelter. Then I got to my feet and threw some lead myself. My aim was better than theirs."

The sheriff had moved back to look at the bodies. "Cripes! It's Joe Frame. And Butch Grier!"

"Danged if it ain't Joe Frame and Butch Grier," Link Dexter said.

"Who do you suppose was back of this move?" Poddy Cameron said.

"Who do you suppose?" Tucson replied grimly.

The sheriff looked at Tucson. He didn't say anything. Link Dexter watched the sheriff anxiously, but, as the sheriff didn't say anything, Dexter contented himself with a feeble gulp.

Some distance down the street, high-heeled boots clumped on the plank walk. Tucson roused himself, "Well, Poddy, what do you want done with the bodies?"

"Why, er, take 'em to the undertaker's, I reckon. It's just a few doors down the street."

"Sure, sure," Link Dexter nodded vigorously, "take 'em to the undertaker's. Only place for 'em. It's just a few doors ——"

"Link," Cameron cut in testily, "one of us is enough to do the talking. You hightail it down to the Gunsight. I think Regan is still there, if he hasn't closed up. Tell him there's business waitin' ——"

"— he hasn't closed up," Dexter was

mumbling. "There's business ——"

"Do you know he hasn't closed up?" Cameron demanded sharply.

"No — er — no, I guess not ——"

"Oh, for the love of Hanner," Cameron begged plaintively, "will you please go and find out? Tell Regan I want him. We'll be waitin' in front of his place."

"Sure, sure, in front of his place —" the deputy began.

Cameron suddenly lost patience: "Go on now! Git! Scat!"

Link Dexter turned hurriedly and started off toward the Gunsight. Poddy Cameron mopped his brow. "That Link certainly is a trial and a tribbalation, sometimes," he said wearily. "Can't seem to think for himself. Always repeatin' me."

The sheriff led the way to Regan's establishment, Tucson following behind with the horses and their lifeless burdens. While Tucson and Cameron waited, the sheriff asked for further details regarding the attempted ambushing. Tucson gave the information briefly, then asked, "Where's Stony and Lullaby, do you know?"

"Around town, someplace," Cameron shrugged. "I saw 'em come into the Gunsight once, tonight. Didn't notice 'em leave. I wasn't payin' much attention. I got to talkin' with a feller that raises chickens, and he was tellin' about some sort of feed that'll make hens lay right straight through the winter months. Not that I believed him, but I wanted to get the details for Martha — that's my wife — 'cause she's interested in scientific doin's ——"

A sudden hail from the other side of the street caught Tucson's attention. Lullaby and Stony came hurrying across, asking questions. "What you got there?" Stony exclaimed.

Lullaby put in, "Looks like dead meat to me. Who are they?"

"Joe Frame and Butch Grier," Tucson replied. He told his story again. When he had finished, Stony said, "Just my luck. We stay in town and you go out and find all the *real* excitement."

"What you waitin' here for?" Lullaby asked.

"Waiting for the undertaker to come and take charge of these bodies," Tucson replied.

Lullaby started to laugh, but checked himself suddenly. A broad grin had appeared on Stony's face. Lullaby said gravely, "Were you lookin' for some *real* excitement, pard?"

Stony nodded, chuckling, "I hope it's still there to happen."

"What you two chucklin' about?" Tucson asked.

Lullaby said promptly, "We were just thinkin' how surprised Grier and Frame must have been when you started throwin' lead."

Tucson looked sharply at Lullaby, then changed the subject, "Did you fellers take care of that business, tonight?"

"You'll be surprised when we tell you," Stony grinned.

"We'll talk it over later," Tucson nodded. "Get these bodies off'n our hands first."

Poddy Cameron looked curiously at the three men, but didn't say anything.

A knot of men was approaching from down the street. In front walked Link Dexter and Regan, owner of the hardware and undertaking establishment. Regan proved to be the tall skinny man with the scanty hair and long red nose who had come running into the Gunsight, with his talk relative to a "plague of locusts," on the heels of the fly-trap episode.

At Regan's other side was Quint Sheridan. Sheridan's face was working angrily as he strode up to Tucson.

"Am I to understand, Smith," he demanded hotly, "that you confess to the murder of Butch Grier and Joe Frame?"

Tucson jerked one thumb over his shoulder, said coolly, "Take a look at 'em. They're dead, if that's what you mean. But it wasn't murder. They tried to dry-gulch me. The dirty scheme didn't work. I beat 'em to it. How much do *you* know about this business, Sheridan?"

"Not a thing."

"No?" Tucson eyed the man steadily. "I heard Frame say you'd be pleased to hear I was dead. I been wonderin'."

"Cripes! I don't know nothin' about it." The man backed away a step.

Sheriff Cameron said, "I thought you left for your ranch, with the rest of the boys, Quint?"

Sheridan shook his head. "Me and Scorpio stayed in town. I figured Grier and Frame went to the Circle-Cross with the rest. They were headed that way. I been down in the Faro Saloon all evenin' waitin' ——"

"All alone, too, I bet," a man exclaimed. Loud laughter followed the words.

Sheridan's face got red, but he ignored the remark, not wishing to enter into conversation regarding a place that was supposed to be full of flies. He said to Cameron, "I've been waiting for Scorpio to show up. You seen him?"

"Once or twice tonight," Cameron nodded. "He was doing a heap of drinking with some hombre named Kellogg. I don't know where they went."

"I figured Scorpio might be in the Gunsight," Sheridan said, "and I got there just as your deputy come with the news of this killing. Cameron, I demand that you put Smith under arrest. I charge him with murder ——"

"Maybe you'd like an inquest held too," Tucson suggested quietly.

"What in hell would I want an inquest for?" Sheridan snapped. "You've admitted the killings. An inquest ——"

"An inquest," Tucson cut in sternly, "might bring out a lot of information. For instance, what Grier and Frame were doing on the trail to the 8-Bar, what I was doing there. I'll tell you what I was doing at the 8-Bar, Sheridan. I was discovering what had become of those cows you sold 'em — those cows that disappeared. I've got nearly all the information I need, Sheridan. Want to hear it now, or shall we wait for some sort of inquest?"

"You're crazy," Sheridan growled. His eyes weren't meeting Tucson's. "I don't know what you're talkin' about."

"You'll find out," Tucson laughed coldly, "if you don't shut your trap about murders and inquests. Your record won't stand up so good where either one is concerned ——"

Regan's voice from the doorway of his store interrupted the words. Regan was holding the door open, by this time, a lighted kerosene lamp held in one hand. "Well, bring 'em in, bring 'em in," he said impatiently. "I can't stand here all night."

Tucson and Lullaby were already unlashing the ropes that held the dead bodies across saddles. Poddy Cameron gave orders. Some men stepped out of the crowd, lifted the bodies and carried them to the store entrance.

Regan led the way to his "undertaking parlors" partitioned off in the rear, passing through a small doorway cut in one side. Behind the bodies followed Tucson, Stony and Lullaby, the sheriff and his deputy. Sheridan, with several other men at his heels came pushing in behind.

Regan indicated two canvas cots open along one wall. "Just put them bodies on those cots," he said, placing his lamp on a table. The lifeless bodies were deposited as ordered. Regan went on, "I won't start on 'em until mornin'. Now, who is going to pay for these burials?"

"Well," Cameron commenced hesitantly, "they worked for Sheridan ——"

"I ain't goin' to pay for buryin' 'em," Sheridan exclaimed. "I ordered 'em to go to the ranch. If they got into this mix-up, it ain't my fault. I wash my hands of the whole business."

"Without any murder charge or anythin'?" Tucson asked softly.

Sheridan uttered an oath, but didn't say any more.

"In that case," Cameron said sarcastically, "if a man's employer is too cold-blooded to bury his own pals, the state will have to stand the expense."

"Sure, that's it, the state will have to stand the expense," Link Dexter parroted solemnly.

"Will you shut up, Link?" Cameron roared exasperatedly.

Link looked sheepish and shut up.

Lullaby and Stony had been watching the coffin on the wooden-horses across the room. Beneath the faded wreath of pink and white roses there appeared to be slight movements. No one else had looked in that direction. Now, the noise of the voices in the room was commencing to arouse Scorpio. He had already regained consciousness once, but in his dazed state had imagined himself in his bunk and immediately gone back to sleep, cursing the headache he had but remembering nothing of what it had come from.

Scorpio cursed at the voices, tried to roll over in the casket. His bed was soft, but seemed to be a trifle cramping. The rose wreath suddenly flew into the air and rolled to the middle of the room.

Regan said, startled, "What the hell!"

Men turned and looked across the room. Abruptly, Scorpio came to a sitting position in his coffin, rubbing his eyes. "Time to turn out?" he asked bewilderedly. "Geez! What a head ——!"

A startled yell greeted his words. Several men turned and dashed toward the doorway. Regan commenced to swear. Lullaby and Stony were laughing openly now.

"What — what — what —— ?" Scorpio stammered ineffectually. "Where in the devil am I? What's up —— ?" His mouth dropped open as he gazed down and saw where he'd been sleeping.

"Scorpio! You danged fool!" Sheridan yelled disgustedly. "You're drunk!"

"I am not," Scorpio denied indignantly. "Oh, geez, how my head aches."

Sheridan cursed the man. "Where you been?"

"How did I get here?" Scorpio asked blankly.

"You're drunk, that's what," Regan snapped. "That's just the way with you cowhands — get drunk and then look for a place to sleep! Too damn tight-fisted to buy a decent bed in the hotel. No, you ain't satisfied to soil my good casket. You have to break in here and —" Regan choked, sputtered. "It's an outrage!"

"Wait a minute, wait a minute," Scorpio groaned. He started to crawl gingerly over the side of the casket, to the floor. The others waited for explanations.

Scorpio's head was clearing now. "It was this way," he commenced uncertainly, "I was walking along with Kellogg. Just as I was passin' your place, Regan, somebody roped me and hoisted me up to the roof ——"

A sudden howl of laughter greeted the statement. Scorpio looked hurt. "Don't you believe it?"

"No," Sheridan rasped, "and nobody else does, either. Up on the roof! How did you get in here — in that thing?"

Scorpio shook his head. "Dam'd if I know," he confessed. "Whoever roped me, must have dragged me in here."

"What a story, what a story!" Regan said furiously. "How could anybody get in here? The front door was locked. You can see the rear door, there, is bolted. You're drunk, that's what! You probably picked my lock and come in to get a quiet sleep to sober up on. Cripes! You cowhands ain't got any respect for other folks' property. I got a good notion to have Cameron take you up, on a charge of breakin' and enterin' ——"

"I tell you, I didn't," Scorpio said lamely. "If you knew how my head ached, you wouldn't pester me with questions ——"

"I don't doubt you got a head," Sheridan said sarcastically. "Where's Kellogg?"

Scorpio looked blank. "Kellogg? Oh, yeah, Kellogg. Dam'd if I know where he went, Quint."

"Nor you don't know anythin' else," Sheridan raged. "Dang drunken sot! C'mon, let's get back to the ranch."

"Who's goin' to pay for the damage to my casket?" Regan said shrilly. "I'll pro'bly have to have that box re-lined ——"

"Charge it to the county for all I care," Sheridan snarled. "It ain't any of my business. Take it up with Scorpio, some time when he's sober. C'mon Scorpio."

Seizing the still-dazed man by the arm, Sheridan propelled him savagely through the knot of men clustered at the doorway, and thence to the street. A roar of laughter followed the departure. Regan was still

278

spraying profanity about the room: "It's a dirty shame, that's what it is. Those Circle-Cross hands think they can break all the laws of the county and nothin' won't be done. Poddy, I insist you arrest Scorpio ——"

"Aw, you better forget it," the sheriff advised. "Go home and sleep on the matter, Regan. You'll feel better in the mornin'. Add the cost of re-linin' your box to the burial expenses of them two would-be murderers."

That somewhat pacified Regan. He nodded and fell silent.

Tucson said, "C'mon, Lullaby, Stony, let's get out of here."

The Three Mesquiteers pushed through to the street, followed by Sheriff Cameron and his deputy. Cameron said, "There's Frame's and Grier's horses. I reckon I'd better put 'em over in the livery, until we see if Sheridan wants to claim 'em."

"I've got to put my horse up," Tucson offered. "You and Link run along to your beds. I'll take care of those Circle-Cross broncs."

"I'll be much obliged if you'll turn 'em over to the livery for me," Poddy nodded. "I got a ride between me and my bed yet. Martha — that's my wife — will be wonderin' why I ain't come home. Link, you better come along down to the office and turn in."

The deputy and his chief said good-night and walked down the street. Tucson and his companions turned the horses in at the livery stable, then started across the street towards their hotel. The instant they were alone, Tucson said,

"Well, what about Kellogg? 'Course I know who's responsible for Scorpio bein' found in that casket, but how did you fellers work it?"

Grinning widely, Lullaby told how he had captured Scorpio. Stony took up the story and related how he had caught up with Kellogg and gained his friendship.

"Where's Kellogg now?" Tucson asked.

"After Lullaby arrived, we pumped him plenty. 'Course, we had to buy a few drinks now and then. By the time he'd reached the point where he couldn't talk any more, we took him down and left him to sleep it off under the horse shelter, back of the hotel. There's straw there; by the time the mornin' stage gets in and starts to make their change of horses, Kellogg will either be awake or they'll wake him ——"

Lullaby put in, "We considered takin' him to the hotel, but we didn't want too many people to see Kellogg with us."

The Three Mesquiteers paused on the sidewalk before the hotel, twisted and lighted cigarettes. Tucson went on, "Well, what did you find out about Kellogg?"

"He's a solid citizen of Marnsville. That's a sizable town t'other side of the Santa Madrazas. Kellogg is in the beef business and has a contract to supply the butchers of Marnsville with their meat. There's also an army post over that way, and Kellogg furnishes some of the post's beef too." Stony paused to drag on his cigarette.

"Which same, I'm guessin'," Tucson put in, "he gets from Sheridan."

"Part of it anyway," Lullaby nodded. "It seems Sheridan promised to deliver him two hundred head day before yesterday, but Sheridan didn't arrive with the beef. Kellogg came to Godwin to learn why. Kellogg got shunted off by Sheridan, when Sheridan got sick of arguin' with him. It looks like Sheridan put it up to Scorpio to get rid of Kellogg."

Stony put in, "Kellogg couldn't understand why Sheridan didn't deliver the beef."

Tucson said slowly, "Mebbe Sheridan has been too busy with some bigger project. Now, the last few days, things in this section have been stirred up proper, and Sheridan doesn't want to have anything to do with Kellogg. That's my guess leastwise. Of course, we're pretty sure Sheridan rustles the cows he sells Kellogg. Do you think Kellogg is aware of that?"

Lullaby shook his head. "I doubt it. He's just a big, dumb windbag, but I figure him as honest enough."

"How did he happen to make this connection with Sheridan?" Tucson asked next.

"About a year and a half back," Stony explained, "Sheridan and some other Circle-Cross riders came driving one hundred sixty-five head of stock to Marnsville, looking for a buyer. The price was below the regular market and Kellogg jumped at the chance to buy. Sheridan promised more cattle later ——"

"Wait!" Tucson said quickly. "Year and a half back. That's just about the time Clem Hayden discovered the loss of the one hundred sixty-five cows he'd paid Sheridan for."

"Right," Lullaby nodded.

"Did you ask Kellogg how that hundred-sixty-five head was branded?" Tucson pursued.

Stony nodded. "The cows had Sheridan's earmark. They'd been branded Circle-Cross, but the brand had been vented. Sheridan gave a bill-of-sale ——"

"Don't tell me," Tucson interrupted, "that those cows also were burned with the 8-Bar iron."

"No, dammit!" Lullaby grunted disgustedly. "Just the vented Circle-Cross, that's all. Stony and I were plumb elated at first; we thought sure we'd located where Hayden's cows went to. But Kellogg insisted the vented Circle-Cross was the only mark on them.

"That," Tucson laughed softly, "is perfectly grand news!"

"Huh?" Stony said blankly. Lullaby added, "You think those cows were Hayden's after all?"

"I'm pretty sure of it," Tucson chuckled.

Stony and Lullaby set up a clamor for explanations. Tucson shook his head. "You hombres try to dope it out. It'll be good brain exercise ——"

"Aw, Tucson ——" Stony commenced.

Tucson shook his head. "If I start talkin' now we never will get to bed. I'm plumb weary. The bank here is tryin' to run a whizzer on Nancy too, regardin' her father's note. I'll explain that later. I want to hit the hay."

"But, Tucson," Lullaby persisted stubbornly, "those cows. Nancy saw 'em branded with the 8-Bar."

Tucson laughed wearily. "All right, wise man, have it your way. Mebbe she did. I'm too tired to argue. Look, I'll give you a clue — remember when your cigarette end burned my hat?"

"Huh, what about it?" Stony asked blankly.

"That's your clue," Tucson laughed. He turned and stepped into the hotel, headed for his bed. Stony and Lullaby looked blankly at each other. They were still talking an hour later, when they, too, sought their beds.

XX. PISTOL PALAVER

The following morning, during breakfast in the hotel dining room, Lullaby and Stony were still discussing the problem, and were no nearer the solution, already reached by Tucson, than they had been the previous evening. Tucson had left the hotel some time before and gone to the Godwin Savings Bank where he was to meet Nancy Hayden.

". . . what I'm maintainin'," Lullaby was saying earnestly, through a mouthful of pancakes, "is what has a cigarette burn on a Stet hat got to do with brandin' cows?"

"I've given it up," Stony growled. "What

284

I'm maintainin', do you intend to sit here and eat all mornin' —— ?"

"I ain't eatin' any more than is normal ——" Lullaby commenced in aggrieved tones.

"No more than is normal for an elephant," Stony put in quickly. "You've had three cups of coffee, a double order of flapjacks ——"

"Whoever heard of an elephant eatin' flapjacks, let alone drinkin' coffee?" Lullaby sneered.

Stony could have found an insulting retort for that one, too, but for once he passed up the challenge. "Listen," he begged, "will you please hurry up?"

"I'm hurryin' as fast as I can. Just as soon as I have some ham and eggs ——"

Stony groaned and got to his feet. "I'll meet you later, cowboy. After what Tucson told us about that note of Clem Hayden's bein' for five thousand instead of five hundred, I'm curious to see what they found out at the bank. Nancy should be in town by this time."

"All right, I'll meet you someplace near the bank," Lullaby nodded. Stony donned his sombrero and left the dining room. Lullaby settled down peacefully to his fourth cup of coffee. . . .

Meanwhile, Nancy Hayden, escorted by

Micky Callahan, had already reached town. Tucson was seated in the shadow of the wooden awning fronting the sheriff's office, which stood next door to the bank, talking, or trying to talk, to Deputy Link Dexter. Inasmuch as Poddy Cameron had not yet reached his office, Dexter was pretty much at a loss as to how to proceed with a conversation.

Bright morning sunshine drenched the dusty street. A few customers had already entered the bank, but for the most part activity, in the morning heat, was at a minimum. Tucson, glancing along the thoroughfare, saw two horses drawing near; Nancy rode one, Micky maintained an awkward seat on the other, and was talking earnestly to the girl. Nancy was smiling. Tucson chuckled at the sight, "Looks like the runt is makin' hay while the sun shines."

Dexter brightened a trifle. "The sun shines right hot this mornin'," he stated.

"Sure does," Tucson smiled. He rose to his feet and went to the edge of the sidewalk to greet the approaching pair.

"Hi-yuh, folks!" he called.

"Hello, Tucson," from Nancy.

"We got here," Micky grinned.

"So I see. Light and rest your saddles. The bank's been open about fifteen minutes.

We'll go in and see what's what."

Nancy swung down easily from her mount, tossed her reins over the hitchrack. Tucson did the same with Micky's reins and smiled inwardly as he watched Micky half slide, half fall, from the horse's back. Micky glanced at Tucson's bronzed features, guessed what was passing through Tucson's mind and smiled sheepishly, "I'm makin' progress in my ridin' anyway, Tucson."

"That right?" Tucson said gravely.

Micky nodded, "Yep. I already know that the hardest part about learnin' to ride is to stay on the horse's back."

"Never you mind, Micky," Nancy said sympathetically. "You're getting along fine. Don't let anybody josh you about your riding."

Micky looked gratefully at the girl. Her cheeks flushed a trifle at the reporter's ardent gaze. Tucson looked at the two, whistled softly under his breath, and wondered if Micky was the only one who had been "makin' hay while the sun shines."

The two were still lost in each other's eyes, when Tucson broke in, "Well, let's get inside the bank and see what this Hodge hombre has to offer."

A trifle red-faced, the two followed Tucson into the bank. The Godwin Savings Bank had pretty much the appearance of all small cowtown banks. A partition, in which were placed a couple of grated windows, reached half way to the ceiling. At one side was a swinging gate which allowed access to the rear half of the bank in which was a desk, vault, filing cabinets, etc. In one corner a door, at present closed, had "PRIVATE" painted across the panels. This, Tucson judged to be the entrance to Fulton Hodge's office.

A client of the bank was just leaving one of the wickets, which was presided over by a chinless, pale-featured individual, whom Tucson judged to be the cashier. Tucson approached the window and spoke through the grating.

The cashier shook his head. "Mr. Hodge is out of town, at present. Anything I can do for you?"

Tucson replied in the negative. "I wanted to see Hodge personally."

Nancy Hayden cut in, "It's about father's note which Mr. Hodge is holding."

"Oh, good morning, Miss Hayden," the cashier smirked. "The note? Oh, yes. I remember Mr. Hodge had me get it out of the files for him two days ago."

"Is it in the bank, now?" Nancy asked.

The cashier shook his head. "Mr. Hodge

must have it with him. He didn't return it to me."

"Just where is Hodge?" Tucson asked. "When will he return to Godwin?"

The cashier replied, "Mr. Hodge is in Herrero — over at our branch bank. I don't know just when he'll return. He spends most of his time in Herrero these days ———"

"You mean," Tucson frowned, "Herrero — that little Mex settlement across the border."

"That's it, sir," the cashier replied respectfully. "Mr. Hodge established a branch bank for the convenience of Mexican depositors a year or so back."

"I shouldn't think," Tucson said shrewdly, "there'd be enough business in Herrero to warrant that."

"Personally, I couldn't say," the man behind the grating drew himself up a trifle stiffly. "I've never been over there. However, Mr. Hodge thinks Herrero has a great future. His opinion is good enough for me. I'd never think of mistrusting his judgment."

"I'll bet you wouldn't either," Tucson nodded, smiling. "All right, thanks. I reckon we'll just have to wait until we can see Mr. Hodge."

He stood aside to let another client approach the window. Nancy and Micky followed him outside. They found Stony waiting in front of the bank, talking to Sheriff Cameron who was just dismounting. Tucson spoke to the sheriff, then asked Stony, "Where's Lullaby?"

"Stowin' away fodder at the hotel, last I seen him," Stony replied. "How that hombre can eat! . . . Say, how'd you come out regardin' that note of Nancy's father's?"

"Hodge has the note with him," Nancy put in. "He's in Herrero."

Tucson asked, "Poddy, what do you know about Hodge?"

The sheriff shrugged his shoulders, tugged at his close-cropped mustache a moment. "We-ell," he said at last, "I don't know anythin' against him. We never got friendly. At the same time, we never had any disagreements. Fact is, I haven't seen much of Hodge for more than a year back, except to say 'Howdy' to, now and then."

"He's been spending most of his time at a branch bank in Herrero," Micky started. "Thinks business over there ——"

"Yeah, I heard somethin' about that," Cameron nodded disparagingly. "Never did think the idea was sound ——"

"How large a town is Herrero?" Tucson interrupted.

Cameron considered. "Pro'bly about five hundred population. Not much of a town. Sort of hard, I'd say. Half the population is made up of tough hombres from this side of the line, or almost. You know — the sort that find it unhealthy to buck the law in the States."

Tucson narrowed his eyes thoughtfully. "There's somethin' dang queer about Hodge settin' up a bank in Herrero. Mebbe Mister Fulton Hodge will bear investigatin' ——"

The words were interrupted by the sounds of gunfire up the street about a block and a half. There were two shots, close together, then a third. Wild yells ran along the street.

Cameron said, "What the devil!" and leaped back into his saddle.

"Tucson, Stony!" Nancy cried. "Take our horses. Micky, you climb up behind Tucson."

Micky hesitated. Stony and Tucson were already putting feet in stirrups. "C'mon, Micky!" Tucson exclaimed.

"Go on. Hurry!" the girl urged the reporter.

"Gee whiz!" from Micky, "I hate to leave you ——"

"Never mind me," the girl cried. "I'll be all right. You've got to get news for your paper! I'll see you later."

Micky grinned widely. "You're one grand acushla," he said, low-voiced.

The girl crimsoned. "You're not so bad yourself, Irish," she laughed.

Micky was already scrambling up behind Tucson. The horses were under way. Passing the Faro Saloon, Tucson caught a brief glimpse of Quint Sheridan and a couple of other Circle-Cross men pushing through the swinging doors. He drove in his spurs, pounded on. . . .

Stony's first thought when he heard the shooting was of Lullaby Joslin. And sure enough, Lullaby was playing a part in the affair. After finally finishing his lengthy breakfast, Lullaby had left the hotel and stepped out to the street.

Lullaby had intended to head toward the bank, but, happening to glance in the opposite direction, he noticed Tate Scorpio just stepping out of the Gunsight Bar. From that point, Scorpio had moved along the plank sidewalk toward Regan's undertaking establishment. The fact that Scorpio was bareheaded caught Lullaby's attention.

Lullaby grinned. "What's Scorpio up to, I wonder? Pro'bly headin' down to the undertaker's to see if he can learn what happened to him last night. Reckon I'd better drift down that way. I might get another laugh."

By the time Lullaby reached the undertaking establishment, Scorpio had moved out to the road, and was walking in circles, scrutinizing the earth near the hitchracks. Lullaby noticed that Kellogg's horse was gone and guessed correctly that Kellogg had left for his home in Marnsville.

A few pedestrians sauntered past on either side of the street. Lullaby smiled to himself, took up a position under the wooden awning fronting the restaurant operated by the Chinaman. There wasn't any awning in front of Regan's and Lullaby preferred to watch from the shade.

Scorpio was muttering to himself, walking back and forth near the hitchrack. So far, he hadn't noticed Lullaby.

Lullaby laughed softly and asked, "What's the matter, Scorpio, lose your dawg?" The tones were gentle, politely curious.

Scorpio replied, without looking up, "Lost my hat along here some place, last night. It was too dark to find it then." He hadn't recognized Lullaby's voice.

Lullaby smiled sleepily, moved out a few steps and leaned against the hitchrack. He pointed to a crushed and dirty object a few feet away. "That," he said gravely, "looks as though it might have been a hat, once."

Scorpio glanced along the ground, started for the hat. Stopping, he looked up at Lullaby. His features went red with anger. "You, eh, Joslin?"

"That's my name."

"I want to talk to you."

"I'm not leavin'."

Scorpio swore under his breath, edged over and picked up his sombrero. It was nearly buried in dust. Scorpio cursed as he picked it up. The hat was a sorry sight. Wagon wheels had passed over it. It was cut by the sharp shoes of passing horses. Scorpio eyed the ruined sombrero a moment, then, carrying it in his left hand, rounded the hitchrack and confronted Lullaby.

Neither man spoke for a few minutes. Lullaby eyed Scorpio with a sleepy, indolent gaze. Scorpio was breathing hard, trying to get himself under control.

"Some measly coyote," he grated at last, "crept up behind me last night, and slugged me with a gun barrel."

"That so?" Lullaby yawned. "Tough."

"I'm goin' to make it plenty tough when I find him," Scorpio snapped.

"That so?" Another yawn. Lullaby didn't seem interested. He smiled lazily. "I suppose it was the same hombre that put you in that casket of Regan's."

"It must have been," Scorpio growled. He was gazing steadily at Lullaby. Lullaby's eyes were half closed. "Thought you were going to the Circle-Cross last night," Lullaby said.

"We come in this mornin' ——" Scorpio started.

"To hunt for your hat?"

Scorpio bridled and called Lullaby a name.

Lullaby said reprovingly, "That ain't any way to talk. You might get in trouble." Another wide yawn stretched his jaws.

Scorpio looked contemptuously at Lullaby. "I reckon you won't make said trouble," he sneered.

"Pro'bly not," Lullaby agreed placidly. "I'm peaceable, I am. I don't like trouble ——"

"You wouldn't," Scorpio growled. "Not unless you had your friends with you. I figure you as yellow, Joslin." He backed a step, tensing.

Lullaby didn't accept the challenge. "I often wondered about that, myself," he said agreeably. "Most fellers have a streak of yellow at some time or other ——"

"And yours is showin' now!" Scorpio snapped triumphantly. "Joslin, I aim to ask you some questions."

Lullaby waved one hand in a lazy gesture. "So you said."

"Joslin, I was in the Gunsight a few minutes back ——"

"Nice clean place," Lullaby drawled. "No flies ——"

"Cut that!" Scorpio snarled. "A feller in the Gunsight said you and Brooke left right after me, last night."

"Mebbe we did. Sometimes we ain't particular who we follow. Did this feller say where we went?"

Scorpio shook his head. "He didn't see you leave. Just looked up and noticed you were gone."

"Sort of vanished like, huh?"

"You're not funny, Joslin. I want to know where you went, what you did."

"Any particular reason?" Lullaby said softly.

"Somebody done me dirt last night. If I find the feller, I'm goin' to give him a good pistol whippin' and then boot him out of town. I'm goin' to fill him so full of slugs on the way out that he'll look like a sieve. I'm goin' to rub his nose in the road and ——"

"That sounds plumb harsh," Lullaby said gently. He scratched his head and yawned lazily.

Scorpio swore at him again. Half a dozen passersby hearing Scorpio's angry tones had stopped and were looking around. No one was in the immediate vicinity of the two. Scorpio's voice rose. The words that fell from his mouth weren't pleasant to hear.

Suddenly Lullaby grinned. "Do you know," he said gently, "you're not going to have to buy a new hat after all."

Scorpio halted his cursing. "What do you mean by that?"

"You ain't goin' to have any chance to wear one. Listen, Scorpio —" and Lullaby straightened to his full height, the sleepy look passing from his eyes, "— you've done a heap of talkin' about what you're going to do. You laid your tongue to some names I didn't like. Now don't you think it's just about time you cut out the pistol palaver and did something about it —— ?"

"Huh!" Scorpio was a trifle taken aback by the abrupt change in Lullaby's bearing.

Lullaby's voice didn't raise above normal: "I'm tellin' you, scut. You've found your hat. Now, you've found the hombre that's responsible for your losin' it, the hombre that roped you and socked you with a gun barrel, the hombre that put you in a coffin and made you a laughin' stock in Godwin. Yeah, I'm the man you're lookin' for. And if you want to make anythin' out of it, you don't have to look an inch farther, I'm waitin', sidewinder!"

Scorpio choked. For just one instant he hesitated, then his right hand flashed to his hip. Lullaby laughed, his own arm darting down with the speed of lightning. He swayed slightly as he moved.

Two guns flashed from holsters, Lullaby's six-shooter roaring a split instant before Scorpio's. Scorpio's shot flew wild as his muscular form was smashed against the front of Regan's building. Lullaby had scarcely changed position.

Scorpio cursed, righted himself, swung his gun for a second shot. The hammer of Lullaby's forty-five slipped smoothly from under his thumb. White flame darted from the muzzle.

The Colt gun flew from Scorpio's clenched fist. His fingers spread widely. A look of amazement, clouded with pain, passed across Scorpio's eyes.

"By — God — you're — fast," Scorpio muttered unbelievingly. His form sagged. He slid to a sitting position, back against Regan's front wall, his glazing eyes still fastened on Lullaby's grim features. Two wide stains of dark crimson were spreading across his shirt front.

And there, in a sitting position, Tate Scorpio died, his chin dropping slowly to hs chest. Powder smoke lifted along the street, vanished. Startled yells sounded from all directions. Men came running. Lullaby plugged out his spent shells, shoved fresh cartridges through the loading gate of his Colt gun. Then he replaced the gun in holster after a quick glance at the gathering crowd.

Hoofs drummed along the street. Poddy Cameron, followed by Tucson, Stony and Micky, came pushing through the knot of men about Lullaby. Everyone was talking at once.

"You hurt, pard?" Tucson cried.

"Not none," from Lullaby.

"Hurt?" a man in the crowd laughed scornfully. "I saw it all. Scorpio never had a chance. Joslin waited for Scorpio to start his draw before he moved. Hell's bells! Joslin didn't even go for that gun on his left hip. One cutter was enough."

Lullaby heard the man, said level-voiced, "Scorpio only had one gun on him."

Poddy Cameron was asking for details. Lullaby was talking quietly. There came a rush of fresh footsteps. Sheridan, followed by three Circle-Cross hands came running up.

"My Gawd!" Sheridan exclaimed. "It's Tate Scorpio. Who done this? If I catch the skunk that shot Scorpio, I'll ——"

"Sheridan," Lullaby snapped, "you're lookin' at him now. Scorpio made a heap of pistol palaver before he passed out. Do you want to try his game? I don't advise it, but it's your play!"

XXI. "DON'T JERK THAT HARDWARE!"

Sheridan tensed, his three followers ranging at his back. Stony and Tucson took quick steps to back up Lullaby. The hands of the Three Mesquiteers weren't near their guns, but they were alert for the first hostile movement on the part of the Circle-Cross men.

Silence had fallen over the crowd. At one side, Micky Callahan was writing furiously, making notes, with a stub of a pencil on a sheet of folded paper. He paused, his eyes expectant, as Tucson and his men stood facing the Circle-Cross cowboys. Two or three men near the belligerents commenced to edge uneasily back, out of range. The crowd waited, expecting every second to hear the roaring of heavy guns.

"It's up to you, Sheridan," Lullaby said sternly. "You never had a better chance to take up Scorpio's fight. What you aimin' to do?"

"Think fast, Sheridan, think fast," Tucson said softly.

Stony's words held contemptuous tones: "What'll we do, pards, concentrate our fire on Sheridan first, and finish the other coyotes later?"

Sheridan paled a trifle. His men were waiting for him to make the first move. Suddenly, Poddy Cameron found his voice. "Don't you hombres jerk that hardware — not any of you! We've had enough bloodshed hereabouts. Tucson! I'm lookin' to you and your pards to help me keep the law!"

That broke the spell. Sheridan flung his arms in the air. His henchmen with audible breaths of relief followed their chief's example. "I'll do my part to keep peace," Sheridan said quickly. "If there's any shootin' now, it'll be murder. You see how it is, Cameron. We're not startin' anythin'."

"Cripes! What a lucky break for Sheridan and his crew," Stony sneered. Tucson and Lullaby laughed softly, turned away.

Micky Callahan, looking a bit disappointed, jotted down a few more notes. Sheridan was still a trifle pale. He said to Cameron, "Sheriff, you figuring to arrest Joslin for Scorpio's death?"

"Don't be a fool, Sheridan." Cameron grunted. "There's several witnesses here saw Scorpio draw first. It's a clear case of self-defense."

"It was self-defense with Joe Frame, too, when he killed Clem Hayden ——" Sheridan commenced a protest.

"Hayden didn't go through with his draw," Tucson cut in sternly. "Scorpio did. Sheridan, you'll note the difference there. I'd be glad if you'd explain it."

Sheridan said, "Oh, hell!" and turning, left the crowd, followed by his henchmen. Immediately conversation sprung up on all sides. The crowd commenced to disperse, when Regan emerged from his store and, with the help of another man, lifted and carried the dead Scorpio into the undertaking establishment.

Poddy Cameron said, "I think I'll drift down the street — sort of keep an eye on Sheridan and his men for a spell. No tellin' what they may start. If they take this up with Judge Tibbetts and try to get a warrant swore out for Lullaby's arrest, I'll have to serve it, of course, though there's no doubt as to the eventual outcome. If I see 'em headin' for the court house, I'll get in and tell Tibbetts a few things myself."

"There was no warrant sworn out for me,

when I finished Frame and Grier," Tucson pointed out.

"That was different," Cameron pointed out. "Scorpio's killin' has hit Sheridan hard. Scorpio was his right-hand man."

The sheriff sauntered off. Micky Callahan drew Tucson off to one side, saying, "What are you planning to do now, Tucson?"

Tucson smiled, "This for publication?"

"No, for my own information. It's this way, Tucson, I'm in a tight spot." Micky flourished a handful of pencil-written notes before Tucson. "I've got to write my story of this gun fight for the *Clarion*'s readers. If I get busy right at once, I can get my story off on the noon stage, leaving for Rankintown. Then it can be telegraphed to Los Angeles and my editor will get it ——"

"Want me to write your story?" Tucson grinned, "while you go take care of Nancy Hayden?"

Mickey reddened. "You're about fifty percent correct, Tucson. It's this way. I brought Nancy in to town. If I ride back to the 8-Bar with her, I won't get my story off in time. 'Course, Nancy is most important. At the same time, I got to hang on to my job. The way things are shaping up, I may need my salary ——" Again he broke off, looking a trifle foolish.

"Don't you think Nancy can get home alone?" Tucson asked.

"I think she could. At the same time, I'm afraid of Sheridan and his men. I think somebody should ride with her. No telling what Sheridan might try to do."

"Mebbe you're right at that, son," Tucson nodded slowly. "All right, you hightail it for the hotel and take care of your story. I'll find Nancy and explain things to her. You go right along; I'll take care of this."

"You're a great guy, Tucson Smith. I hope you weren't planning anything important."

"As soon as I get a chance I'm figuring to drift over to Herrero and talk to Fulton Hodge."

"But you'll take care of Nancy first, eh?"

"I'll see that she's looked after. Don't you fret your head about her, son."

"That's great." Micky turned and dashed toward the hotel.

Stony and Lullaby were looking curiously after Micky as Tucson rejoined them. "What's Irish up to now?" Stony asked.

Tucson explained the situation. "Gosh," Lullaby said, "I'll bet that runt has fallen in love."

"You don't know the half of it," Tucson chuckled.

"You mean," Stony asked, "that Nancy

has fallen for Micky?"

"I wouldn't bet against it," Tucson said dryly. "If you'd seen the look on her face when she and Micky come ridin' in to town, this mornin', you'd known at once the runty Irishman wasn't repulsive to her."

Stony said, "Well, I'll be damned."

"Look," Tucson said, "I planned to ride to Herrero today."

"We're goin' with you," Lullaby said.

Tucson shook his head. "You've got to stick around town, Lullaby, in case Sheridan does decide to swear out a warrant. I don't think he will, but if you left Godwin, it might look to the judge like you were tryin' to make a getaway. Stony, I want you to stick with Lullaby, in case Sheridan and his skunks get an idea they want revenge ——"

"Cripes! I wish they would," Stony said enthusiastically. "We'd show 'em some *real* excitement."

"I don't think they will," Tucson frowned, "but you know — just in case. Now, here's what I want you to do for me. See Poddy Cameron and get him to have Link Dexter ride to the 8-Bar with Nancy. I figure Poddy will be glad to do it. You'll probably find Nancy down near the bank, or at the general store. She said something about wanting to get some dress goods or curtain material or somethin'."

"The homin' instinct," Lullaby drawled. "Yep, Micky looks like a goner."

"All right, we'll take care of things for you, pard," Stony nodded. "You line out for Herrero whenever you get ready."

Ten minutes later, Tucson, having gone to the livery to get his horse, was riding past the Faro Saloon on his way to Herrero. As he passed, Quint Sheridan was standing just inside the doorway of the saloon, gazing moodily over the swinging doors. Tucson didn't notice Sheridan, but Sheridan eyed Tucson thoughtfully as his gaze followed the lean, bronzed figure down Main Street. He saw Tucson's horse turn south at the edge of town, then disappear from sight.

Sheridan swung back from the entrance. The only men in front of the bar were Gabby Emmett, Frenchy Duproix and Soapy Randle. Sheridan called the three men to his side. They came quickly in response to his snapped command.

Emmett said, "What's up, boss?"

"Tucson Smith just rode past. He turned south."

"Do you reckon he's headin' for Herrero?" Duproix asked.

"That's what I want to know," Sheridan replied, cold-eyed. "We know he was over

306

to the bank, askin' for Hodge, this mornin'. That cashier told him about Hodge's bank in Herrero."

"Do you think that cashier knows what Hodge knows what we know?" Soapy Randle frowned.

Sheridan shook his head. "No, Hodge just keeps him here to run this bank straight — he does a good job, too."

"Good thing he's good for somethin'," Duproix laughed. "Otherwise I'd say he was right dumb."

"That's the way Hodge likes 'em," Sheridan grunted. "Look, Emmett, you and Frenchy, get your horses and trail Smith. Learn what he's up to if possible ——"

"And let daylight through him, eh?" Gabby Emmett said eagerly.

"Not unless you get a chance with no risks. Don't get outsmarted like Frame and Grier were ——"

"Joslin didn't outsmart Scorpio," Emmett interrupted. "That damn sleepy-eyed cowhand just plain outshot him ——"

Soapy Randle cut in, "I betcha Scorpio would have beat him to the shot if he'd had his other gun. Hey, Quint, why'n't you make Cameron give that gun up?"

"Why don't I make him?" Sheridan snapped testily. "I can't make him do nothin'. But I'll get that gun, yet. I got to get it. Only things been movin' so fast, lately, I haven't had a chance. If I only knew where Cameron kept that gun ——"

"There's somethin' damn funny about that gun," Duproix said, "somethin' that you fellers never let me and Soapy and T-Bone Hinkle in on. We know it's got some connection with Hodge, that Quint takes a lot of orders from Hodge, but what's the tie-up? With Frame, Grier and Scorpio gone, seems to me Soapy and I ought have your full confidence, Quint ——"

Sheridan scowled and started an evasive reply, but Randle cut in with, "I been thinkin' about that gun myself. It pro'bly shoots just like any other gun, but why you have to have that particular ——"

"Mebbe it don't shoot," Emmett started. "Mebbe that gun ——"

"Gabby!" Sheridan thundered, "keep your mouth shut. We'll tell Frenchy and Soapy about that later, if it works out."

Emmett gulped and fell silent. Randle said, "Why won't that gun shoot? That Irish reporter shot it once. I ——"

"What!" Sheridan exclaimed. "Callahan shot Scorpio's gun?"

Emmett burst out, "The gun that Hayden had when Frame killed him? The gun that

Bogart stole from the 8-Bar and brought to us that night — the gun Tucson Smith and his pards took away from us?"

"Sure," Randle reiterated. "What's funny about that?"

"How do you know Callahan shot that gun?" Sheridan demanded.

"That day of the inquest on Hayden," Randle explained. "I overheard Joslin and Brooke kiddin' Callahan about dropping the gun when it went off. It seems Callahan had never shot a forty-five before. They didn't notice me listenin' in on 'em ——"

"It can't be the same gun — not Scorpio's gun." Both Sheridan and Emmett looked worried as Sheridan expressed his doubts.

"I dunno." Randle shrugged his shoulders. "That's what I understood 'em to say."

"What's the excitement about anyway?" Duproix asked.

"I'll tell you some other time," Sheridan evaded. "Frenchy, you take Soapy with you to follow Smith, instead of Gabby. I want to talk a couple things over with Gabby."

Duproix nodded. "C'mon, Soapy, we'll show these hombres how to put Smith out of the runnin' if we get a chance."

"But don't take any risks," Sheridan reminded. "Our crew is pretty much whittled down now."

The instant Duproix and Randle had left the saloon, Sheridan swung on Emmett: "How do you figure it, Gabby?"

Emmett shook his head. "It's got me beat. That gun just couldn't shoot."

"It didn't shoot for Clem Hayden," Sheridan said.

"Hayden didn't even try to shoot it," Emmett pointed out.

"Lemme see," Sheridan frowned. "Scorpio had it, then Hayden. Bogart stole it at the 8-Bar. We had it, but Smith and his friends took it away before we had a chance to ——"

"Mebbe Smith learned ——"

"Callahan shot it that night ——"

"Do you suppose Poddy Cameron ——"

"Oh, hell!" Sheridan snapped. "It couldn't be the same gun, that's all. Soapy Randle didn't hear all of the conversation; mebbe he misunderstood Callahan's remarks. You can rest sure if Smith had learned anythin', we'd heard about it before now. The first thing for us to do is to get rid of Smith and his pards. After that, I'll work on Cameron in my own way and I'll either get that gun, or else — well, no use fussin' about it now. Let's have a drink. Barney ——" to the bartender slumbering on a stool behind the bar, "— set out a bottle pronto!"

"And with Duproix and Randle on the trail," Emmett put in, "mebbe we can drink to the end of Tucson Smith, eh, Quint?"

"To the finish and the damnation," Sheridan growled, reaching for the bottle.

XXII. THE BANKER OF HERRERO

The sun stood well past meridian when Tucson neared the International Border Line between United States and Mexico. At this point on the Border it was necessary to cross a long plank bridge, placed above a deep ravine, to gain entry into Mexico. On the United States side, to one side of the entrance to the bridge was a small shanty, with a pole corral at the rear containing an unsaddled horse.

As Tucson rode up to the shanty a man in the uniform of a United States Customs Officer stepped out of the doorway. As Tucson drew nearer he recognized the man as an acquaintance of former years. He pulled to a stop, grinning widely, "Bill Wyatt! Well, I'll be danged!" and put out his hand.

"Tucson Smith! What you doin' down here?"

"I was just goin' to say the same to you.

311

Last time we shook hands, you were over Utah way, working out of the office of the U. S. Marshal ——"

"That's all of eight years ago. I transferred to the Customs Bureau sometime back. Then I was sent down here. What you doin' these days?"

"My pards and I are hanging around Godwin ——"

"Lullaby and Stony with you?"

"You bet. They'll be driftin' down your way to say hello, when they hear you're here."

"I'll be dang glad to see them. See anybody, in fact. This is just about the dullest job I've had. My pardner who 'shifts' this job with me, was taken sick and headed for his doctor in Rankintown. I've been holdin' the fort with twenty-four hour duty, when I wasn't sleeping. Haven't been up to Godwin in ten days. Heard there'd been a killing up there. Man named Clem Hayden. I didn't know him."

"There've been a couple more since then — three in fact — not to mention a couple from Herrero — names of Bogart and Manning - ——"

"That so? Give me the news. I used to see Bogart and Manning come through here. Come to think of it, they rode through just a few days back. Trouble is, nobody wants to take time to talk when they do go through here, and there aren't many go through."

Tucson gave brief details of the doings of the past few days. When he had finished, Wyatt said, "There always seems to be something unusual afoot wherever you are, Tucson. What is it this time?"

"I'm not sure yet," Tucson laughed. "If it turns out to be anything connected with your line, I'll give you details. How about you, they keepin' you busy?"

"Not very. This is supposed to be a port of entry, but very little passes through. Once in a while I catch a Mexican trying to smuggle something in, but it never amounts to anything. There've been quite a few Chinks run into the States the last few months, but none of 'em have come my way — not since I been on this job, anyway."

"If I see any in Herrero," Tucson laughed, "I'll shoo 'em your way. See if I can't make you earn your money."

"What you headin' for Herrero for? Nothing to see there. It's a sort of tough town, if you ask me."

"I want to see Fulton Hodge."

"Oh, the banker. . . . Yes, he comes through here, once a week or so. Spends most of his time in Herrero. Him startin' a bank over there doesn't look like he showed sound judgment. Still, you can never tell what a banker will do. Some of 'em are pretty slick, and know their business better than I do."

The two men talked a few minutes longer, then Tucson gathered up his reins. "I'll see you on my return trip, Bill."

"Don't forget."

"I won't. S'long."

Tucson cantered his horse across the plank bridge. Another mile's ride through low hills would bring him to Herrero. At the opposite side of the bridge was another small building from which stepped two officers in Mexican uniforms. Tucson spoke to them in Spanish, explained that he was crossing on business, and was given permission to proceed. Apparently, examinations here weren't very strict. A good many cowmen made trips between Godwin and Herrero from time to time, during the course of a year. Suspicious-looking packages and loaded wagons were what caught the customs men's attention.

Tucson spurred his pony into a swift, ground-covering lope that carried him rapidly between the cactus-dotted hills. The road he was following was rough and full of chuck holes. Finally, rounding a shoulder of rock at the side of the trail, Herrero came into view.

It was a rather squalid-looking town, composed of adobe buildings, set down helter-skelter. A sort of rough street, unpaved, coursed a winding way between the structures. There were several *cantinas,* a few shops. Men drowsed in the shade between houses; an odor of stale liquor permeated the atmosphere in the vicinity of the *cantinas.* Tucson saw nearly as many *Americanos* as he did Mexicans. The *Americanos* were, for the most part, rough-looking individuals.

Finally, Tucson found what he sought. To his right was a small adobe building with a sign over the doorway stating it to be the *Banco Herrero.* There weren't any signs of activity about the bank; the hitchrack in front was bare of horseflesh. A small door was open, as was a window set to one side of the entrance.

Tucson pulled his pony to a stop, dismounted and tied his reins to the hitchrack. He crossed the dirt pathway and stepped to the entrance of the bank, pausing before he went in, to look the place over.

Inside was a wide desk and a couple of straight-backed chairs. In one corner, back of the desk, was a small steel safe. Near the other corner was a closed door which Tucson judged led to Fulton Hodge's living quarters. The place, Tucson decided mentally, didn't look much like a prosperous savings bank.

His eyes went to the man seated at the desk. He hadn't yet noticed Tucson, standing near the doorway. He was a man of middle age, with iron grey hair and sharp features, smoothly shaven. He had bulky shoulders and arms but didn't appear to be fat. He was dressed in a neat suit of grey clothing, the coat of which hung on the back of his chair as he sat in his vest, frowning over a sheet of figures spread on the oak desk in front of him.

Tucson stepped inside. The man looked up, still frowning. "Howdy," he nodded shortly.

Tucson said "Howdy" adding, "You Fulton Hodge?"

"I'm Hodge. What's your business?"

"Name's Smith — Tucson Smith. I'd like to *habla* with you a few minutes."

"Tucson Smith?" Something akin to an expression of anger flitted across Hodge's face, then vanished. "I've heard of you," he said slowly. "From Godwin, aren't you?"

"Stayin' there for a few days."

"Not permanently?"

"Hadn't figured on it."

Hodge laughed harshly. "Sometimes a man's plans go all awry."

"Meanin' just what?" Tucson asked coolly. "That you'd like to see me planted permanently, perhaps?"

"I didn't say that."

Tucson didn't like the man at all. At the first mention of his name he'd noticed that expression of mingled fear and hate flash across Hodge's features. More than ever, now, Tucson decided there was something decidedly queer about this banking business in Herrero.

"Well, what's your business?" Hodge asked crisply. "I'm a busy man — haven't any time to waste on idlers."

"Yeah," Tucson drawled, "I noticed how busy the place looked when I come in. I sure was afraid I'd get lost in the stampede when that big crowd of Mexicans came rushin' to deposit their savin's. Seems like you should hire a couple extra clerks."

"No sarcasm, please," Hodge said, flushing deeply. "I asked what your business was."

"You'll get your answer. Hodge, you hold Clem Hayden's note for five hundred dollars ——"

"Five thousand," Hodge snapped.

"Miss Hayden says five hundred."

"The girl's a fool —— !"

"Go easy, Hodge!"

"Miss Hayden's mistaken," Hodge corrected himself lamely. "She's seen the note ——"

"I know," Tucson nodded. "To be frank with you, I suspected forgery, but Nancy Hayden says the signature is genuine. But there's something off color about it. I'd like to see the note myself."

Hodge hesitated, then, "I'd just as soon show it to you, but it happens to be at the Godwin bank ——"

"Your cashier says different."

"He's a liar!"

Tucson shrugged his shoulders. "I can advise Miss Hayden to go to law about the matter. Sooner or later you'd have to produce that note, Hodge. All I ask is to see it."

Hodge hesitated again. Finally he said, "All right, I'll show it to you, but you'll have to give me your word not to attempt to destroy it."

"You've got my word."

Hodge twisted in his chair, reached to the inner pocket of his coat. Removing a wallet, he opened it and extracted a folded slip of paper which he tossed on the desk. Tucson took the paper, unfolded it, read it through. He felt Hodge's eyes on him while he read, could sense the hate springing from their depths. Finally, he tossed the paper back on the desk.

Hodge said, "Well?" triumphantly.

Tucson shook his head. "It's not well at all. You might bluff a girl that isn't accustomed to cow country ways, but you can't make that note stick with me."

"What's wrong with the note?" Hodge asked belligerently. "It's just as I wrote it out for Hayden. He signed it. What's wrong with it?"

"Well," Tucson said easily, "my guess is that you added an extra *naught* to that five hundred, changing it to read five thousand. Oh, it's neat work, but there you are ——"

"Bosh!" Hodge exploded.

"An honest man," Tucson pursued quietly, "would not only have put down the figures but spelled out the amount as well. You didn't do that."

"Hayden didn't have to sign that note either," Hodge said angrily.

"Uh-huh," Tucson nodded. "I can't imagine you sayin' somethin' like that to him, in just those tones. Hayden couldn't afford to quibble. He needed money desperately. He was a stranger, you might say. He trusted

319

you, Hodge. And now you're trying to do his daughter out of her property."

"Smith, are you insane?"

"You know damn well I'm not, but *you are* if you try to collect on that note."

"You won't stop me!"

Tucson laughed softly. "Them's my plans. If I can't do it any other way, I'll give Nancy the money to pay it off ——"

"You haven't got it ——"

Tucson's smile broadened. "I'll make you a proposition. I'll take that note off of your hands. I'll pay you five thousand, plus interest. Are you willing?"

"Certainly not," Hodge growled. "I take care of my own notes. You better leave, Smith. I'm busy ——"

"I'll leave when I get ready. I know why you won't turn that note over to me. You plan to take Nancy's property — which is worth several times the value of that note. You want her ranch. That leads me to wonder just what your tie-up is ——"

"My tie-up?" Hodge snapped.

"With Quint Sheridan," Tucson explained.

"I haven't any tie-up with Quint Sheridan. I know him, of course. He's done some business with my Godwin bank, but ——"

"Don't lie, Hodge! You hold a note for the 8-Bar. Sheridan rustles 8-bar cows. You planned to beat the Haydens out of their property — you and Sheridan together. What do you want with that ranch? There must be a pretty good reason when you'll war on a woman. There's a reason back of your schemes, and s'help me when I learn what they are, I'll send you and Sheridan to the penitentiary so fast ——"

"You're crazy, Smith!" Hodge had moved back in his chair, one hand resting on a drawer in his desk.

"I'm not too crazy to demand an investigation into your affairs, Hodge. I got a hunch this bank, in Herrero, is all a bluff to cover some other game. I'm makin' it my business to learn what that game is ——"

Hodge jerked open the desk drawer, leaped from his chair, a revolver clutched in his hand. "By God —— !"

And then he stopped short upon seeing the six-shooter in Tucson's fist.

"Better drop it, Hodge," Tucson advised sternly. "You've overplayed your hand. I asked a few simple questions and you pulled a gun on me. No honest man would do that. You're coming to the end of your rope."

Hodge gulped and dropped his gun to the floor. "Put — put your gun away," he said hoarsely. "Perhaps you and I can do business after all."

Tucson shoved the Colt gun back into his holster. "Talk fast," he said, cold voiced. "What sort of proposition you aimin' to make?"

Hodge's eyes strayed uneasily away from Tucson's hard gaze. Suddenly his face changed. He laughed shortly, "A proposition I don't think you'll want to agree to," he half snarled.

Too late Tucson caught the abrupt change in the man's manner. Footsteps sounded at his rear. He started to turn, then went rigid as Frenchy Duproix's voice sneered:

"Hold it, Smith! Put 'em high!"

And then Soapy Randle's hateful tones: "Go on, make just one move, Smith. I'm fair itchin' to bore you!"

Tucson raised his arms, crossed his fingers on top of his hat, then turned to see Duproix and Randle covering him with six-shooters. Fulton Hodge, a look of triumph and anger contorting his features, was on his feet now. He rounded the desk in three swift steps.

"Good work, boys," he smiled nastily. "You keep him covered, while I unbuckle his gun belts. He was getting a bit too inquisitive for comfort. There's only one answer to a man of that type. And Smith is due to get his answer mighty soon!"

XXIII. MICKY COMES CLEAN

Tucson paced restlessly up and down his prison. The single wooden-barred window let through the last rays of the setting sun. The building in which he was confined was built of thick adobe, the one door of stout oak, locked on the outside. It was to this place of confinement Tucson had been brought by Frenchy Duproix and Soapy Randle, after the pair had covered him with their guns in Hodge's office. The small building was generally used. Tucson guessed, as a sort of a storehouse; it was located only a short distance to the rear of Hodge's bank building, if bank it may be termed.

The door had resisted all of Tucson's efforts to force it open. He had studied the wooden bars in the narrow window and figured that, given time, he could wrench them from their sockets, but from the time Tucson had been made prisoner in this place, either Randle or Duproix had been watching that window and had warned Tucson to keep away from it. Six-shooters clenched in their fists had spoken more plainly than their words what Tucson's fate would be should he attempt an escape by the window.

The afternoon had dragged slowly on, with Tucson wondering just what was to happen. Now, with the sun near setting, he had begun to feel hungry and wondered if his captors intended to starve him to death. Of Fulton Hodge he'd had no further sight. Luckily, his captors hadn't taken away his Durham or cigarette papers, and a litter of brown stubs cast about the floor showed how Tucson had occupied his time. Mostly, he was waiting for night to come, hoping, under cover of darkness, to make some sort of a break for freedom, regardless of the menace of enemy guns.

There wasn't a stick of furniture of any sort in the small room. Just a dirt floor, a ceiling, and four walls in which were set the single door and one window. Tucson pondered, "Once it gets dark, mebbe I can yank those bars out of their sockets, and take a chance on those skunks missin' me when they cut loose with their hawg-laigs. Cripes! I wish now I hadn't told Stony and Lullaby to stay in town. But it looks like I'd have to get out of this jam under my own power - - if I'm goin' to get out." That thought wasn't pleasant, either.

Loud voices were heard outside, the sounds indicating a tussle. Duproix and Randle were cursing. There was further movement. The door was suddenly flung open. In the dying light from the sun, Tucson saw a small figure propelled with no little force through the opening and go sprawling to the floor.

"There's company for you, Smith!" Duproix snapped.

The door was quickly slammed shut, the padlock replaced and secured. From outside rose jeering remarks from Duproix and Soapy Randle. Tucson ignored the voices and went toward the small form that was just rising, stiffly, from the floor.

"Micky!" Tucson exclaimed.

"Sure and you've named me," Callahan panted groggily. He staggered a trifle as Tucson caught his arm, led him to one side and made him sit down on the floor.

"How in Hades did you get into this?" Tucson asked.

The light was fading fast, but Tucson could see the little Irish reporter had met some hard going. Ten minutes passed, and at the end of that time Callahan had somewhat regained his composure, though he was still a trifle winded. A few moments more and his voice came easier, "Those blackguards certainly play rough when they get started," he commented wryly.

"But what happened to you? I thought you

were in Godwin."

"I was. I wrote up the story of the gunfight between Lullaby and Scorpio and put it in the mail. I hung around with Lullaby and Stony for a while, then got to thinking about your coming here, after they told me how you'd had them arrange for Link Dexter to escort Nancy home. I figured maybe I'd better come over here too, and see that you didn't put anything over on me."

"What do you mean?"

"You didn't have any special reason for seeing Hodge?"

"Just what I told you," Tucson replied puzzledly. "I wanted to see him about that note of Nancy's father's."

"But you don't know who he is?"

"Fulton Hodge," Tucson growled, "a banker — with a bank that I think is just a cover for some other sort of game."

"Uh-huh," Micky nodded. "What did you learn about that note?"

Tucson told him the result of his visit with Hodge, ending, ". . . and after they got the drop on me, they brought me in here. I've been here ever since. I'm still wonderin' how you got into this jam."

"I looked around Herrero after I got here," Micky said, "trying to catch sight of you. Finally I saw your horse standing in front of Hodge's bank — anyway, I thought it was your horse. It looked like the same animal to my unpractised eyes. So I went into the bank, if that's what it is, and asked Hodge if you'd been there ——"

"And of course he denied it."

"Said he'd never even heard of you. Well, he almost had me convinced. I'd only seen him once before, in Godwin. Today when I got a better look, I recognized him ——"

"Who is he? What is he?"

"Let that pass now. Anyway, I felt he was lying. About that time I saw a couple of belts and guns hanging on a hook in one corner. Well, those sort of looked like the guns you wear. I told Hodge I figured he was lying, and dropped a hint about his past life that made him go green around the gills. Anyway, he tells me to wait while he went out to see if anybody had ever heard of you. He was gone about five minutes and when he returned Frenchy Duproix was with him, and Frenchy Duproix was holding in his hand what looked like a cannon ——"

"A forty-five looks that way, sometimes, when you're lookin' at the wrong end."

"Well, I clinched with Duproix, figuring to get past him. He sidestepped me, hit me a wallop on the head with his gun. About the time I got up from the floor, Hodge swung a right to my head. All this, you might say, lowered my resistance, so it wasn't any trick to force me in here with you."

"You're lucky you got off as easy as you did."

"I don't imagine they're through with us yet, Tucson. I heard Hodge drop something about finishing you off tonight, after the town has quieted down. From what he said, I judge they intend taking you outside of town some place and ——"

"We'll worry about that when the time comes, Micky. Just who did you recognize Hodge to be?"

"We-ell —" Micky hesitated, then, "well, back about five years, there was a picture of him or his double in the California papers. At that time, he was wanted for being the head of an opium smuggling ring. Somehow, he'd escaped the net thrown out for him ——"

"And came here and got into banking," Tucson cut in. "Do you know if Hodge is his name?"

"As I remember it, the pictures in the papers carried another name, but what it was, I can't say. What do you know about him?"

"No more than I've told you."

"Is that straight goods?"

"Micky, I'm tossin' a straight loop. Look here, you've asked me before what brought me to this neck of the range. I told you the truth. You always seemed to doubt me. Once you dropped something about a reward. I've asked you what brought you here, but you've sidestepped answering that. Don't you think it's about time, Micky, that you came clean with me?"

Micky hesitated. It was dark now, but Tucson guessed that the runty Irishman was smiling. Micky said, after a time, "You sure you're not after that reward?"

"I don't even know what you're talking about."

"Never even heard of the Pinchot diamonds, I suppose."

"You're talkin' Greek as far as I'm concerned. What's the story?"

Micky said, "By geez! I believe you are telling the truth."

"I certainly am," Tucson said earnestly.

Micky laughed softly. "And all the time I thought you were holding out on me." He heaved a long sigh, "All right, here's the story. There's a multi-millionaire in Los Angeles, named Ygnacio Pinchot. This Pinchot is a collector of valuable jewels. His collection is worth millions, but the prize of his collection is what he calls his rose diamonds ——"

"Rose diamonds. Never heard of 'em."

"Rose colored. Really a sort of pink. There's ten of 'em, they're perfectly matched and cut. They're sort of freaks in the jewelry world and worth big money because of that, rather than because of their size. Pinchot had them set in a brooch for his wife. One of the Pinchot servants stole the brooch. The police eventually caught him, and he confessed to having turned the brooch over to a fence — you know, a man who disposes of stolen goods ——"

"I know what a fence is," Tucson said impatiently.

They were holding their voices low now, in case Duproix or Randle might be listening. Micky went on, "The police traced down the fence, but he'd disposed of the rose diamonds some place else. Swore he didn't remember where. He's serving a sentence now, but his memory hasn't returned. Sometime later, the setting for the diamonds was picked up in a pawn-shop, but the proprietor didn't know where it had come from. From that point on, the police were up against a blank wall."

"And the diamonds were never recovered?"

"You said it. Of course, my paper was interested in those ten sparklers as news. My editor gave me the job of seeing what I could find out. Well, a reporter can sometimes learn things that the police never hear of. I finally received information, from one source and another, that the rose diamonds had been taken across into Mexico. You may not know it — a reporter gets lots of information that outsiders don't get — but right now there are quite a number of diamonds being smuggled through this part of the country. The Government hasn't been able to stop it, either."

"You mean the smugglers are operating from this part of the country?"

"Somewhere around here. I played a hunch. Crooks always know where to dispose of stolen goods. I figured maybe those rose diamonds might have been brought over this way, and would re-enter the United States in this vicinity. I put the proposition up to my paper, and the editor sent me to Godwin to sort of look around and see if I could learn anything. Then, Clem Hayden got shot and I've been sending him a different sort of news ever since. You've sort of kept news coming for the *Clarion*'s readers."

"You mentioned something about a reward?"

"Oh, yes, old Ygnacio Pinchot is offering ten thousand dollars reward for the return of his diamonds. You see the layout, Tucson? If I can recover 'em, my paper gets the news and I'll get the reward."

"Whew!" Tucson whistled softly. "That's a nice reward, Micky."

"Enough to pay for a printing press and let me set up a paper in Godwin," Callahan grinned.

"But you haven't got a trace of the rose diamonds yet?"

"Not a smell. Though, since I've had a good look at Hodge, I've been thinking I'm on the right track. He may use this bank, in Herrero, as just a blind for his real business — you know, a sort of clearing house for stolen stones. He is, unless I'm guessing wide of the mark, a fence. And the more I think about it, the more I figure I'm right."

Tucson nodded slowly. "Mebbe you're on the right track, son."

It was pitch dark in their prison now. Occasionally sounds from the town reached their ears: drunken voices, boisterous singing, now and then a woman's high-pitched squeal of fright or merriment. An hour passed, while Micky went over his story, Tucson listening closely. Micky finally said hopefully, "You never heard of those diamonds, or that reward, eh, Tucson?"

"It's all news to me, Micky. If we ever get out of this, and get Nancy's business cleared up, I'd admire to take a hand and see if I can help you locate 'em. I'd like to see you get that reward."

"I'd split with you."

Tucson laughed softly. "Forget it. I got enough to get along on now. Nope, Micky, we'll just have to forget those ten rose diamonds for a spell. We got more important work ahead, the same being to get out of this dump."

Tucson rose and softly approached the window. His hands wrapped around two of the wooden bars, his muscles tensed for the pull. There came a sharp sound of splitting wood, as one of the bars commenced to give.

Wham! A leaden slug crashed into the wall, not far from the window. Abruptly, Tucson dodged back. Then came Duproix's voice from the darkness a few yards away.

"Don't try that again, Smith. We'll be borin' you. If you know what's good for your health, you and Callahan will keep away from that window."

"Just as you say," Tucson replied easily. "How about some grub?"

"Aw, you don't need any grub," Soapy

Randle cut in. "Take it easy for a spell."

Tucson retreated back into the room. "I was afraid they'd be watchin'," he said quietly.

"Maybe," Micky suggested, "we could pull off one bar at a time and then take a chance on getting through."

Tucson shook his head. "That'd be sheer suicide. They'd just pick us off. That window is too tight a squeeze to get through in a hurry."

Tucson dropped down on the floor beside Micky, his back to the wall, and started to roll a cigarette. The minutes drifted along, extended into quarter hours and then hours. There weren't so many sounds to be heard from outside now; the town was evidently quieting down.

Tucson struck a match, looked at his watch. "Gosh, it's after ten," he announced. The match flickered out, leaving them once more in darkness.

"It don't look like we'd get out of here tonight," Micky commented. "I thought they'd be up to something by this time."

"Mebbe mornin' will bring some change. I reckon to stretch out and see can I get some sleep. I wish to cripes I had a gun ____"

"Now, if I could get that reward," Micky

was saying absent-mindedly, "I could ——"
He broke off suddenly, then, "Cripes! I've got a gun!"

"You have!" Tucson sat up straighter.

"Sure, that gun of Bogart's. I'd forgotten about it. I've been so darn busy thinking of those diamonds and the reward and Nancy ——" Micky broke off suddenly.

"You mean to say those skunks didn't take that gun when they captured you?" Tucson demanded unbelievingly.

A sort of giggle escaped Micky's lips. "They looked for it in my waistband, but when it wasn't there, they figured I didn't have any."

"But where was it?"

"After that day when I got the drop on Sheridan and his two plug-uglies, I figured I better not wear it, or they'd be forcing a fight on me. I hated to give it up, so I took a length of cord and hung it down my trouser leg, inside my pants."

"Cripes Genimy!" Tucson exulted. "We've got a chance, son. Let me have that hawg-laig."

Micky's fingers trembled as he untied the knot after hauling the gun from his pant leg. Tucson was laughing softly, as he took the gun in the darkness. He scratched a match, examined the gun. The examination was only a cursory one before the match flickered into blackness. Tucson's voice came through the gloom, "The hammer is restin' against a shell. I figure Bogart must have fired once, that night he was shot. There's an empty shell in the cylinder. Well, that leaves four loads, anyway."

Both men were on their feet now. Micky asked softly, "How do you figure to get the drop on 'em, Tucson?"

Tucson replied grimly, "There won't be time for any drop business. If I can get 'em to open the door, they'll be holdin' guns, expectin' trouble. I'll just have to start slingin' lead. You stay out of range, then duck out at the first chance. If I get detained, you keep goin'. Get to Godwin, then bring Lullaby and Stony back with you. Gosh! This is a break for us." Tucson was laughing softly as he cradled the Colt's forty-five in his hand. In this gun — Bogart's gun, carrying the cylinder from Scorpio's weapon — Tucson now placed all of his rising hopes. He whirled suddenly toward the window, called out, "Hey, Duproix — Randle!"

"What you want?" Duproix's voice sounded through the gloom.

"I got a proposition for you, if you'll open the door. Look, I've got a money belt under my shirt. I've got important business in

336

Godwin. Let me out and maybe we can strike a bargain."

"Aw, I don't bite easy ——" Duproix started scornfully.

Tucson heard Randle cut in, caught the words "money belt," then Duproix's low tones, "He might be bluffin' — just trying to get us to open the door ——"

"Suppose he is," Randle said harshly. "We'll both open the door and let him have it! It'll save takin' him out in the hills later — him and Callahan — and finishin' 'em off. Go on, what you afeared of? 'Tain't as if they had guns. And he's pro'bly speakin' the truth about that money belt. Smith and his pards are supposed to make good profits from their 3-Bar-O spread."

Impatiently, Tucson called out, "You two goin' to debate the matter all night?"

There was some more low muttering between Duproix and Randle. Tucson couldn't catch what they were saying this time. Finally, Duproix raised his voice, "Smith, toss that money belt through the window, and we'll talk about it later."

"Nothing doing," Tucson refused. "If you want this money belt, you've got to let me out and talk to you. Or go get Hodge. I'll put my proposition to him. In that case, though, Hodge might keep it all for himself.

It's important that I get to Godwin, so you can make some easy *dinero* if you think fast."

There was more low conversation, then Duproix said, "Okay, Smith, we'll let you out. Callahan has to stay there. If you make any phoney moves when we open that door, we aim to bore you."

"Come ahead," Tucson called back. Then, lowering his voice, he said to Micky, "They aim to bore us anyway. The dirty skunks don't figure to give us a houn'-dawg's chance. At the same time, they're too yellow to let us both come out. I'm not kickin', though. All I want is for 'em to unlock that door."

Footsteps sounded outside, then fell silent for a moment. Tucson tensed, near the door, the forty-five clutched in his right fist, the hammer pulled back under his thumb.

"They're comin', son," he whispered through the darkness. "Get ready to follow my lead. I aim to crash that door the instant they take that padlock off."

"I'm ready, Tucson. Give the scuts hell!"

Footsteps sounded on the gravel outside, whispering voices. Silence again. Tucson commenced to wonder if they were planning to shoot him and Micky through the window. He called softly to Micky to hug the floor. Flattened against the wall, near the door, Tucson waited, every nerve in his body quivering with suspense.

XXIV. Thundering Hoofs

Minutes passed while Tucson and Micky waited, tense, in the darkness. There wasn't a sound to be heard now. Micky's breath came faster with suppressed excitement. He cleared his throat nervously; the sound in the silent room appeared to be unusually loud. Tucson shifted one foot slightly, and at the scraping of the boot against the bare dirt floor, Micky jumped as though a gun had been exploded near his ear.

"What — what they cooking up?" Micky whispered hoarsely.

"I — don't — know." Tucson's words were harsh with the strain of waiting.

"God! I wish they'd hurry."

"I don't like it either, son. But don't let your imagination stampede you. Keep cool, steady. You'll be needin' all of your wits."

"Uh-huh." Micky's voice shook a trifle, and he swore under his breath.

Five minutes more dragged past. Tucson was near the door, but keeping an eye on the window now, half expecting to see the flash of a gun stab redly between the wooden bars.

The tension ceased abruptly. Quick steps sounded on the gravel outside. There was a noise of fumbling at the padlock. Tucson braced himself, raised the gun in his fist. Then ——

"Tucson!" came a voice, as the door was swung open. Tucson relaxed, spun the gun cylinder, eased the hammer to an empty shell.

It was Lullaby speaking!

"Lullaby!" Relief tinged Tucson's tones. Micky was at Tucson's shoulder. Lullaby's form was framed against the door opening. His hand sought Tucson's and Micky's. "Lullaby, you ol' gay-cat!" Tucson said gladly. "Cowboy, you got here in time. Where's Stony? What's become of Randle and Duproix —— ?"

"Here's your guns and belts," Lullaby was saying hurriedly.

"You got Hodge —— ?"

"We took all three prisoners," Lullaby was speaking swiftly. "Stony and me got to worryin' about you when you didn't return to town. We thought we'd come over and have a look-see ——"

"Did you see Bill Wyatt?"

"Yeah, he's in the Customs Service now, ain't he? He said you passed him —— Anyway, when we got into Herrero the first thing we saw was your horse, standin' in front of that bank. We didn't want to start anythin' in this town, without locatin' you first. We left our horses in the street, snuck around back here, just in time to hear you talkin' through your window to Duproix and Randle. About the time they started for here, Stony and I put our guns on 'em, told 'em if they made a sound we'd bore 'em pronto —— "

"Where's Hodge?" Micky cut in.

"We tied up Randle and Duproix," Lullaby explained. "Then I went around to the bank and put the drop on Hodge, got Tucson's guns and brought Hodge around back here, tied him tight, too."

Tucson was buckling on his guns and belts, laughing softly. He shoved Micky's gun toward the reporter, saying, "I won't need it after all, son, thank the powers that be."

Micky shoved the Colt gun into his waistband. Lullaby went on. "We got the horses saddled — Micky's was standin' not far from your bronc, Tucson. Hodge, Randle and Duproix are in saddles, their hands tied to the saddle horn. Stony's watchin' 'em, threatenin' 'em with instant death if they make a sound. You see, we figured them skunks have friends in town, and we don't want a battle on our hands, right now, if it can be avoided. At the same time, I figured you might want to take them three back to Godwin."

"Good. You had the right idea. You're lucky you didn't meet more resistance."

"Resistance?" Lullaby laughed. "Duproix handed over the key to this shack, meek as a lamb, when he felt my Colt barrel borin' into his back."

"C'mon, let's get going," Tucson said. "We'll have to slip out of this town the back way, if we want to take prisoners with us. If we tried to ride along the street, somebody might see us and start a fuss."

The three men quickly walked away from the adobe hut. In a few moments they heard soft sounds. Horses and men loomed out of the darkness. Stony laughed genially, "Nice night for a ride, pards. Is the little reporter gettin' news at first hand?"

"Aw, you go to hell," Micky said good-naturedly. "At the same time, much obliged for this nick-of-time rescue."

"Don't mention it, sweetheart. Me'n Lullaby always aims to please. That's our motto in this vale of tears."

Randle, Duproix and Hodge were tied into saddles. The first two sat in sullen silence. Hodge started to talk when he saw

Tucson and Micky. "This is an outrage," he declared venomously. "I protest this treatment. I'm a decent citizen ——"

"Protest and be damned," Tucson snapped. "You're going back to Godwin. I'm aimin' to prefer charges ——"

"The sheriff at Godwin has no authority on Mexican soil, Smith," Hodge said angrily. "I demand to be released. If you have charges to make, you can make them to the local authorities. I'm licensed to conduct a business here ——"

"You might as well shut up, Hodge," Tucson said sternly. "We're takin' you back to the States. There's a lot of your movements won't stand investigation ——"

"You'll never take me past the Mexican Customs men," Hodge snapped. "I'll tell them you have no right. Later, I'm willing to appear in Godwin, providing you do this legally ——"

"And get out extradition papers to bring you back, eh?" Tucson laughed. "Hodge, that isn't going to work. Too much red-tape. We never would get our hands on you again. I'm glad you mentioned those Mexican Customs men though. I'd plumb-forgotten ——"

"How about those fellers?" Lullaby asked worriedly. "Mebbe we should tie a gag in

Hodge's mouth ——"

"Hell! A gag would be noticed," Stony objected.

"We're going to have to run for it," Tucson said seriously. "We can't afford to be stopped by those Customs men on this side of the line. They'll tie us up in legal tangles. Now, get this — we approach that bridge at a normal speed. When I give the signal, we make a run for it. The Customs men will open up with their guns, but we've got to chance that —"

"I can stop *that* ——" Stony commenced.

"Nothin' doin'," Tucson shook his head. "They'll only be doing their duty. We don't want to get mixed up in any international squabbles. If Hodge or Randle or Duproix open their mouths, we'll just have to bore 'em."

The three men concerned looked rather worried in the gleam from Lullaby's match as he hastily lighted a cigarette. It was mostly bluff on Tucson's part, and while the bluff didn't quite go down with Hodge, Duproix and Randle shivered in their saddles.

Tucson and his pardners climbed on their horses. The animals set out, Tucson and Lullaby leading. Next came the three prisoners. Micky and Stony fell in at the rear.

There was little talking as the horses

moved away in the darkness. The street was given a wide berth, as Tucson cut toward the hills at a tangent. In a few minutes the town had been left behind, and Tucson swung his pony back toward the road leading to the international bridge between the two countries.

The horses' hoofs drummed softly along the road, as it wound through the hills. Tucson spoke to Lullaby, as the string of riders commenced to draw near the Border line. Lullaby dropped back to the rear with Stony. Micky pushed his horse up beside Tucson's.

Abruptly as the riders circled a shoulder of rock, a light came into view. A few minutes more and it was seen to be shining from a window in the hut of the Mexican Customs officials. Tucson — and the rest caught Tucson's low-spoken orders — slowed pace as they approached the long, plank bridge across the ravine. At the opposite end of the bridge, a light shone in Bill Wyatt's shanty.

"Hodge," Tucson spoke sternly over his shoulder, "if I hear one yelp out of you, you'll be plumb sorry."

Hodge didn't say anything. Tucson added to Lullaby and Stony, "If Duproix and Randle hold back, let 'em have it."

"We're holdin' guns on 'em now," Lullaby called softly.

"Hell, we won't squeal," Randle whined. Duproix made some similar remark.

The two Mexican officials came stretching and yawning out of their shanty. One of them carried a lantern. They stood waiting in front of their shanty, peering through the darkness at the approaching riders. The horses drew nearer the bridge. Tucson whispered to Micky to push ahead a little. Micky moved into the lead while Tucson dropped back and reached one hand to the bridle of Hodge's mount. Hodge glared through the darkness, but with his hands bound to the saddle-horn there was nothing he could do to prevent Tucson's action.

One of the Customs men called out an order to halt.

Tucson said genially, *"Buenas tardes, amigos."*

"Good evening, *senores,"* the Mexicans commenced in reply.

At that moment Hodge raised his voice in a cry for help: "Stop these men! They are bandits! They are taking me —— !"

"Cut for it!" Tucson yelled.

Knee-guiding his pony, he struck Micky's horse across the haunches with his rope, tightened his grip on Hodge's bridle.

Lullaby and Stony let out wild yells, plunged in their spurs. Electrified by fear, Randall and Duproix put their ponies into a run, realizing that bullets would be humming in the next instant.

Micky nearly fell from the saddle as his horse jumped ahead. The yelling startled Hodge's horse into movement. There came a rush of hoofs, as the ponies thundered over the plank bridge. The Mexican officials cursed in excitable Spanish and fell back, while the riders pounded past them. The horses were half way across the bridge before the Mexicans recovered their senses sufficiently to draw their guns.

A bullet whined overhead, then two more. A fourth bullet nipped the ear of Hodge's horse. The beast plunged frantically, and was nearly knocked down as Randle's horse collided with it, but Tucson held firm to his grip on the bridle, and dug the spurs into his own pony.

Leaden slugs whined viciously about the riders. At the opposite end of the bridge, Bill Wyatt came running from his hut, waving a lantern and yelling orders to stop. A six-shooter was raised in his right hand.

"Hold your fire, Bill!" Tucson yelled. "It's us. It's all right!"

Wyatt lowered his Colt gun as the horses

came thundering on. "That you, Tucson?" he shouted.

"Yeah — and my pardners. We're takin' prisoners across. Explain to those Mexicans that we're all right. I'll be back to see you when we get settled."

"Right! Keep goin'! I'll square it."

The horses clattered across the planks, struck solid earth again in a burst of dust and gravel, continued running at top speed. Once more, they were on United States soil.

Glancing back over his shoulder, Tucson saw Bill Wyatt run to meet the Mexican officials who had started across the bridge. The firing died out. The horses thundered on for another mile, before Tucson gave the order to slow the pace.

"We did it, cowboy!" Lullaby exclaimed.

"Anybody hit?" Tucson called back.

"Reckon not," from Stony. "All present and accounted for."

Micky's horse dropped back beside Tucson's. Micky laughed a trifle shakily, "There's nothing like a pursuing bullet to make a man stay with his horse."

"You'll learn to ride yet, son," Tucson chuckled dryly.

Randle and Duproix rode in sullen silence. Hodge cursed bitterly, until Tucson, growing weary of the vile tirade, ordered the man sternly to keep his mouth closed.

"I demand a lawyer when we get to God-win," Hodge snapped.

"You'll get a lawyer," Tucson promised, "but only when we get ready to let you have one. You've had things your own way for quite a spell. It's our turn now. I aim to keep you coyotes out of sight, until we see how Sheridan reacts to your disappearance."

"What are you planning, Tucson?" Micky asked.

"If Sheridan doesn't hear from his pards," Tucson said, "he's going to start worryin'. When he gets good and worried he's likely to start something that will tip his hand. When he tips his hand, maybe we'll learn a few things."

"How are you going to keep Sheridan from seeing his pals?" Micky asked, his voice sounding above the drumming hoofs of the horses.

"I'm expecting Poddy Cameron to help us on that," Tucson explained. "Poddy's home is on this trail we're following. We'll stop by and see him. I figure the town will be wrapped in sleep, when we hit Godwin. It shouldn't be hard to put these three coyotes into jail without the news getting out ——"

Hodge roared a vigorous protest, but

Tucson shut him up with, "You kick up a row, Hodge, and you'll find it tough going. Behave, and I'll see that you get a lawyer within a reasonable length of time." Hodge's better judgment forced him to fall silent. Randle and Duproix had nothing to say. The horses pounded on.

Within a half hour Tucson had roused the surprised Poddy Cameron from his bed and explained what he wanted. Cameron agreed to help, got dressed quickly and mounted his horse, then accompanied the riders into Godwin. The streets were dark and silent. Deputy Link Dexter was aroused from his cot. The jail door was thrown open and Hodge, Duproix and Randle were locked in cells. No one had witnessed the arrival of the prisoners, except the men who had a part in their incarceration.

"Well, that's that," Tucson said wearily, on the dark street a few minutes later. "And Micky and I haven't even had supper yet. I'm goin' to wake up that cook at the hotel and demand food or his life. Then a bed is sure goin' to look good to me."

"Hear that, Stony?" Lullaby asked.

"What about it?" from Stony.

"I ain't the only one that likes food," Lullaby grinned.

Stony sneered, "You want to remember,

cowpoke, there's a heap of difference between *likin'* and *worshippin'*."

XXV. A Rustling Charge

Nine o'clock the following morning. Bright
sunshine along Godwin's Main Street.
Tucson, Stony and Lullaby were seated on
the railing'd porch of the hotel, digesting
their breakfasts and talking. To the west, the
rugged peaks of the Santa Madraza Mountains lifted craggy heads against the sapphire
sky. Tucson shifted his feet on the porch
railing, tilted back his chair.

"That's the story, cowhands," he concluded. "You've got it all."

Lullaby whistled softly, "What a yarn.
Rose diamonds. I never heard of such a
thing."

Stony put in, "And you think Hodge
knows where they are?"

Tucson shrugged his muscular shoulders.
"We don't know about that. We're just
guessing. It's my hunch — and Micky's —
that he does."

The three men smoked in silence for a
few minutes. Stony said suddenly, "Where'd
Micky go to?"

Tucson jerked his head toward the hotel
entrance. "Micky's writing up some stuff

for his paper, wants to get it off on the noon stage ——"

"Gosh!" Lullaby interrupted. "He isn't spilling the information regardin' your suspicions of Hodge, is he?"

Tucson shook his head. "He's not spilling a thing. He won't until we've got more definite proof, one way or the other."

"But what became of those rose diamonds, if Hodge had 'em?" Lullaby pondered.

"You tell me, and I'll tell you," Tucson said quietly. "Just as soon as we can open up a mite and get proper authority, from the Mexican Government, I'm goin' to see if we can't go back to Herrero and search Hodge's safe. Right now, for a few days —" and Tucson laughed softly with the activities of the previous night in mind, "— I don't figure it would be healthy for us to return."

Poddy Cameron came walking down the street, stepped up to the hotel porch and said good-morning.

Tucson said, "What's on your mind, Poddy?"

"Just thought I'd let you know," the sheriff explained, "Quint Sheridan is plumb worried. He was talkin' to me a spell back, asking if I'd seen Randle or Duproix. I sidestepped the question and dropped a hint that you were in Godwin. I could see that bothered him plenty. Since then, he and Gabby Emmett have been going around Godwin asking everybody if they've seen Randle and Duproix. Nobody has, of course."

"Link Dexter won't tell anybody about our prisoners, will he?" Tucson asked.

Cameron shook his head. "Link can't say anythin', unless I say it first. Otherwise he's just plain dumb, and nobody bothers to talk to him. But I been thinkin' about those prisoners, Tucson."

"What about 'em?"

"It ain't legal, holdin' 'em in jail, 'thout a warrant and reg'lar arrest bein' put through. Unless we can get somethin' on 'em, and make it stick, I stand to lose my job — maybe worse."

"They kicking up any fuss?"

"Duproix and Randle are quiet enough. Hodge keeps protestin' and demandin' a lawyer. I told him if he didn't shut up, I'd put him in irons. That quieted him down, but I'm afeared it won't be for long. You see, anythin' they done to you happened on Mexican soil. I haven't the authority to hold 'em for that."

"Sure, I get your slant, Poddy," Tucson

remarked quietly. "You can hold 'em the rest of the day, can't you?"

"Sure I can. Or if you'll swear out a warrant chargin' 'em with plottin' against your life, I can make regular arrests. In that case, though, Hodge would get a lawyer and get out on bail."

Tucson nodded. "Hold 'em as long as you can. With Sheridan bothered about the disappearance of his two hands, maybe he'll come asking me questions. He might drop something that would give us a reason to swear out warrants. I'm hoping he'll be just worried enough to get careless and tip his hand."

"Just as you say, Tucson. I'll hold 'em in their cells."

"I'll drift down and talk to Hodge in a little while," Tucson said. "I'll drop a coupla hints about what we suspicion. Maybe I can bluff him into keeping quiet a spell longer."

The sheriff nodded, stepped down from the porch and sauntered off down the street.

"You told a story, Tucson," Lullaby said, after a time, "but there's one point you didn't clear up."

"What's that?"

"Stony and me are still puzzlin' our heads over what happened to those rustled cattle of Hayden's. We've gone nigh batty tryin' to

354

dope out the connection between a cigarette burn on your Stetson and a bunch of missin' cows."

Tucson grinned. "Reckon I'll have to clear that up, too, if you can't figure it out. Look, the other night when the end of your cigarette fell on my hat brim, I half expected it would burn right through the felt. Do you know why it didn't? Because the fine nap on the felt kept the fire from going too deep. You know, that sort of hairy surface on felt. I scratched off the burned nap, and there was just a little scorched spot left. That started me to thinking. Suppose, in branding a cow, I didn't press the iron down hard _____"

"Cripes A'mighty!" Lullaby leaped to his feet, a dawning light in his eyes. "That's what happened! Sheridan and his men just pressed that iron down hard enough to burn the hair — the hot iron never got to the flesh _____"

"And when the hair growed out again," Stony exclaimed, "there wasn't any brand to show! Judas priest! But, say, Tucson, how do you account for the thirty-five cows that were branded all right?"

Tucson explained, "Like I said, Sheridan and his men just branded the surface hair. That made a brand good enough to convince Nancy Hayden, who was new to range ways. She thought she was seeing her cows branded correctly. She was riding back and forth between two brand fires, watchin' as close as possible and counting her cows. Just brandin' the hair like that, Sheridan and his men had to work slower, be a little more careful. They couldn't just slam the hot iron against the cow's hide, like you and I would do. Prob'ly, once in a while, when Nancy was watching closer than usual, those coyotes were actually forced to burn a genuine brand. Or they may have actually branded a few by going at the work careless. Anyway, there were one hundred sixty-five head that were just hair-branded."

"The Circle-Cross mark was vented in proper shape, wasn't it?" Lullaby asked, slowly seating himself again.

Tucson nodded. "Sure, Sheridan saw to that, so that a few months later, when he came to get Hayden's cows, he wouldn't get 'em confused with any of his own."

"Then," Stony put in, "when Sheridan had rounded up those hair-branded cows, he drove 'em over the mountains to Marnsville and sold 'em to that Kellogg hombre at a cheap figure. The dirty, billy-be-damned scut —— !"

"You got proof of all this?" Lullaby asked

suddenly.

Tucson shook his head. "But it all works out. When I go down to the jail to see Hodge, I'm aimin' to talk to Randle and Duproix about those cows. I think mebbe they'll admit that I'm right."

Lullaby gazed at Tucson and shook his head. "Dam'd if you ain't got a noodle on you. And you doped that out just because my cigarette burned your Stetson."

"It was that got me thinkin' along the right lines," Tucson nodded.

Lullaby said, "Well, I'll be hornswoggled!" And in the next breath, "Gosh! I wish it was time for dinner."

That started the usual argument between Stony and Lullaby. Tucson rose and, unheeded by the two, started down the street toward the jail.

An hour later, he left the jail feeling considerably elated: he had succeeded in bluffing Hodge into a state of extreme fright. On top of that he had gained a confession from Duproix and Randle, who now were willing to do anything to please, regarding the hair-branding of the one-hundred-sixty-five head of stock stolen from Clem Hayden. The branding had been carried on just as Tucson had surmised. This much, Randle and Duproix had stated freely. But of Sheridan's connection with Hodge, they either wouldn't, or couldn't, state, and Tucson gathered an impression that neither of the men was any too familiar with Sheridan's activities. They were, apparently, accustomed to carry out Sheridan's orders blindly.

Standing in front of the sheriff's office, Tucson told Poddy Cameron what he had learned. When he had finished, Cameron swore long and deeply: "The dirty, unprincipled sidewinders. Well —" squaring his shoulders, "— we can put a rustlin' charge against Sheridan and his crew, anyhow. That'll take care of two of those coyotes in the jail. I reckon I'll go find Sheridan and Gabby Emmett now. We can see to warrants later."

"I'll go with you," Tucson said.

But now Sheridan and Emmett weren't to be found in town. A thorough canvass of the town stores and streets failed to produce any sight of them. After an hour's fruitless search, Cameron and Tucson returned to the sheriff's office.

"Where in time could he have gone to?" Cameron growled.

"I just happened to think," Tucson replied. "Maybe Sheridan and Emmett have gone to Herrero to see if they can locate Duproix and Randle, see if Hodge can tell 'em anythin'."

"By Cripes! I'll bet that's just what they've done. I remember now, I didn't see their horses standin' in front of the Faro Saloon when we passed. And the barkeep in the Faro didn't know where they were. Well, they'll have to return to Godwin. I'll be watchin' for 'em, and put 'em under arrest the minute they show up."

Tucson nodded a bit disappointedly. "That's all you can do. Well, I reckon I'll slope along and pick up Lullaby and Stony. It's gettin' nigh time for dinner. I'll see you later, Poddy. And you better look me up before you start to arrest Sheridan and Emmett. They might prove hard to handle."

"I'll do that, Tucson. Thanks."

A short time after Tucson's departure, Cameron said to his deputy, "Link, you look after things here. I'm going to ride to the Circle-Cross and get Sheridan's cook. Old T-Bone Hinkle may be able to furnish some information on Sheridan's rustling. Anyway, he's one of the crew and pro'bly smeared with the same tarbrush. . . . No, no need for me to take Tucson. He's been helpin' to shoulder enough of my duties. If Sheridan happens to be at the Circle-Cross, I don't look for him to kick up a fuss about a few cows. If he's in Herrero, I'll pro'bly be back here as soon as he is."

"G'bye," Dexter grunted.

Cameron mounted and rode away.

Tucson, approaching the Gunsight Bar, saw Nick Fitch standing before the entrance, and said, "What's up, Nick? No business?"

"Plenty business," Fitch smiled. "I just had to come out and get a breath of air for a minute. I took on another bartender this mornin', you know."

"Good. . . . Stony and Lullaby inside?"

Nick nodded. "They been there a half hour or more."

Tucson entered the saloon. Nick turned and followed him in. Tucson found Lullaby and Stony seated at a table across from the bar, a couple of bottles of beer in front of them. Tucson dropped into a chair and gave an order. Nick went to fill it. The bar was lined with men. Tucson said, "You haven't seen Sheridan or Emmett, have you?"

Lullaby and Stony shook their heads, asked why.

Tucson explained. Lullaby said, "So you did turn up the right card on that hair-brandin'. And Duproix and Randle owned up to it?"

"We got a rustlin' charge against Sheridan

anyway," Tucson nodded. "Say, where's Micky?"

"Micky left for the 8-Bar about an hour ago," Lullaby said. "He explained that he felt he should ride out and see if Nancy got home all right, yesterday. Gosh, love don't give a feller any peace."

"Between Sheridan and Nancy," Stony grinned, "Micky sure manages to keep busy. I wonder if Sheridan did go to Herrero."

At that moment, Nick Fitch came up with a bottle of beer for Tucson. "Did you say Sheridan went to Herrero?" Nick asked.

Stony shook his head. "We were just wondering where he was."

"I saw him and Emmett ride past here a short time back ——" Nick commented.

"When was this?" Tucson asked quickly.

Nick considered. "Oh, pro'bly fifteen minutes before you come in, Tucson."

Tucson swore softly, "Cripes! They were up at this end of town while Poddy and I were down at the other. Nick, did you notice what way they were headin'?"

"They come ridin' along Santa Fe Street ——" jerking one thumb toward the corner street, "—— swung into Main Street and turned west. They were pushing right along."

Nick left the table. The Three Mesquiteers

stared at each other seriously. Tucson said, "I wonder if those two rattlers could be headin' for the 8-Bar?"

"I don't know what for," Stony frowned. "Still —

"Somehow, I don't like it," Lullaby grunted. He got to his feet. "Mebbe we better go to the livery for our horses and saddle up ——"

" 'Course," Stony put in, "Pete Blair and Stew Trumbull are at the 8-Bar, in case ——"

"I don't think so," Tucson shook his head. "They wouldn't be at the house, anyway. They located a quicksand on the Sereno River, and have been putting a fence around it. If Sheridan and Emmett do go to the 8-Bar, they'll find Nancy and Micky alone, except for that Mex girl servant of Nancy's. Yep, I sort of feel we should saddle up and ride a mite."

They left the saloon, went to the livery and procured their horses. Just as they turned the corner on Main Street, Tucson heard someone call his name. He pulled to a halt and looked around.

"Tucson!" the man repeated. It was Doctor Noah Perkins, running along the plank walk. "Tucson! Wait!"

Perkins came panting to a stop, swayed a

little. He looked badly disheveled. "Where's Poddy Cameron?" he panted.

"I left Poddy at his office a short spell back," Tucson replied.

"He ain't there now. That dang deputy won't say where he is, though he did drop something to the effect that Poddy might be at the Circle-Cross."

Tucson's eyes narrowed. "He might have gone there looking for Sheridan," he mused. Then, "What's wrong, Doc?"

"Sheridan — Emmett —" Perkins gasped. "They come to my house, held me up, demanded to see Bogart. Sheridan said he had to talk to Bogart, had some questions he wanted to ask him ——"

"Bogart isn't conscious, is he?" Tucson said quickly.

"He wasn't. I told Sheridan that. He and Emmett pushed inside the house and covered me with their guns. My wife was away. Sheridan asked if I couldn't give Bogart a stimulant to return him to consciousness. I could, of course, but it was dangerous — and then there was nothing certain about the drug doing the work. Sheridan insisted that I try. I warned him it might kill Bogart ——"

"They made you go ahead, anyway, eh?" Tucson said grimly. Lullaby and Stony were listening intently.

Perkins nodded. "They threatened to kill me if I didn't. I had to try." The doctor paused, wiped one hand across his glistening forehead. He gulped and went on, "It didn't do much good. I managed to rouse Bogart, but he was out of his mind. He babbled something about stealing a gun at the 8-Bar and swapping cylinders with it and his own gun. Sheridan seized Bogart by the shoulder and shook him savagely. Bogart commenced to bleed at the mouth, and then he died suddenly, muttering something about his own cylinder being defective. Then ——"

"Good God!" Tucson exclaimed. A sudden thought had flashed into his mind.

". . . Sheridan and Emmett tied me up, and left the house in a hurry." Perkins stumbled on. "If my wife hadn't come home sooner than expected, I'd still be there, trussed up like a captive hen."

Tucson was only half listening to the man now. His eyes had narrowed in thought. His face was stern. Lullaby said, "What's it mean, pard?"

Tucson swore bitterly, "I've been a fool not to guess it before this. Sheridan must have guessed at the connection. That's why he had to talk to Bogart. He saw Micky take

Bogart's gun, that night. He knows Micky has been carrying it ever since. Yes, we know now that Sheridan and Emmett are heading for the 8-Bar. We've got to ride, pards. It means trouble."

Stony snapped, "What are we waiting for? Mebbe Micky can stand 'em off with his gun until we get there ——"

"Sure, he should savvy shootin' by this time ——" Lullaby commenced.

"Dammit! That gun won't shoot, if it's carrying the cylinder out of Scorpio's six-shooter. It wouldn't shoot for Clem Hayden; he knew better than to try to shoot it. Joe Frame knew it wouldn't shoot. That's why he had the guts to work Hayden into a fight ——"

"What's this all about?" Perkins cut in curiously.

"No time to tell you now, Doc," Tucson sang out, whirling his horse. "We're going to get Sheridan and Emmett for you. C'mon, pards."

There was a rush of hoofs as the riders got under way and thundered along the street, riding west.

Five miles out of town the horses were covered with lather. The Three Mesquiteers pressed mercilessly on and on, urging their mounts to the utmost in speed. Tucson was in the lead, then came Lullaby; Stony was pressing closely behind.

Three more miles drifted past. Lullaby's horse stumbled suddenly and went down. Lullaby went sprawling over its head, rolled over and came up limping. The horse was still down. Tucson and Stony pulled rein, jerked their horses around.

"Go on, go on," Lullaby yelled. "My bronc stepped in a gopher hole — broke his leg. I'll have to shoot him. Keep goin'!"

"I'll take him up behind me, Tucson," Stony snapped. "You got the best horse. Keep pushin'!"

Tucson nodded, grim-faced, again put his pony to the spur and lined out, like an arrow's flight, for the 8-Bar. Once he looked back over his shoulder. He saw Lullaby climbing up behind Stony, saw Lullaby draw his gun. A shot echoed flatly across the hills, but the sound was almost lost in the rush of wind ripping against Tucson's body.

"On, horse, on," Tucson muttered. "Keep goin'. Good little horse."

And, as though the horse understood Tucson's pleading words, it responded nobly and lengthened stride in a distance-devouring gait that carried its rider through a swiftly-unreeling kaleidoscopic blur of grass and brush and swirling skies. Twenty minutes later, topping a low rise, Tucson glanced down the long slope to see the 8-Bar Ranch buildings, with Sheridan's and Emmett's horses waiting not far from the kitchen doorway. . . .

XXVI. FIGHTING BLOOD

Micky had said for the twentieth time, "Nancy, I'm certainly glad to see that you got home all right, yesterday. I sure intended to bring you back, but . . ." and for the twentieth time Nancy had replied, "Certainly, I realize how it was, Micky. Your work simply had to come first."

And Micky would respond, "Oh, no, you come first, of course."

They were both a bit giggly and self-conscious and their faces would flush suddenly crimson at some unintended remark. Watching them, Berta, the Mexican servant girl, would nod knowingly and remain out of earshot. Nancy had eventually remembered an apricot pie baked that morning. Coffee had been put on to brew. With the kitchen table between them, Nancy and Micky had almost arrived at certain decisions regarding their future existence. Micky had related the story of his previous night's

367

adventure in Herrero, and seen sudden fear enter Nancy's eyes.

Micky's heart had thumped madly as he read the concern in Nancy's face. From that point on, affairs really progressed. Time flashed by while Micky spoke of his ambitions, telling the girl about the newspaper he hoped to establish in Godwin. All in all it was very pleasant, with a cool breeze lifting across the range to flutter the curtains at the windows and the sunlight streaming through the kitchen doorway.

Pete Blair and Stew Trumbull were away, engaged in building a fence about the quicksand that had been found in Sereno River. Conversation went on, and when Micky, finally, felt he should take his departure, he was urged to stay for supper and say "hello" to Pete and Stew. Incidentally, Micky didn't require much urging.

Berta appeared at the back door, suddenly, announcing, "Two hombres com' rideeng."

Nancy rose from the table and glanced out. In a moment she turned back into the room, "It looks like Quint Sheridan and one of his hands," she told Micky. "I wonder what they want."

"Probably nothing important," Micky said calmly, though, inwardly, he didn't feel so secure. Unconsciously, his hand strayed to the six-shooter in his waistband; he wished now he had again fastened it to a cord and allowed the weapon to dangle down his trouser leg. On the other hand, he might be called on to use the gun. He rose and stood at Nancy's side, looking out the back way at the approaching riders. They were loping easily, taking their time. Micky saw Gabby Emmett take a last pull from a flask and toss the bottle to one side. Sheridan was riding slightly in the lead, swaying a little in the saddle.

After that, things happened pretty quickly. Sheridan and his companion pulled to a halt near the kitchen door, dismounted and started toward the door. Sensing trouble, Berta had screamed and darted quickly for another part of the house.

Micky stood in the doorway, half a head shorter than Nancy, who had now moved behind him. There wasn't any fear in the little reporter. The fighting blood of Irish warriors coursed his veins. He had realized quite suddenly that he was in for it. His one thought was to save Nancy from any harm.

Sheridan came on, scowling, followed by Emmett. Instinctively, Micky pushed Nancy back into the house, hoping to close the door and step out to meet this danger. But

Nancy refused to release the grip on his shoulder. Somehow, before he could understand just how it had happened, Micky and Nancy were at the other side of the kitchen, the table between them and the door.

Sheridan and Emmett were rocking through the entrance.

Micky said, "What do you fellows want?"

Sheridan snapped one word, "You!"

A soft laugh rose in Micky's throat. "You black-guards, you wanted me once before — but you didn't like what you got."

Sheridan and Emmett had paused just inside the entrance. At Micky's words, Sheridan's face flamed. "If I'd known then, what I know now, you'd never have got the drop on us that day, runt."

Micky said quietly, "All right, you want me. I'll go with you, if you'll promise to leave here at once."

"I want you and I want that gun you're carryin'," Sheridan said slowly. "I've got a score to settle with you, Callahan."

Nancy spoke bravely, "Sheridan, you and your employee are on 8-Bar property. That trespassing rule still holds. I'd advise you to clear out — pronto!"

A guffaw of laughter left Emmett's mouth. "Listen to the gal talk," he sneered.

"You keep your mouth shut, Emmett,"

Micky said savagely, "or I'll shut it for you."

"That'll be right hard with a forty-five slug in your guts," Sheridan growled.

Micky's lips tightened. "Any time you want to finish this conversation outside, Sheridan, I'll go with you. There's no use of Miss Hayden ——"

"You're not going to leave here, Micky," Nancy cried. "Sheridan is planning to kill you ——"

"You're a good guesser, gal," Emmett snarled. "Only you're included in the plans. We got to make a clean sweep. We'll find your greaser gal, later, and ——"

"Shut up, Gabby," Sheridan spat out of the side of his mouth.

He stood looking at Micky and the girl. His hand was resting on his six-shooter butt now. Emmett started for his gun.

Micky jerked the six-shooter out of his waistband, cocked it. He hardly heard the roar of Emmett's and Sheridan's forty-fives. Something struck his shoulder a powerful blow, slamming him up against the wall. A leaden slug ripped into the boards near his head.

Dimly he heard Nancy's smothered scream of fright. Bracing himself against the wall, he deliberately raised the cocked gun he held in his hand, pressed the trigger.

The hammer fell with a dull clicking sound. Blindly, Micky cocked the gun again. A second time it failed to explode when the trigger was pulled. Micky took one step and slid to the floor. Nancy was bending over him as he fought to get up.

He heard Sheridan's triumphant laugh as the man leaped around the table, shoving Nancy to one side. Outside, hoofs drummed frantically across the sod.

Then, Emmett's voice, tinged with fear: "It's Tucson Smith!"

Sheridan cursed and ran back to the doorway. His gun kicked in his hand as Tucson sprinted toward the entrance. Dust spurted at Tucson's feet. With a bellow of rage, Emmett swung his weapon, pulled trigger. But Tucson was moving too fast to make a good target. A shot snapped from near his hip as he moved. Emmett yelled with pain and clapped one hand to his neck. Blood spurted through his fingers.

Micky was up now, staggering across the room. He propelled his body in a low dive, clutching at Emmett's legs. Emmett pitched forward, colliding with Sheridan, spoiling Sheridan's next shot.

Sheridan shook the man off, backed into the room. Tucson came plunging in, running low. He felt the breeze of a bullet cut past his face. Emmett had rolled over and was shooting from the floor, his shots going wild. The room was thick with powder smoke. Micky came scrambling up through the swirling drifts.

Tucson's right hand jerked, then his left, then his right again, each jerk bringing the accompanying roaring white flash that shook the rafters of the building. Emmett coughed and sank down on his face. Sheridan whirled half around, crashed into a chair and went sprawling to the floor.

Tucson was crouched, legs wide, guns ready. After a moment he relaxed. Micky had found his gun, cocked it a third time. Slowly, he lowered his hand, as he looked down on the two motionless figures on the floor. Grimly, Tucson holstered his Colt guns.

Nancy's face was ashen as she moved across the room. One protective arm was around Micky's slim shoulders.

Tucson said quietly, "That's all, I reckon. You weren't hurt, were you?"

Micky shook his head. Nancy said, "I thought sure he was hit — he — he went down." Her voice trembled.

Micky shook his head a trifle bashfully. "I — I guess I slipped — or something." He didn't feel any pain. There was a sense of numbness in his left shoulder, his head felt strangely light. He held out the gun to Tucson, saying earnestly, "I cocked it — just like you told me — but it wouldn't shoot."

"And a good reason, unless I miss my guess," Tucson said quickly. He took the gun from Micky's hand, removed the shells. His knife came out and was opened. He commenced working the leaden bullets from the brass containers. A bullet rolled to one side unnoticed as two strange objects tumbled from a shell.

Micky emitted a gasp of surprise. Tucson was working on the other shells. In a few minutes ten, perfectly matched, rose tinted diamonds glittered and sparkled in the sunlight that lay across the table!

"And — I — had — them — all — the — time," Micky muttered thickly.

"We know now," Tucson nodded, "why Clem Hayden didn't go through with his draw. Well, Micky, there's your reward and your printing press ——"

"Tucson!" Nancy cried.

Tucson turned, caught Micky in his arms as the little reporter pitched toward the floor. A dark, spreading blot showed through his coat shoulder now.

There came the staccato beating of horse's hoofs. Lullaby's and Stony's excited cries.

But Micky was beyond hearing now, as he plunged down and down through the sea of darkness. . . .

The news of Sheridan's and Emmett's deaths was the last straw necessary to break Fulton Hodge's nerve. Two days after the fight in the 8-Bar kitchen had taken place, the Three Mesquiteers, Poddy Cameron and Nancy, were seated around Micky in the main room of the ranch house. Micky was reclining on a couch, one shoulder swathed in bandages. The little Irishman looked pale, but a cheerful grin illuminated his face. Somewhere at the back of the house, Berta softly hummed a Mexican love song. Sunshine streamed in through the windows. Stew Trumbull and Pete Blair strode in to ask after the wounded reporter's welfare, before starting to work.

". . . and Hodge's confession," Tucson was saying, "dovetails in with the things we've been suspecting. Hodge was set to go into smuggling in a big way. He wasn't just satisfied to deal in stones. That required capital. He and Sheridan — though Hodge was the leader — planned to smuggle Chinamen into the States. That would have netted around a thousand bucks a head ——"

"Nice profits," Stony commented, with a

low whistle.

"Dang nice," Tucson nodded. "But with Customs officers at the international bridge, it would be difficult to get them across. That's why Hodge wanted the 8-Bar, the southern boundary line of which runs right along the Mexican Border for several miles. It would have been a cinch to shove a bunch of Chinks through that wire fence. Well, you know how they rustled 8-Bar cows and planned to ruin Nancy's father and get control of the ranch ——"

"Not to mention raisin' a note for five hundred," Cameron growled, "to five thousand."

"Yes," Tucson said, "Hodge admitted doing that too. As for the Pinchot rose diamonds, Micky was correct in his hunch that Hodge might have received them. He and Sheridan were afraid to take a chance of carrying them past the Customs man, so they had Scorpio hide the stones in his forty-five shells, after removing the powder. Then the slugs were put back. Scorpio rode west along the border, cut the 8-Bar fence, and started to cross toward Godwin. That morning he ran into Clem Hayden. Clem roped and tied him, as you know, but was puzzled as to why Scorpio hadn't gone for his gun. Well, Clem was shrewd. He examined the gun and the shells, and discovered the diamonds; guessed, at once, that they were being smuggled."

Tucson paused to roll and light a cigarette, then continued, "Clem replaced the stones and slugs in the shells, went to Godwin, and threatened to reveal his discovery to the sheriff unless Sheridan repaid him for the cattle that had disappeared. Sheridan refused, then told Frame about the gun Clem carried. It was Frame's chance to square accounts for the wound Clem had given him the previous time they had met. Frame leaped at the chance. Sheridan had already imported one gun fighter to finish Clem, but Clem had killed the feller, though wounded himself ——"

"Being laid up with that wound," Nancy said ruefully, "was what enabled Sheridan to slip that hair-branding stunt over on me, while Dad was recovering."

"Frame tried to kill Clem next," Tucson went on, "and got shot himself. Then, when he heard that Clem was carrying a gun that wouldn't shoot, it was too good a chance to pass up. He went to the Gunsight Bar, picked a fight with Clem. For just an instant, Clem lost his temper and started to reach instinctively for the gun at his hip. That was what Frame had been waiting for, and he cut loose."

Tucson caught the look in Nancy's eyes and quickly changed the subject. "By hook or crook, Sheridan had to get that gun. The diamonds it was carrying were worth big money. You know what happened. Manning and Bogart came here, stole the gun. Bogart replaced the cylinder in his own gun with the one in Scorpio's weapon. For a time Bogart carried that fortune in jewels on him. When he was killed, we took Scorpio's gun, not knowing that the cylinders had been exchanged. Micky grabbed Bogart's six-shooter, and from then on, Micky was carrying the diamonds ———"

Micky laughed suddenly. "And to think that I once got the draw on Sheridan and two of his men with that worthless gun ———"

"Did you say worthless?" Lullaby chuckled.

"I was plannin' to use it myself, that night in Herrero," Tucson said wryly. "It would have been worthless that night, if Lullaby and Stony hadn't arrived in time ———"

"And it was dang worthless to me, too," Micky said, "when I tried to use it against Emmett and Sheridan. Only for Tucson getting here in time ———"

"Don't talk about it." Nancy shuddered.

"You're right, Nancy," Tucson agreed, "we should forget all of that business now. Micky has managed to write the whole story up for his paper and sent in his resignation. He'll get the reward and then his printing press. Godwin will have a real newspaper, I'm betting."

"There's certain, very important news will appear in the first issue," Micky grinned. "Shall we tell 'em, Nancy?"

Nancy laughed. "They probably know, already, that something of the sort is due to happen — unless they're blind."

"And we've already picked Tucson for best man," Micky went on. "As for Lullaby and Stony — well, they've kidded me a lot. The only way I know how to get even is to demand that they act as ring-bearer and flower girl ——"

"My Gawd!" Lullaby exclaimed. "Which am I?"

Nancy giggled. "We'll have food instead of flowers."

Stony rose, laughing. "Well, that settles that. I reckon I'll go out and practice my ring bearin'."

"All of which looks to me," Tucson smiled gravely, "like the start of another story, instead of the finish of one."

And that is exactly what it was. . . .

We hope you have enjoyed this Large Print book. Other Thorndike, Wheeler, Kennebec, and Chivers Press Large Print books are available at your library or directly from the publishers.

For information about current and upcoming titles, please call or write, without obligation, to:

Publisher
Thorndike Press
295 Kennedy Memorial Drive
Waterville, ME 04901
Tel. (800) 223-1244

or visit our Web site at:

http://gale.cengage.com/thorndike

OR

Chivers Large Print
published by AudioGO Ltd
St James House, The Square
Lower Bristol Road
Bath BA2 3SB
England
Tel. +44(0) 800 136919
www.audiogo.co.uk

All our Large Print titles are designed for easy reading, and all our books are made to last.